"If he has done your hand, I wi..." he promised, his voice a guttural bark.

His gaze never left her, bright and probing and denying her innocence. "Perhaps you did not realize that 'tis not wise to be alone with a man!" He spat the words out as if they tasted foul upon his tongue.

"We were talking, nothing more!" Gillian protested, alarmed by the look in his glittering depths. "Trust you not your own guard?"

"Nay! I trust no one when it comes to you!" Nicholas growled, taking a step toward her.

Comprehension dawned slowly, laced with so much disbelief that Gillian shook her head, as if dazed. Regarding him with wide-eyed wonder, she whispered the truth. "You are jealous."

He flinched, but did not deny it. "You are mine, body and soul, and you had best remember it!"

Dear Reader,

Whether writing atmospheric Medievals or sexy Regencies, Deborah Simmons continues to delight readers with her romantic stories, be they dark and brooding or light and full of fun. In this month's *Maiden Bride,* the sequel to *The Devil's Lady,* Nicholas de Laci transfers his blood lust to his enemy's niece, Gillian, his future wife by royal decree. Don't miss this wonderful tale.

Fans of *Romantic Times* Career Achievement Award winner Veronica Sattler will be thrilled to see this month's reissue of her Worldwide Library release, *Jesse's Lady.* We hope you'll enjoy this exciting story of a young heiress and her handsome guardian who must survive the evil machinations of her bastard brother and a jealous temptress before they can find happiness.

Beloved Outcast by Pat Tracy is a dramatic Western about an Eastern spinster who is hired by a man with a notorious reputation to tutor his adopted daughter. And our fourth book this month is *The Wager* by Sally Cheney, the story of a young Englishwoman who reluctantly falls in love with a man who won her in a game of cards.

We hope you'll keep a lookout for all four titles wherever Harlequin Historicals are sold.

Sincerely,

Tracy Farrell
Senior Editor

Please address questions and book requests to:
Harlequin Reader Service
U.S.: 3010 Walden Ave., P.O. Box 1325, Buffalo, NY 14269
Canadian: P.O. Box 609, Fort Erie, Ont. L2A 5X3

Deborah Simmons

MAIDEN BRIDE

Harlequin Books

TORONTO • NEW YORK • LONDON
AMSTERDAM • PARIS • SYDNEY • HAMBURG
STOCKHOLM • ATHENS • TOKYO • MILAN
MADRID • WARSAW • BUDAPEST • AUCKLAND

ISBN 0-373-28932-4

MAIDEN BRIDE

Books by Deborah Simmons

Harlequin Historicals

The Fortune Hunter #132
Silent Heart #185
The Squire's Daughter #208
The Devil's Lady #241
The Vicar's Daughter #258
Taming the Wolf #284
The Devil Earl #317
Maiden Bride #332

DEBORAH SIMMONS

Deborah Simmons began her writing career as a
newspaper reporter. She turned to fiction after the
birth of her first child when a longtime love of historical romance prompted her to pen her own work,
published in 1989. She lives with her husband, two
children and two cats in rural Ohio, where she
divides her time between her family, reading and
writing. She enjoys hearing from readers at the
below address. For a reply, an SASE is appreciated.

Deborah Simmons
P.O. Box 274
Ontario, Ohio 44862-0274

Special thanks to Linda Hoffman, Laurie Miller and Jennifer Weithman for their insistence upon and assistance with Nicholas's story

Chapter One

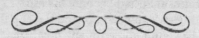

Nicholas de Laci leaned against the wall of the great hall, brooding over a cup of ale. He was not drunk; he never drank too much. It dulled the wits, and he had honed his to a razor sharpness. As if to prove his skills, he lifted his head at a sound from the arched entranceway, his eyes alert for any sign of danger, but it was only his sister, Aisley, and her infant son.

Hexham would not pass this way again.

The thought slipped into his mind like a dark phantom, despite his iron-hard discipline, and for just a moment Nicholas let himself dwell upon it. His enemy was dead. The neighbor who had waylaid him in the Holy Land, abandoned him there and returned to try to steal his lands had been cut down in this very hall by Aisley's husband, Piers, who had deprived him of his revenge in one fell swoop.

Nicholas glanced toward two heavy chairs near the front of the hall. That was where they said it happened, by Aisley's seat, but the tiles had long been scrubbed clean, and Hexham's blood was gone. Forever. Nicholas would never see it spilled, never know the satisfaction of vengeance in the depths of his hungry soul.

He had tried other killing in the year since, hiring himself out as a soldier, but the deaths of strangers meant as little to him as the coins he received in payment. Nicholas already had great wealth and a prosperous demesne to call his own. Built by his father, Belvry was a modern castle and the envy of his peers, and yet it gave him no pleasure, either. And so he had returned here, to the scene of his bitter disappointment, vainly searching for a respite from the gnawing emptiness that had become his life.

Nicholas's fingers tightened around the cup that held his ale. In truth, he found contentment nowhere, for nothing held meaning for him anymore. His sister was so much changed over the five years he had been in the Holy Land that he knew her not, and he resented her husband for taking what he had most wanted: Hexham's life.

"Nicholas! I did not see you there against the wall. What are you about this afternoon?" Aisley asked, with that half welcoming, half wary smile that he had grown accustomed to seeing directed toward him. His lovely fair-haired sister was not sure what to make of him, but that hardly surprised him. Nicholas was no longer sure what to make of himself.

"Nothing," he answered, brushing her query aside with a flick of his eyes. He nodded toward a long bench, and Aisley sat down, baby in her arms. "Look, Sybil, 'tis your uncle Nicholas," she cooed. "Uncle. Uncle Nicholas," she babbled, crooning in a way Nicholas would never have thought possible.

The Aisley he had known had been an aloof child-woman, a skilled chatelaine, but certainly not the sort to lavish affection upon anyone. Now, instead of handing the infant over to a nurse, she dragged it around with her most of the time, carrying on over it in a way he found hard to fathom.

A sound from the entranceway drew his swift attention, and Nicholas saw Piers stride into the hall. A huge man,

Aisley's husband was capable of intimidating others, but rarely did so. Instead, he seemed to take infinite delight in the world around him, from which he had been briefly cut off during a bout with blindness.

"Piers!" Aisley's voice rose in excited pleasure. "Look, Sybil, 'tis your father!" she said, waving the baby's tiny fist toward the great knight. Perhaps something about the birthing process had damaged her wits, Nicholas wondered, not for the first time during his visit. "Here, go to your uncle while I greet your father," Aisley cooed.

To his utter horror, Nicholas found the infant thrust into his arms. It was small and fat and bald, and it smelled, with an odd sort of milky, soapy odor. He had known it to reek more foully. The thought made him rise to his feet and glance down suspiciously. If it soiled his tunic, he might have to strangle it. Cup in one fist, babe in the crook of his arm, he glanced helplessly toward his sister, but she was already beyond his reach.

With a happy smile, Aisley threw herself at her husband's tall form, while Nicholas watched in amazement. He would never get used to *that* behavior. The two of them kissed passionately, just as though they were in their own chamber and not standing amid the rushes of the open hall. Nicholas found the display positively sickening.

He would have thought that Piers only indulged his daft wife at such moments, but for the fact that the knight sought her out with the same enthusiasm. Perhaps Piers's sightlessness had left him sadly addled, too.

"Waaah!" The babe in Nicholas's arms seemed suddenly to realize where she was and started screaming shrilly in protest. Nicholas's gut churned in response to the hideous noise, and he wondered if he ought to depart Dunmurrow soon. He felt apart and alien among this strangely happy threesome who made his own life seem even more barren and aimless.

"Here!" he said, standing abruptly and holding out the child to its mother.

"There, there, Sybil, 'tis time for your nap, perhaps?" Aisley whispered, and Nicholas stared, astounded at the way she talked to the thing, just as if it might understand her. His sister was beyond him now, as was everyone, everything, everyplace.... His stomach twisted, reminding him that he ought to eat something, but food held no interest. Instead, he focused on the giant blond man who would call him brother.

"Nicholas!" Piers greeted him with the warmth that continued to annoy him. How dare the Red Knight eye him with that knowing look, as if seeing right through Nicholas's skin to his hollow insides? How dare he tender advice, when his keep was shabby compared to Belvry?

Dunmurrow was old, and its residents were far from wealthy, and yet they seemed to possess some treasure that Nicholas lacked, which only frustrated him further. The ache in his belly clawed at his vitals until he nearly winced, but he did not waver under Piers's steady regard.

"I came to find you, brother," the older knight said. "A messenger from the king has arrived, seeking you." Nicholas glanced quickly behind his sister's husband, to where a man sporting Edward's device stood not far away. How had Nicholas missed him? His attention had been diverted by babes and amorous displays, that was how! Deflecting his anger inward, Nicholas calmly placed his cup upon the great table and stepped forward to greet the stranger.

Finally. It had been a year since Hexham had made war upon neighboring Belvry, and all this time the fate of the bastard's lands had remained unresolved. Piers claimed that Edward would decide in Nicholas's favor and award the property to Belvry's heir in reparation, but Nicholas had a deep-seated mistrust of kings and princes, gained in a folly called a holy war. It would not surprise him if Edward confiscated Hexham's demesne for the crown.

Nor did it matter to him. Hexham had no issue, so either way, the land would leave the man's line forever. That was small satisfaction for Nicholas, but he took it. It was all the revenge left to him.

"You are Nicholas de Laci, baron of Belvry?" the king's man asked.

"I am," Nicholas said.

"I have a message for you from your sovereign."

Nodding, Nicholas gestured for the man to take a seat on the long bench beside the great table. As the messenger found a place, Nicholas caught a glimpse of Aisley's anxious face and realized that his sister and her husband wanted to hear the news, too. Their interest startled him. Was it curiosity? He supposed they had little enough excitement in their dreary keep.

"Shall I fetch some refreshment for you?" Aisley asked hopefully, and Nicholas was again amazed by the transparency of her thoughts. The Aisley he had known would never have shown emotion—or felt it, either. 'Twas the birthing, no doubt, he thought again. It had changed her, and not for the better.

"That would be most welcome, my lady," the man said. "But my message is brief. Care you to hear it first?" he asked Nicholas. His gaze traveled from Nicholas to the lord and lady of Dunmurrow, and Nicholas felt a smart of annoyance at those who sought to know his business. He had kept his own counsel for years, and had learned to rely solely upon himself, because it was necessary. It was the only way to survive.

To hasten his audience's departure, Nicholas gave Piers
an inquiring look, but he received a flash of warning from
the Red Knight's blue eyes in response. Piers coddled his
wife, and he seemed to feel that Nicholas owed Aisley
something for her wardship of Belvry. Nicholas did not care
for the debt, nor for the reminder of it, and he stiffened
slightly. He had the feeling that someday, for all Piers's attempt at friendship, the two of them would come to blows.

This time, however, Nicholas gave way. What was the
harm in them hearing, after all? It was a matter of little
enough importance to him. "This is my sister, and you have
met her husband, Baron Montmorency," Nicholas said with
cool disdain. "You may speak freely before them."

The man glanced again toward Aisley, as if seeking the
resemblance between the delicate lady with the silver-blond
hair and Nicholas's tall, dark form, but he said nothing.
Presumably he was too eager for his supper to care.

"I have come about the dispensation of the lands adja-
cent to Belvry, property of Baron Hexham, now deceased," the man said, and both Piers and Aisley nodded,
worry apparent in their eyes. Did they hide nothing from the
world? Nicholas thought with contempt. And what did it
matter to them what happened to Hexham's land? Had they
not had the pleasure of watching the villain die?

Nicholas felt the familiar clenching of his stomach at his
lost vengeance, and pushed the thought aside, concentrating on the messenger instead. He was reading from a royal
decree, couched in fancy wording, about Edward's desire to
bind people to their lord with strong ties and to cement loy-
alties through marriage whenever possible. *Yes, yes,* Nicholas thought, impatiently. *Get on with it!*

"As Baron Hexham has been found to have a living female relation, a niece, it is our wish that you take this

woman, Gillian Hexham, to wife, thereby joining the two properties and taking lordship over all."

Although the man continued reading, Nicholas heard him not, his interest focused solely on one piece of information: *Hexham had a living relative.* Nicholas's blood, long dormant, surged through him at the knowledge, and the hatred he had nursed so bitterly sprang to life once more, filling the emptiness in his soul with renewed purpose.

"A niece? Hexham has a niece?" Aisley's voice, oddly strained, pierced the haze of blood lust that gripped him. "I knew of no niece."

"Apparently she is the daughter of his younger brother, long dead," the messenger said. His words fell into a silence so heavy with tension that the very air seemed to vibrate with it, and he shifted uncomfortably, glancing anxiously at the stunned faces that surrounded him.

Nicholas paid him no heed, for he was consumed once more with thoughts of the revenge he had been forced to abandon. It was Aisley who broke the quiet, a soft sound of agitation escaping from her slender throat. "Nicholas . . ," she whispered. "Oh, Nicholas, please . . ."

He glanced over at her in surprise. She was still standing, her daughter in her arms and her husband beside her, and she wore a stricken expression at odds with her cool beauty. "I know what you are thinking, but do not even consider it," she begged.

"You know what I am thinking?" Nicholas echoed, his tone heavy with contempt for her audacity, his eyes daring her to go on. But he had forgotten how strong she was, and she reminded him by meeting his cold glare and holding it until he turned away, revolted by her entreaty. Even that outright dismissal did not stop her, however.

"This poor woman is not to blame for her blood," she said. "Indeed, she has probably already been punished for

it, by Hexham himself. Think of how he would destroy all
those he touched. Think of his own wife, locked away in her
tower!''

His sister was babbling now, and even through the primitive heat raging through him, Nicholas noticed it. So unlike Aisley, he thought dispassionately, and vowed that he
would never display himself so openly.

''Why, this innocent girl has probably been locked away,
too, else why would I never have met her?'' she asked.
Growing desperate now, she whirled toward the king's man,
and the baby in her arms began fussing. ''She cannot have
stayed with him, for we would have heard something of her.
Where has she been all this time?''

''She has lived in a convent for many years—since her
youth, I believe,'' the messenger answered.

''A convent?'' Aisley gasped. ''By all the saints, she is a
nun?''

Aisley bit her lip as she paced back and forth across the
great chamber, her hands knotted into tight fists at her sides.
''You saw him! You saw the look on his face! He will cru-
cify her!'' she cried.

''Nonsense,'' Piers said calmly. ''Nicholas is a hard man,
but not cruel.''

''You think you know him?'' Aisley asked, turning on her
husband. ''Well, I do not. Even in our youth, he was distant, unfeeling, and when he returned from the Holy Land,
so cold and hard, and his eyes so...so...'' Aisley shuddered, unable to go on.

''War changes a man, Aisley,'' Piers said gently, but she
would take no comfort. Her thoughts were on her brother,
who had made hatred his life's blood, vengeance his only
joy, and on the poor innocent who would be forced to suffer for it.

"What could Edward be thinking? He knows how Nicholas was obsessed with Hexham, chasing him down like a dog and driving him to madness."

"I think the king knows what he is doing," Piers said with a pensive air. "You must admit that this is the first time Nicholas has shown an interest in anything since Hexham's death."

"Yes, Nicholas finally responded to something, but 'twas horrible to see it." Aisley shuddered at the recollection of how those gray eyes, so like her own, had sprung to life with the fire of his malice.

"Edward is no fool," Piers said. "He would not put the girl in danger, and I seem to recall one marriage he arranged to the good."

Aisley stopped pacing to glance at her beloved husband, her thoughts diverted momentarily by their own hard-won happiness. "But that was different," she protested. "Edward told me to choose one of his knights, and I picked you. 'Twas my own good judgment that founded our marriage."

"I do not think you felt that way from the first," Piers said in that familiar dry tone of his, and Aisley could not help but smile.

"Oh, Piers," she whispered, her voice breaking. "But I was strong and world-wise, while that child is innocent—a nun, by all the saints! My brother would abuse a holy woman!"

"Nicholas is not going to abuse her, and she cannot have taken her vows yet, or she would not be made to wed," Piers protested.

"But she has grown up in a convent, a gentle, delicate thing, most likely, sheltered from the hard ways of the outside, and certainly unused to men and their brutality. Oh, Piers, what shall become of her in Nicholas's hands?"

"Have faith, Aisley," Piers answered.

"Yes, faith," Aisley echoed. "I shall pray for her, as she will need it, and may God have mercy on the poor girl."

Nicholas rode away from Dunmurrow without a backward glance. Nothing held him there, but something, finally, waited for him ahead. Though he feared no one, Nicholas kept enough men with him at all times to provide good escort, so he was well equipped for a new journey. Pausing only long enough to learn the location of the convent where he would find her, Nicholas had set out to fetch his bride.

He did not care what she looked like. Whether she was old or young, crone or beauty, she was of Hexham's blood, and his hatred drove him on toward this new object of revenge. In fact, Nicholas was so eager to reach his destination that he hurried his men needlessly, the patience and discipline that had ruled his life for years loosening its tight hold upon him.

"Where go we?" A deep voice, low and melodious, sounded beside him, and Nicholas flicked a glance to the man who spoke. He wore a long, flowing robe, as did several others in Nicholas's company who disdained the traditional knight's mail coat.

"Darius." Deep in thought, Nicholas had not noted his companion's approach. Although annoyed at his own inattention, he was not surprised to be caught off guard, for Darius had the ability to seemingly appear out of nowhere. Some of the others called him Shadow Man and feared his stealth, but Nicholas was not so foolish. That skill had saved their lives more than once as they roamed strange cities throughout the East.

Although he was called a Syrian, Nicholas had no idea where Darius came from originally. The population of Syria was diverse, with Greeks, Armenians, Maronites, Jacobites, Nestorians, Copts, Italians, Jews, Muslims and Franks coexisting, along with a few Germans and Scandinavians.

Darius's name was Egyptian, and Nicholas could well picture the tall, dark man as a direct descendant of some powerful pharaoh. He had a noble look about him, and a confidence not born of the gutter. His skin was a deep gold, but light enough to suggest a mixed parentage, and Nicholas often wondered if Darius was some sultan's cast-off son. Or perhaps he was simply the product of a knight who had raped a local woman in a crusading frenzy.

Nicholas had never asked, and Darius had never offered. Since their precipitous meeting several years ago, they had kept to an unwritten rule between them: no questions about the past. When the time came for Nicholas to return to Britain, Darius had come along, and Nicholas had shared what needed to be known with the man who came closest to being a friend to him. But that was as far as it went. They held each other to no oaths, shared no future beyond the day, and passed no judgment upon each other.

"We go to a convent," Nicholas replied. "A holy place for women," he added when Darius sent him a questioning look.

The Syrian still appeared puzzled as he struggled with such a foreign concept. "The women live alone together?" he asked.

"Yes, they have pledged themselves to God."

"What do we there? I am surprised they allow men in such places."

"We go to find a kinswoman of my enemy. Hexham's line lives on, Darius, and I would have my vengeance upon it, at last."

"This kinswoman is a holy one?" Darius asked.

"Nay. She but lives there with those who are."

Nicholas saw Darius relax slightly. Although, as far as Nicholas knew, the Syrian did not practice any religion, he had a high regard for the places he deemed holy, both Christian and Muslim. "Ah," he said softly. "And what shall you do with her?"

Nicholas did not answer immediately, for he was still considering his plans. The future, which had only a few hours ago seemed so bleak and senseless, now held endless possibilities. Nicholas tried to tamp down the clamor in his blood to a dull roar, but the patience that had been his mainstay seemed to elude him now. Thwarted by Hexham's death, and the long, hollow months that had followed, he craved immediate recompense. Now. At last.

"I would make her suffer as Hexham did me," Nicholas finally replied.

"You mean to leave her to bleed to death in the desert sun?" Darius asked.

Nicholas ignored the Syrian's sarcasm, for he did not wish to be reminded of the torment of those burning days and freezing nights, or of the slow year of recovery that had followed.

"Nay," he said. "But I would find out that which she cherishes most, and I would take it from her, just as Hexham tried to do to me and mine. I would discover what she most fears and reviles, and I would present it to her. I would torment her and take pleasure in it. I will have my revenge."

In the ensuing silence, Nicholas felt Darius's hard stare upon him. Although the Syrian's dark eyes held no censure, he knew that Darius had a deep-rooted respect for women. More than likely he did not approve of Nicholas's plans, but he would not interfere.

For a long moment, neither of them spoke. Then Darius dropped his gaze. "You go to kill her, then?" he asked, his exotic features, swathed in cloth, revealing little of his mood.

"No," Nicholas answered, as he let a slight smile play upon his lips. "I go to marry her."

Chapter Two

Nicholas was vaguely aware of the rapid rise of his pulse, but he did not seek to slow it with his usual discipline. Not this time. He had pushed himself and his men to reach the nunnery in ten days, and he was going to savor the small surge of satisfaction that filled him as he awaited his bride.

Victory was nearly his! Victory over the demons that had haunted him for years, that had destroyed the life of an optimistic young knight, changing his path forever. Finally, he would claim his revenge, and then, mayhap, he would be whole again.

Darius settled in behind him, and Nicholas slanted a glance at the Syrian. As usual, Darius's face was an enigmatic mask, but Nicholas sensed his disapproval. Darius was far more chivalrous than any knight, and Nicholas knew he did not care for a scheme that involved a woman. Already he had pushed the boundaries of their relationship by asking Nicholas what came after the vengeance. Nicholas had not deigned to answer; he did not let himself think that far ahead. She was to be his wife, and unless she proved herself too frail for that task, he would have many years in which to exact payment from the last of Hexham's line.

Gillian, she was called. Nicholas pictured her in his mind—a smaller, female version of his enemy, with Hex-

ham's blue-black hair and the pasty-white skin of the idle.
Convent-bred she was, too, Nicholas thought with contempt. He knew the type: delicate and helpless. He had only
to look at the woman who headed the order to confirm his
beliefs. Small and bent, the abbess moved with the slow-
ness of age, but had risen to do his bidding immediately. It
would be easy enough to shape such a creature to his will,
and he looked forward to it.

"I would wed as soon as she arrives," Nicholas said,
hiding his eagerness behind an impassive expression.

"But that is impossible, my lord!" the abbess protested,
her lined face easily showing her dismay. "Father Goode has
gone to visit his ailing sister, so the nearest priest is in Lit-
ton, a good day's ride from here."

In deference to the nun, Nicholas bit back his oath. Then
he turned to the burly man who flanked him, along with
Darius. "Renfred, fetch the priest," he ordered tersely.

"Aye, my lord."

"And have him back here tomorrow."

"Aye, my lord," Renfred said, grinning evilly. He moved
quickly, ducking through the arched entranceway just as
three more women appeared.

"Ah, Gillian," the abbess said, and Nicholas felt a rush
of excitement. She was here! But which one was she?

All three wore the black robes and white wimples of their
calling and kept their faces lowered in a deferential manner
that made it hard to see their features. The only apparent
difference between them was the height of the middle one,
who towered over the other two. Studying her closely,
Nicholas was startled by her sudden, sharp glance of curiosity as she and her companions filed in and took seats on
a worn bench.

"Gillian, dear, I have good news for you," the abbess
said, and again the tall one lifted her head, her bright eyes

shifting quickly toward the speaker. Surely that brazen creature was not his bride, Nicholas thought. Perhaps she simply lacked the manners that the other two exhibited with their discreet silence.

"The king has sent you a husband," the old woman continued, her voice trembling with age—or was it trepidation? Nicholas glanced back at the bold one again. Her gaze was fixed firmly on the abbess, and what he could see of her face showed not meek submission, but determined dissent. She certainly did not act like any nun he had ever seen.

"I do not believe it. Why would Edward have any interest in me?" she said, and Nicholas felt a sharp stab of awareness. This tall, rebellious creature was Gillian Hexham?

"'Tis true, my dear," the old woman said, speaking gently. "The king sent word of your uncle's death, and that you were to marry Lord de Laci to unite the lands."

The girl's gaze swept over Nicholas in a swift assessment that he found both unseemly and oddly exhilarating. Aye, Gillian, know your master and weep, he thought grimly, and he let her see a glimpse of his triumph.

She did not flinch, but met his hard look with one of her own, and he saw that she was younger than he had expected. No child, to be sure, but neither was she old. Eighteen years, Nicholas judged, give or take, and she was not ugly, or even plain. Her face was a creamy oval, her skin clear, her nose small and pert, her mouth well formed. And her eyes... They were not Hexham's black, but a deep green, and they were burning with a cold fire. Abruptly she glanced away, dismissing Nicholas with a contempt that stunned him.

"You knew of this, but informed me not?" she asked, turning on the abbess. Her voice betrayed strong emotion that Nicholas could only guess was despair, but that, oddly enough, sounded more like repressed fury. This female was convent-bred?

"Now, Gillian..." the abbess said, and Nicholas's attention was caught by the movement of the two other women, who exchanged wary glances, just as though they expected some outburst from his bride.

They were not to be disappointed. "Do not patronize me!" Gillian said, rising to her feet. "You received word, but you failed to tell me. Were you afraid that I would run away and lose you a fat purse from this popinjay?" she cried, pointing a finger at Nicholas.

Popinjay? The casually flung insult inflamed Nicholas, and he had to gain control of himself, lest he beat her here and now, when she was not yet his wife. Only great strength of will kept him from moving, but he held still, his features impassive, while his blood boiled and his hands itched to reach for her. Later. Later she would suffer for her words, and more...

The nuns gasped in horror, while the old woman stepped forward with a placating smile. "Gillian, you know that gold holds no sway with me. If you would but take the time to think, you would see that I have your best interests at heart. You have not been happy here, but now you have a chance for a new life. Take it, child, with God's blessing."

"I would be more inclined to view this news as good fortune if you had deigned to share it, instead of keeping it from me. I suspect that you did not let me know the truth for fear I would try to escape."

Escape? What kind of woman was she, to babble such nonsense? Did she truly think to defy the king? "Enough!" Nicholas said sharply, astounded that she dared raise her voice in a convent. "It matters not when you were told. We are to be wed, and you have no choice."

She whirled toward him, and the other nuns reached out for her, murmuring soothingly, but she shook them off and walked forward until she stood directly in front of Nicholas.

"There are always choices, my lord," she snapped, and Nicholas was stunned to silence by the enmity flashing in those green eyes. What cause had she to hate him? *He* was the one who had been ill-used, first by her uncle and now by her sharp tongue! Then she turned and stalked from the room, without waiting for the dismissal of her lord or her abbess.

Nicholas was not even aware that he moved, but suddenly he was at the door, Darius holding firm to his arm. "Let her go for now," the Syrian said, his voice low and pleading for reason.

Startled by his own loss of control, Nicholas drew back. His blood was pounding so fiercely that it took an effort for him to gain mastery over it. And so it became a small victory simply to hold his position and not give chase to Gillian Hexham like some herder after an errant pig.

"Forgive her, my lord," the abbess urged. "Gillian is impetuous, a bit headstrong, even, but she will come around. She simply needs some time to grow accustomed to the idea."

Amazed at the depth of his rage, Nicholas breathed slowly, seeking his vaunted discipline before he spoke. "Why did you not let her know that I was coming, so that this display might have been avoided?"

The abbess did not meet his penetrating stare, but turned her head away, forcing Nicholas to wonder whether Gillian had spoken the truth. Would she flee, rather than wed him? But why? She had no notion of his hatred or of what lay between her uncle and himself. The abbess had told him that Hexham had taken no interest in his niece save to tuck her away in the convent, and that no communication had passed between them in the years since. Gillian could hardly be devoted to a man she had never even met.

An oddly unsettling notion took root in Nicholas's fevered brain, and he watched the abbess closely for her response. "Has she a lover nearby? Or some tie that would make her refuse to leave here?"

The nuns gasped at his plain language. "No, no, my lord, I assure you that Gillian has nothing holding her here. 'Tis only her own strong will, my lord," the abbess answered. Her reply filled him with a strange relief, which Nicholas put down to a desire not to be cuckolded.

"She is stubborn, my lord," one of the nuns whispered.

"She dislikes anything that is not her idea," the other one said, her face pinched with disapproval.

"She has had a hard life, my lord," the first nun added.

"In a convent?" Nicholas asked, not bothering to hide his disbelief.

"After her father died, she and her mother were forced to live very meagerly, and then her mother, too, passed on. She was cast adrift until her uncle finally sent funds for her to join us here," the abbess explained.

Cast adrift? "What do you mean? Where did she live?"

"She took shelter with a burgher's family, as little more than a servant."

Wonderful. His wife had been as one lowborn. Oddly enough, the thought of her trials did not give Nicholas pleasure, perhaps because they had been brought on by fate, and not by himself. Perverse as it might seem, he wanted to be the sole source of distress to Gillian Hexham.

"She hardly seems subservient," he commented dryly.

"She is a good girl, my lord, but lacks the proper disposition for the holy life. Perhaps she is better suited to be a chatelaine," the abbess suggested, with a gleam in her eye.

Nicholas frowned. If the old woman was likening Gillian's behavior to that of her betters, she was sadly mistaken. The ill-mannered creature little resembled any lady he knew. His sister, Aisley, never raised her voice, and she was the most regal of females.

Nicholas nearly laughed at the comparison. His tiny, fairhaired sister was nothing like this green-eyed jade. Convent-bred, indeed! Obviously, the old woman could not control her flock, but Nicholas would put the fear of God into Gillian Hexham quickly enough.

The ghost of a smile flickered at the corners of his mouth as he contemplated his revenge. By faith, by the time he was done with her, Gillian would look back on her past with longing. Aye, she would envy even a peasant's meager lot!

Gillian rushed to the dormitory in which she slept, frantically wondering how much time she had. Soon it would be time for vespers, and her absence from prayers would be noticed. Oh, why her? And why now, when she had finally resigned herself to the convent? Suddenly the existence she had viewed as stifling and regimented seemed wholly satisfying.

It was her own fault. She had become complacent and bored with her lot, forgetting that the very same walls that hemmed her in kept the outside world at bay. She had never fit in here, lacking the patience and commitment that was needed to answer a holy calling, but she had been clothed and fed and, most of all, kept safe.

Too late, she remembered that a life outside the convent was fraught with dangers. Poverty, starvation, degradation and horrors too evil to contemplate lay but a short walk down the road. And Gillian knew most of them well. Swiftly she considered her choices while she gathered together her bedding—small payment for her years of service.

Already she could feel the breathlessness that took her when she was frightened. How long had it been since she had been forced to struggle for air? It all came back to her now: the hunger that had gnawed at her belly too often, the cold that had chilled her to the bone, the grimy smell of a body too long between baths and the frustration that had never found surcease.

Gillian's hand stilled as she sucked in a harsh breath. It did not have to be like that again! She was older and wiser now, with many skills to her name. Surely she could become a servant in a respectable home. No, she thought, with a shudder, it would have to be something else. Although the guilds kept a stranglehold on most of the trades, the city must have other jobs that would keep her out of harm's way.

Tossing in her meager belongings, Gillian yanked the linens into a knot, then slipped out of her room. Although she knew she ought to take food with her, she could hardly dare the kitchens. Obviously, several of the nuns were aware of her situation, and they might expect her to bolt. Unfortunately, she was not known for her cool head, and now she rued her reputation.

Deciding that the doorways might be watched, Gillian snuck toward a window. It was a good drop to the ground, but there was no help for it, she thought, gazing down at the grass below. She had no time to dither; she had to get away before *he* came after her.

Long ago, she had dreamed of a family of her own, of a husband who did not waste his coins, as her father had. A shopkeeper, a knight... Gillian smiled humorlessly. Even then, she had not aspired as high as the de Lacis, famous throughout the country for their wealth!

Gillian could still hardly believe that she, lowly daughter to an unsuccessful second son, was betrothed to the owner of Belvry. Although she had long since changed her mind about marriage, still Gillian might have been tempted, if the man had been kind and gentle and patient. A man who would not frighten her with his brute strength, or...

Gillian shuddered again, for *he* was none of those things. One look at that face—so handsome, yet so implacable— and those strange eyes filled with hatred had settled her mind. She had no idea why he despised her. Perhaps he did not want to wed her, or harbored some grudge against her uncle; the reason mattered not. She knew only that his icy gray gaze frightened her far more than a flight into the unknown. She had managed once before on her own, and she would do it again, rather than face a life with that one! Tossing her bundle to the ground, she swung a leg over the stone and jumped.

The fall knocked the breath from her, and Gillian lay on her back, gasping for air. Luckily, the grass was soft beneath her, but she gingerly wiggled her fingers and toes, just to make sure that she had suffered nothing more than a few bruises. She was sprawled in an unladylike pose, her legs apart, her gown hiked up to her knees, her wimple askew, yet it hardly mattered. Her days of strict decorum were over, she thought, smiling slightly.

That was when she saw him.

He was standing a few feet from the top of her head, so that he looked upside down to her, and so close that she could have reached out to touch his boots, below the rich material of his long tunic. The thought startled her, and she jerked her eyes upward. His hands were fisted against his slim hips, and above his wide shoulders, his face was dark with contempt, those silver eyes like the points of twin daggers.

"If you were trying to kill yourself, you should have picked a higher window," he commented. For a moment, Gillian could only lie there, staring up at him, so stunned was she by his words. What kind of monster was he to make such a twisted jest?

"I will make sure that the ones in your room at Belvry are barred," he said, the low purr of promise in his voice making the threat sound serious. Gillian sat up abruptly then, tugging at her skirts and twisting around—the better to see her enemy. His lips were curved into the ghost of a smile, as if her discomfiture pleased him well, and Gillian's blood ran cold.

"Resign yourself to your fate," he said softly, "for tomorrow we wed."

He had not locked her in, for there was no need. No woman, not even Gillian Hexham, could get by his men, Nicholas thought with grim satisfaction. He lay with his arms crossed behind his head on a hard pallet in one of the small cells reserved for visitors, content that on the morrow she would be his.

But what a strange creature she was! Nicholas could not understand why she would flee the convent with nothing but a change of clothing rather than marry him. And to jump out a window! The stupid wench could have broken her neck, and then where would he be? She would not rob him of his revenge, as Hexham had done!

Nay, he would see to it that she did not endanger herself again, foolish chit. She obviously needed a firm hand to keep her from such escapades, Nicholas thought, clearly remembering the absurd picture she had made sprawled upon the ground. Some of her hair had escaped, spilling like molten fire from her wimple. Red it was, bright and clean, and Nicholas wondered what it would look like loose. He had yet to really see her, although she had given him a glimpse of shapely calves, the way she had displayed herself on the grass, her legs wide open like a whore's....

Taking a slow breath, Nicholas shifted, bringing his arms down to his sides and firmly crushing such thoughts. What mattered to him the color of her locks or the manner of her form? She was nothing to him but a tool for his revenge.

Yes, Gillian Hexham would soon be his wife, but Nicholas wanted no part of her body. Although he had seen many a man fall prey to that feminine trap, slave to their own desires, he had never let passion rule him. Hexham's niece would not gain mastery over him in any way.

She might as well have taken her final vows, Nicholas thought, his lips curling at the irony, for she would never know his touch, nor any other man's. And that small deprivation would be just the beginning . . .

"My lord?"

The voice broke into his thoughts, seemingly out of nowhere, and Nicholas could have cursed his own inattention. Without a sound, his fingers closed over the dagger at his hip. Although he had removed his tunic, he had left his girdle in place, and now he was glad, for even a convent held its dangers, it would seem. As he had learned long ago, nowhere was safe, and no one—not even a nun, apparently— could be trusted.

Nicholas glanced toward the low opening, which had no door or covering, but he could see nothing in the darkness except the vague shape of a bent figure. He moved swiftly into a low crouch.

"No! Please, stay where you are. It is I, Abbess Wright." The old woman's voice came low and oddly breathless as she stepped back behind the entrance, cold, thick stone separating her from his sight. "I wanted to have a word with you privately."

At this hour? Despite her vows, Nicholas might have suspected her of seeking out his male flesh, but the abbess was far too old for such sport. "What is it?" he whispered.

"'Tis a most delicate matter, my lord, that I could not easily say to your face."

Better to sneak up on him in the middle of the night and risk a knife in her gullet? Nicholas wondered at her reasoning, but did not send her away, for her office allowed her some respect—and some allowances. "Go on," he said.

"It is about Gillian, my lord. I would beg you not to treat her ill."

Annoyance flared. "She is to be my wife, and no longer your concern," Nicholas replied dismissively.

"Yes, my lord, but I would not have you... force yourself upon her person."

What the devil? Was the abbess giving him advice upon his marital duties? "You do not want me to consummate the marriage?" he asked, incredulous.

"Not until your heart has warmed to her, my lord."

"Forgive me if I am confused, Abbess," Nicholas said, not bothering to disguise his sarcasm, "but doesn't the church demand that wedding vows be consummated?"

"I would only remind you that rape is a sin," the abbess said, a bit vehemently.

"There is no such thing as rape between man and wife!" Nicholas snapped. His amusement at lying half-naked in a darkened convent cell, discussing sex with a nun faded, replaced by rising annoyance.

"Nevertheless, the Lord sees and knows all, and he will judge accordingly!" The old woman's voice broke, and Nicholas reigned in his spleen with some difficulty.

"Abbess, what makes you think I would rape my bride?" he asked, as mildly as he could.

"I have seen the hatred in your eyes when you look at her!" The words rang out clearly, an accusation that he could not deny, and then a rustle of skirts signaled the abbess's departure. Astonished by her behavior, Nicholas stared at the opening to his cell, wondering if all holy women were as mad as those to be found here.

Cursing silently at the folly of females, he lay back down upon his hard pallet, struggling against the pain in his belly. If the old woman had not had the effrontery to scold him, Nicholas might have assured her that he had no intention of bedding his wife.

He had much worse planned for her.

Nicholas knew a heady triumph he had not felt since he had destroyed Hexham's army and given chase to his enemy. They had never faced each other, never engaged in personal combat, since Hexham had fled like the coward he was, but now Nicholas stood beside the bastard's niece, before a priest who would make them man and wife. And then she would be his....

She was wearing her black nun's garb, and Nicholas felt a stab of annoyance. Had she no other clothes? Probably not, for she had no money of her own. And then he wondered at his perversity. What cared he what she wore? If she liked fine things, he would keep her in rags, and if she wanted to wear drab garments, then he would dress her in finery. His lips curled in anticipation.

His bride was not as tall as Nicholas had first thought, for the top of her head reached only to his chin. He watched it now, wondering about the hair that lay hidden, and then let his gaze rove over her features: delicately arched brows over thick-lashed eyes, creamy cheeks, and lips of the deepest rose. They were gently curved, and yet, even when she was prompted, they remained silent. With a tingle of surprise, Nicholas realized that she was hesitating over her vows, and he moved closer, menacing her without a word.

Although Nicholas expected her to be firmly cowed by his movement, she glanced up at him in challenge, just as if she dared him to threaten her. Their eyes locked, and he tried to force her to speak through sheer strength of will, but she did not flinch. Nay, Nicholas had the distinct impression that she would have spat in his face, if she could. But she could not, and, ultimately, no matter how fierce her pride, he would be the victor. The knowledge made him smile, and she looked away from his triumph, fairly snarling her vows to the startled father.

Her bravery took him aback, if truth be told, for his years in the East had made Nicholas value courage above all else. How odd to find such a staunch heart beating in Hexham's heir. Nicholas caught himself studying her curiously and glanced away, telling himself that her actions were born of foolishness, not valor.

As soon as the priest had finished, Nicholas turned his back on his bride in blatant dismissal. "We leave at once," he told the startled abbess.

"Come, wife, say your goodbyes," he snapped, hoping to dismay her with their abrupt departure. But she only gave him a stony-faced nod. Nor did she weep any farewells. Indeed, she stunned him, yet again, by walking past the nuns without a word. Faith, she was an unnatural female!

For a moment, Nicholas stared after her as she stepped toward the doors, head held high, but then he returned his attention to the abbess. "Have no fear, I will not touch her," he said, jeering.

The old woman did not seem relieved by his assurance. Indeed, her wrinkled face showed only consternation, and she reached out toward him with a trembling hand. "Now, my lord, I know that Gillian is not as fair as some, but God tells us to go forth and multiply."

Nicholas fixed her with a glare. His bride's beauty, plain for all to see, was not the issue. "That is not what you said last night," he reminded her with a sneer.

"Last night?" The old woman appeared flustered, or was she confused? Perhaps she did not care to be reminded of her unseemly visit to his quarters, he thought, but when she lifted her pale eyes to his, Nicholas saw only bewilderment. Suspicion pierced him like a blade, and without volition, he swiveled toward the doors.

She was standing outside, by her palfrey, her back to him. He knew, without a doubt, that it was Gillian who had come to him in the night. She had snuck through the darkened convent to his cell, pretended to be the abbess and made a fool of him, right enough!

When Nicholas thought of the red-haired minx giving him advice as to the bedding of her, his blood boiled. Faith, was there nothing she would not dare? Slowly, as he gained control of his anger, his outlook altered, his lips curving slightly with satisfaction. Although she was not at all what he had expected, perhaps that was all to the good.

Have at your tricks, then, vixen, Nicholas told her in a silent challenge. *The war has just begun.*

Chapter Three

Nicholas had driven them hard until dusk, and he took satisfaction in seeing the little nun stumble from her mount, barely able to walk after the journey. He and his men were well used to such travels, but Gillian would have done little riding at the convent.

Now her head was bent over her supper in what Nicholas could only assume was exhaustion. In another woman, he would have thought the pose a sign of submission, but not so with this one. He suspected that she would not reveal even this small weakness, if she knew he was watching from underneath the trees.

She was a strange creature, but a worthy opponent, Nicholas decided. Aye, in the brief time he had known her, she had shown more courage by far than her worthless uncle! Nicholas's eyes narrowed. Only her midnight visit to him at the convent smacked of Hexham's deviousness, and he had yet to discover the reason for that foolery. Still, it served to remind him that treachery and deceit ran in her blood, and he had best not turn his back on her, wife or no.

The knowledge fueled his hatred for her, and Nicholas stepped forward, impatient to torment her. She had eaten more than enough already. Indeed, he was beginning to wonder where all that food was going. His bride might be

taller than most women, but she was certainly not 'fat. Yet
he had been finished for some time, and still she continued
to feed. Perhaps she sought to delay speech with him, he
mused, his lip curling. The suspicion urged him on, and he
stalked to where she sat by the fire and stood over her in
purposeful intimidation.

"Have you had your fill, wife?" he asked.

She stiffened and straightened her drooping shoulders,
her chin lifting imperceptibly, and Nicholas spared a bit of
admiration for her strength. It was quickly replaced by annoyance, however, when she refused to look at him.

"No," she answered, sharp as a fishmonger's wife. Then
she took another bite of bread, without even bothering to
acknowledge his lordship over her.

Her impudence made him bristle. "Whether you wished
it or no, I am your husband now, and I say you are finished," he snapped, reaching for her trencher.

She glanced up at him then, her green eyes flashing contempt. "Would you starve me, my lord?" She spat the ap-
pellation at him as though it were a curse.

"Ha! 'Twould be hard to waste away on what you have
put in your belly this night!" Nicholas replied. Then he
paused, as if to reconsider her suggestion. "But 'tis a notion, wife. Perhaps I will, if you do not please me."

Instead of lashing out at him, as he expected, she released the trencher and dropped her gaze to her lap. Did she
think to ignore him? Nicholas would not allow it. He took
her chin in his hand and raised it, forcing her to meet his
eyes. The antagonism he had come to know greeted him, but
something else lurked in those green depths.

Fear. Nicholas could almost smell it. Her nostrils flared,
and her breasts began rising and falling rapidly with the
force of each breath. Despite her bravado, the vixen was
terrified, for the first time since he had met her. Why now?

Nicholas wondered briefly, before the answer came to him, clear and swift.

The bedding. This daredevil who had braved her abbess, his wrath and a leap from a convent window was afraid of doing her marital duty. She had come to him last night begging him to spare her body not out of whimsy, to make him look the fool, but because she was frightened of his lust.

His first reaction was to feel insulted. Nicholas never made an effort to please women, his de Laci looks had always guaranteed female attention, more than he wanted, in fact. And although he did not pride himself on any particular skills, those he took to his bed had never complained of their treatment there.

Nicholas could feel her pulse beneath his finger, racing wildly, but not with anticipation. Why should he be offended? He had sought to torment her, and he had succeeded. His proud, defiant wife was scared to death. Nicholas told himself the means did not matter.

But, somehow, it did.

Nicholas released her chin, and though she made an effort to keep it from falling, her bold stance was gone. Her fists were closed so tightly that her knuckles had gone white from the strain, yet Nicholas took no delight in the sight. Her discomfiture was strangely affecting, and without thinking, Nicholas took her wrists and drew them forward.

She flinched, but he held them fast and gently ran his thumbs across the fleshy part of her palm until her fingers unfurled like a reluctant blossom. Her nails had left marks so deep that Nicholas was surprised they had not drawn blood. Slowly he moved his thumbs over the punctured skin, wondering when last he had touched another person.

He could not remember ever holding a woman's hands, though there was something oddly compelling about the act. Gillian's were soft, yet strong, with blunt-tipped fingers that had seen their share of work. Nicholas stared at them, fascinated by their form and feel, and continued stroking until he heard a strangled sound. He glanced up, startled by the stunned look on her face, and released her abruptly.

"Get to your bed, wife," he snapped. Turning on his heel, Nicholas stalked away, but he felt her gaze following him until he gained the cover of the trees. Then a flurry of noise told him that she ran, stumbling, to her tent.

Stupid wench! Refusing to look at her, Nicholas remained where he was until she had settled down. What the devil had possessed him? His efforts to bully her had turned into something else entirely, although Nicholas was not sure what. She was his enemy! And he had best remember it. He tried, concentrating on the hatred that he had long nurtured, but his stomach rebelled, burning with a fire brighter than that which lit the camp.

Although he wanted to bend over in agony, Nicholas forced himself to remain still. It would be better soon, for he usually gained some ease after eating, and meanwhile he could do naught but wait.

"Why do you not rape her?"

The words, more than Darius's voice, made Nicholas start, and he swiveled to stare at his companion, his eyes narrowing into slits. The Syrian was seated against a tree, blending in with the shadows as if he were one with them.

"Obviously it is the girl's worst fear, else why last night's charade?" Darius asked, his face expressionless.

"You heard her?"

"She made enough noise about it," Darius answered. "I also saw the abbess when you talked with her this morning. The holy woman knew nothing of it, did she?"

Nicholas shook his head, thoughtfully. "'Twas the little nun, masquerading as her better." He sank down to his haunches, trying vainly to soothe the ache in his belly.

"Then why not rape her? You said you would find that which she feared most and make her suffer it. Why do you dally? We are far from any aid. No one will heed her screams. Perhaps you would like the men to watch?"

Nicholas frowned in annoyance, for he was not fooled by Darius's cool suggestions. The Syrian disliked Nicholas's plans for his bride, and so would force them down his throat. "I want her not," Nicholas retorted.

"Why? She has not the beauty of the women of my lands, but—"

Nicholas cut him off, his head filled with the memory of blazing green eyes and slender hands alive beneath his own. "She is comely enough," he muttered.

"Why, then? Does not every Frank sire himself an heir at all costs?"

"I want no child, especially not one with Hexham's tainted blood!" Nicholas snapped. "Nor will I surrender to the vixen any part of me—not even my seed!"

Refusing to elaborate, Nicholas glared his companion into silence. Darius's experience with women was expansive; he loved them freely and then moved on without a qualm. None ever really touched him, so he was not wary of their wiles, but Nicholas had seen other men, seemingly intelligent and reasonable beings, succumb to the pleasures to be had in a woman's bed. A man's body too easily ruled over his head, and Nicholas would never let that happen to him.

Unwilling to share his reasoning with one who would not understand, Nicholas remained sullen and quiet. Beside him, the Syrian was still, his dark expression unchanging, but those eyes, blacker than the night, seemed to probe into Nicholas's soul, seeking out his secrets.

Swearing, Nicholas looked away, unwilling to let the other man see too closely. "'Tis more of a torment to make her

wait and wonder and suffer her fear,'' he said, telling himself, as well, that he took grim satisfaction in her terror.

Married but one day, and he had already found a way to
bring his arrogant bride to her knees! Nicholas sought the
heady rush of victory that he had so coveted, but all he felt
was a twisting ache in his gut that would not go away.

Gillian tried to breathe slowly, concentrating on the air
that moved into her body and out again, lest she become a
gasping wreck, unable to feed her own lungs. Coward, that
she should lie here immobilized by fright! And all over
something that other women did easily enough.

She knew what was going to happen, of course. Her
master, Abel Freemantle, had told her more than once, de-
scribing it in graphic detail as he groped her. Gillian shuddered, gasping at the memory of the fat, dirty burgher
loosening his braies to show off his wick, a horrid little red
thing that Gillian could hardly believe capable of all that he
claimed.

Yet, if what Freemantle had said was true, then she could
expect her husband to bare his part, too, and do more than
talk about it. Gillian tried to imagine Nicholas de Laci pulling down his braies for her, and she shivered, suddenly hot
inside and cold without. Shutting her eyes tight, she hoped
to block out the image of him, so terrible and yet so beautiful.

Oh, she was not oblivious of his appeal! No woman could
be, for though Nicholas de Laci acted like a heartless fiend
there was nothing harsh about his features. His thick sweep
of hair, so dark as to be nearly black, was always smooth
falling perfectly to his shoulders, in sad contrast to her own
wild mane.

His brows were finely arched over eyes the color of silver, his cheeks smooth above the shadow of new beard and

his lips curved nicely under a deep indentation that made her heart trip, whether she willed it or no. His nose, not aquiline, was nonetheless well formed and kept his face from looking feminine, though none would ever confuse him with a woman.

Nicholas de Laci was distinctly, deliberately male, from the way he moved to the hard lines of his strong, tall body, from the deep timbre of his smooth voice to the flicker of his dark lashes. In fact, he seemed to possess more masculine appeal than Gillian had ever imagined possible. She suspected that any number of women had gladly lain awaiting the lord in his bed, for he was not only handsome, but clean, and he smelled not of horses and sweat, but of some exotic essence all his own.

Although he did not fit the descriptions of the flattering, courtly heroes of the ballads, he could be…less severe than she had come to expect. When he grasped her wrists, Gillian had thought for one terrifying moment that he was going to tie her up, but instead he had taken her hands in his, running his thumbs over her palms until she felt a strange quickening. Just the memory of his dark head bent over her and the slow caress of his fingers drew a moan from her such as the one that had erupted from her throat at the time, dispelling the odd mood that had settled over him.

Gillian hugged herself. His gentleness had disappeared as swiftly as it came, leaving her with naught but his usual cold fury. Nicholas de Laci would save his tenderness for other women, while serving her only the icy splinters of his hatred.

And that, Gillian suspected, would be the worst of what awaited her. Not only would he violate her body this night, but he would try to despoil her soul, too, with the force of the malevolence that lurked inside his beautiful frame.

Yet Gillian had no choice but to lie and wait, her fright feeding upon itself, deep into the night. Her exhausted, aching flesh begged for respite from her day of riding, but her eyes remained wide open, her breathing swift and ragged, until finally she heard something above the roaring of her own blood in her ears.

"Rest, my lady, for your husband sleeps. He will not come to you."

Gillian jerked her head up in response, for there had been no footfall, no sound of approach. Was she imagining things, or had someone spoken? It must be the foreigner, she decided, for who else would bring her tidings of peace? He was a strange one, but so were all males, she thought as she finally relaxed.

None, however, were quite as terrible or as beautiful as her husband.

He was watching her. Gillian could feel those silver eyes boring into her, and her cheeks burned with frustration. It was bad enough that she was forced to ride until her muscles screamed for relief, but on top of that misery, she had to suffer his predatory gaze. All day she had felt it pricking her, disrupting her thoughts.

Although aching and weary, she had tried to assess her situation and make some sort of decision about the future, without much success. Gillian was not one for planning; she knew that the best of schemes were all too easily overturned. Life threw things at you, and the most you could hope to do was endure.

And she had. Gillian was a survivor. She told herself firmly that she had already abided worse things than this unwanted marriage. She even knew that some women would be thrilled to find themselves wed to a young, handsome, wealthy knight, despite his evil disposition. Some were even drawn to cold, cruel men, but not Gillian. She recognized the evil fiend lurking beneath that beautiful exterior.

What, then, could she do? Her first instinct to flee returned, but now was not the time to do it, when surrounded by his men on the road, her location unknown. No doubt she would have a better chance of escaping when they reached their destination.

Still, the idea did not sit well with her. Somehow, she felt as if Nicholas de Laci had thrown down his gauntlet in challenge, and she would be a coward to run from it. She had always faced her troubles; it was not her way to hide from them.

All her life, Gillian had tried to make the best of every situation. She was not fatally optimistic or unrealistic, but she was determined not to fall into despair, as her mother had done, wasting away to nothing because of the follies of others.

With a sigh, Gillian realized that she was just going to have to reserve judgment until they arrived at wherever they were going. A lot depended upon *him*. Just how much did he hate her? How badly would he treat her? Perhaps his glares were brought on by her close proximity, and once among his people he would forget her. She shot a glance at him as they sat by the fire, hoping he would do just that.

During the day, he was not so frightening. He was just another mean master, albeit a handsome one, who drove them all on too far, too quickly, and wore his animosity toward her like a shield. All through the long ride, she had known naught but anger toward him, for she had done nothing to earn his enmity.

During the day, she had returned his dark glares with her own, had even possessed the temerity to answer his orders with tart replies. But now that twilight was settling around them, Gillian was not so sure of herself. She felt her nerves grow taut once again and her breath quicken.

During the day, Nicholas de Laci was simply a man, but when night fell, he became her husband and, as such, a creature to be feared for what he might do to her in the darkness. His evil looks took on a more sinister aspect, his face an unholy beauty that both repelled and attracted her.

Shuddering, Gillian nearly dropped the piece of meat she had plucked from the fire. Then, in her haste to retrieve it, she thrust it into her mouth too quickly and flinched as it burned her. Hurriedly she grabbed her cup and drank enough water to soothe her steaming throat.

"By faith, you make a pig of yourself," her husband commented from a few feet away from her. Although she suspected that she did appear unmannerly, Gillian tried to give him a ferocious look, but it was difficult to do while her eyes were watering.

He made a sound of disgust, then suddenly stilled. "You eat enough for two," he whispered, as if to himself. His face grew even more cold and frightful, and his eyes narrowed as they raked her from head to toe. "Are you with child?"

Gillian nearly choked at the question. Truly, he was a madman! "Aye, 'tis the way of things in a convent," she replied.

He stiffened at her snide answer, and she braced herself for his wrath, but he did not strike her. "It has been my experience that some of the so-called holy women wander the halls at night, seeking out male visitors. Indeed, did I not see you involved in such a game?" he asked, fairly purring with superiority.

Gillian's mouth popped open at the realization that he knew of her masquerade as the abbess. Obviously, he was more clever than she suspected, damn the fiend to hell!

"Do not try to lie to me or fool me, little nun," he snapped. "For you shall fail—and suffer for your efforts."

His voice, so deep and smooth in the darkness, sent shivers up Gillian's spine, but it was not his threats that startled her. Little? No one had called her little since she was a child. Yet this lord was a tall one, and she would have to lean back her head to look at him, if she ever desired to get that close....

"Why do you hate me?" Gillian asked, to remind herself just what lay between them. As she eyed him intently, she could tell by the flick of his lashes that her question surprised him, but he quickly recovered his disdain.

"Your blood, vixen. 'Tis tainted."

His forthright response annoyed her, though the answer was what she had expected. "And what manner of man was my uncle, that you worry his heir after his death?"

"He was a base coward, a thief, and a treacherous, murderous villain." The words were spoken with such cool conviction that they nearly took Gillian's breath away, and she watched, horrified, as his silver eyes came to life with the force of an enmity greater than she had ever imagined. Her heart sank under the weight of it.

Entreaty was hopeless, and yet she made the effort anyway. "But I am blameless," she reasoned. "I knew him not. I have never even set eyes upon him."

"He sent money for you to join the convent."

"Yes," Gillian said, bitterness creeping into her voice. "To be rid of me . . . because he did not want me, as no one ever wanted me." Too late, she realized how much of herself she had revealed, and she would have taken back her words. This man seated so close to her might be possessed of an angel's face and form, but he was a devil who despised her. Better not to give him any part of herself, else she find it used to destroy her at the first opportunity.

In an effort to distract him from her slip of the tongue, Gillian threw a stick on the fire and watched it flare, the flames reaching up to light his flawless features. She realized that he could have taken anyone to wife, but now was stuck with her, a stranger who would serve as a constant reminder of some past grievance. No wonder he was angry.

"What of your father, Hexham's brother?" he asked.

"What of him?"

"Did you love him?" His eyes narrowed, as if the thought displeased him, and Gillian did not know whether to give him lie or truth, for she suspected this man was much more adept at twisting words and thoughts to his own ends than herself.

"No," she finally answered, honestly. "He was a wastrel and a spendthrift, losing any coin that he might gain, with no care for his wife or family. So you see, there is nothing between him or his brother and myself. Why punish me for their sins?"

For a moment, he looked uncomfortable, as if something pained his strong warrior's body, but then his eyes glittered with unmistakable malice. "You are his heir. You are all that is left."

The words, spoken so matter-of-factly, made Gillian catch her breath, and the look on his face as he uttered them frightened her far more than any threat. She realized that Nicholas de Laci lived for naught but revenge, and the knowledge filled her with despair.

"What will you do with me?" Gillian asked. Her heart pounded with trepidation, for she knew full well that he could do whatever he pleased—send her away, lock her in a dungeon, starve her, beat her—and no one would say a thing to him. As his wife, she was his chattel.

The convent, with its boredom and toil, was looking better by the minute, and her handsome husband more terrible than she had ever dreamed.

"Do not be in a hurry to discover your future, little nun, for we have many long years ahead of us," he said, smiling grimly at the taunt.

His words, coupled with the promise in his tone, made Gillian's blood run cold, and she put aside her trencher, her hunger forgotten. How could she ever have thought to make the best of this marriage? It was impossible!

"I am tired," she said, suddenly eager to get away from his stifling presence. "You will excuse me?" She expected refusal, for he was nothing if not recalcitrant, yet he nodded curtly. Gillian understood why when she saw the glow of triumph in his eyes. With a gasp of fury, she rose and stomped off, the sound of his laughter following her to the tent.

Gillian's pride smarted at his successful intimidation, and she would have marched right back to face him, were she not so fearful that he would join her soon enough. Each breath became a struggle as she contemplated the ill-usage that she was certain would come this night. Now that she knew the depths of her husband's hatred, Gillian expected the worst sort of violence from him. She knew about rape, had seen its effects, yet she could do nothing but lie waiting for it.

Not until she heard the Syrian's soft assurance did Gillian sleep at last, and then it was only to toss and turn restlessly, caught in dreams of Nicholas de Laci's face, brightened by the fire's flames, just like that of the devil himself.

Chapter Four

For once, Nicholas was rather annoyed by the circumspect greeting he received upon his return to Belvry. Although usually unconcerned with his home or his people, for some reason he now found himself wanting the little nun to be dutifully impressed. He told himself that she should do well to recognize his power and wealth, which was evidenced by the prosperous demesne and modern castle.

He did not bother to note that such things had never mattered to him before. Nor had the behavior of the members of his household, who suddenly seemed distant and wary to his eyes. In truth, they had been more taken with Piers, but Aisley's husband was a showy sort, given to great emotion, Nicholas thought with contempt.

The fools! They had no cause for complaint, for he was a good lord, knowledgeable and just. It was simply not his way to hold speech for the sake of talking or to visit his tenants for no reason or to throw a celebration upon every excuse, as his sister was wont to do since her marriage. Nay, he kept the castle in good repair, protected its residents and had an excellent steward who ran the place well.

And he was certain that was enough. Still, when Nicholas walked into his hall, he was aware of the silence that rippled like a wave through the great room, an odd quiet

that had not been evident in Piers's presence, or even in his
father's time.

Ignoring it, Nicholas stalked across the rush-strewn tiles
with Darius at his side. Refusing to look back to see his
bride's reaction, he told himself that he did not care what
she thought of his holdings. "I am for a bath," he said
without a glance at the expectant faces that surrounded him.

"I, as well," said his companion. "Will your new bride
do the duty? You have driven us hard and long, and I have
a mind to have her wash my weary body."

Darius's words stopped Nicholas in his tracks, and he
turned swiftly to meet the Syrian's inscrutable dark gaze. "Is
not that the way of your people?" Darius asked. "That the
lady of the castle bathe her guests?"

"Not the little nun," Nicholas snapped. "She is unaccustomed to such tasks." Suspecting the Syrian of toying
with him, Nicholas eyed his companion closely, but Darius's face gave away nothing. Nicholas pictured his naked
body, deep gold and gleaming, with Gillian bending over it.
His belly burned.

"She will be busy, attending her lord," Nicholas added,
giving Darius a warning glare for good measure. He glanced
back toward his wife, who trailed behind, gawking like a
peasant.

"Osborn!" he called, so sharply that the servant stum-
bled over himself hurrying to Nicholas's side. "See to my
lady wife!" Nicholas fairly spat the last word as he inclined
his head toward Gillian. At Osborn's startled nod, Nicholas said, "Take her to my chamber and provide her with hot
water."

Then he turned to Gillian. "Get yourself a bath, quickly,
for I want one, too, and I shall have you attend me." The
shock that passed over her lovely features gave him some
measure of satisfaction, but, as usual, she was too much

hidden by her ugly nun's garb for Nicholas's liking. He had
seen his fill of it. "And rid yourself of that black gown.
Osborn, find some of Aisley's old trunks and bring them to
the room. I wish my wife to be properly dressed."

As Osborn hurried her away, Nicholas felt more than a
little relief. She would attend no one but himself, by the
faith! The knowledge stirred his blood, and he watched her
as she left the hall, hips swaying gently beneath her heavy
garments. So intent was he upon his wife that he barely ac-
knowledged his steward, who came forward, offering ten-
tative congratulations.

Accustomed to keeping his own counsel, Nicholas saw no
need to share the facts of his marriage with anyone, so he
accepted their good wishes, but greeted any questions with
a silent scowl that discouraged further curiosity. And although he listened absently to their foolish chatter, his eyes
kept straying to the stairs that led up to his chamber.

A sudden eagerness flooded him at the thought of the
vixen washing his body. Of course, such duties would be
onerous to her, and Nicholas told himself that was why the
notion appealed to him; yet that could not fully explain his
impatience.

When he felt sufficient time had passed, Nicholas dis-
missed his people with a nod and slowly walked to the
curving stair. Once out of their sight, however, he took the
steps two at a time until he reached the top. Although the
great chamber had never held any particular allure for him
before, Nicholas rushed to the door and flung it wide,
without pausing to knock.

She turned, startled by the noise, and he could see that she
had, indeed, completed her toilet. In fact, while he watched,
she finished plaiting her wet locks into a fat braid that fell
over one shoulder. Her fingers were slim and nimble, and
her hair... Faith, even damp, it was a fiery color, like a

bright sunset, and ungodly thick and long, for his eyes followed it down below her breast.

She was wearing one of Aisley's gowns, a dark green that matched her eyes, but it was not right for her by any other means. Crafted to fit his sister's dainty, slender frame, it was too short and much too tight for his wife. Gillian was far more generously endowed, a fact that had been hidden under her shapeless clothing. *Far* more generously endowed, Nicholas realized as he stared at the bodice of the dress, where her breasts were flattened into two great mounds.

She must have hurried, for Nicholas thought he saw a patch of dampness where the linen was stretched taut. It looked as if it could accommodate nothing more without bursting at the seams, and yet Nicholas suddenly saw it ripple as her nipples hardened, creating two tiny points in the fabric.

He whirled away from the sight. "You will make yourself some clothes that fit," he ordered, hoarsely. His plans to robe his wife in rags were forgotten at the swift and sure knowledge that he not want her appearing below in such provocative garb as this.

Eyeing the still-steaming bath, Nicholas yanked off his boots. "Help me from my mail before the water is stone-cold," he snapped, and soon her hands, surprisingly strong, were lifting the coat from him. He tugged off his hose and his braies and stepped into the tub, but when he looked around, his wife was conspicuously absent.

"Well?" he snapped, irritated to discover that she had turned her back in some sort of misplaced modesty. "Get over here and do your duty!"

Her eyes flashed fire at him, and her braid bounced over her shoulder as she grabbed up a swatch of linen and the lump of soap. Well satisfied with his victory, Nicholas leaned forward, only to feel her begin scrubbing his back fiercely enough to take the skin off. What the devil?

His hand shot out to snare her wrist. "Gentle yourself, vixen, or else," he warned. Her green eyes clashed with his for a long moment, as if in a battle for supremacy, but finally they dropped away in sullen acquiescence. With an angry tug, she pulled her wrist from his hold and bent once more to her task yet this time, Nicholas felt no discomfort. Indeed, he began to enjoy himself thoroughly.

It had been years since he had been washed, if one did not count his months of helpless recovery in the Holy Land. He had no use for women, and certainly had never availed himself of their giggling presence in his bath. But this was different. Gillian was no flirting female or simpering maiden. Far from it, he thought with a smile, and he leaned back, taking pleasure in a welcome, though unexplained, respite from his stomach pain.

Obviously, the vixen had been a poor servant, for she made no effort to hide her dislike for waiting on him. Nicholas grinned, reveling in the scowl that marred her face. Although he had thought her skin creamy and clear, he could see now that a few freckles were scattered over her turned-up nose. However, they did not detract from her beauty, which struck him now with astonishing force. Was it the change from her black nun's garb, or had he simply never been near enough to observe it?

Slowly Nicholas let his gaze rove over her features. Her lashes were dark and thick, her cheeks flushed from anger or exertion, and wispy tendrils of bright hair were drying around her face. Amazing that she had turned out to be so lovely... Nicholas's reverie was interrupted by a vicious pull on his arm as she stretched it out and soaped it. Apparently she was trying to injure him, but her puny efforts were laughable.

She moved around him to take his other arm, and Nicholas caught a whiff of her scent. It was clean and heady, like wildflowers. It lingered in the steamy air, fresh and fragrant, teasing at his senses and robbing him of his brief tranquillity. The atmosphere changed, and as she bent close, he was no longer filled with triumph, but with an unnerving desire to reach out and touch the thick braid that fell down her back.

Tearing his gaze away from it, Nicholas looked down, but that view was worse. She was washing his chest, her strong fingers tangling in his hair as she spread the cloth over him, and he drew in a harsh breath as he watched her move lower, across his stomach, kneading his flesh, more slowly, more gently...

How long had it been since someone had touched him like this? He had never felt comfortable with close contact. Even his experiences with women were swift and sure, and yet he knew none of his usual repulsion now. Indeed, Nicholas felt heat spreading through him, filling him with sensation....

When her wrist brushed his upraised thigh, his calming bath suddenly was transformed into something else altogether by the reaction of his body, both immediate and unexpected. His blood ran hot and fierce, and his tarse stiffened and swelled, as if reaching for her, and for a moment he wanted nothing more than to feel those blunt fingers stroking him to release.

"Get out!" he shouted. Unwilling to let her see his response to her touch, Nicholas sat up, sloshing water over the sides in his hurry to hide the evidence from her gaze.

"What?" Gillian lifted her head, and Nicholas looked at her, only to feel himself grow even harder. Her ferocious scowl was gone, replaced by a rather dazed expression. Her skin had gone rosy, her lips were parted, and her green eyes were all soft and dark. Farther down, he could see the rapid rise and fall of her breasts in her too-tight bodice, her nipples outlined boldly by the damp fabric. She resembled nothing so much as a voluptuous dairymaid, ripe for a tumble.

"Get out!" Nicholas shouted again, and this time the order seemed to penetrate her dulled senses, for she dropped the soap and fled. The door slammed loudly behind her, and only then did Nicholas release the breath he had been holding. And only after firmly disciplining his thoughts did he gain control over his own body.

But just as he finally mastered himself, Nicholas realized that his wife was running around the castle in that shamelessly small gown and, if he was not mistaken, bare feet. To some randy knight on the prowl, she might have the look of a bold villein eager for a mounting. Although he had no intention of bedding her himself, Nicholas wanted no other man putting hands on his property. The very thought made his blood boil.

Cursing fluently, he climbed from the tub, dripping-wet, wrapped a linen cloth around his waist and flung open the door. His usual alertness was abandoned as he took after her, heedless of the slippery tiles beneath him. Without a thought as to how he might appear, Nicholas raced along the passage as fast as he could manage while still clutching his scant covering.

Suddenly, nothing else mattered but that he find her before someone else saw her as he had, before another man was tempted by her vixen's face and voluptuous body. As for himself, Nicholas put his own reaction down to exhaustion and the unusual circumstances of the bath.

He refused to consider the mortifying notion that he might be attracted to his wife.

* * *

Gillian ran into the first room that stood open. It was smaller than the great chamber, of course, but like all else here at Nicholas's home, it was quite luxurious. For once, however, Gillian did not stare in awe at the furniture and tapestries, but went straight to the window, where a lovely seat had been fashioned with brightly colored pillows. Throwing herself on them, Gillian put her head down upon her crossed arms and burst into tears.

She had not cried during her long years without privacy at the convent, but now, unleashed, Gillian's misery poured forth in wracking sobs. And it might have continued un-abated, if she had not heard a noise in between her gulps for air. Lifting her head in cautious curiosity, she was horrified to see an older woman, short and rounded, standing right beside her, cooing to her gently.

"There now," the woman said, reaching out to pat Gillian's shoulder consolingly. "Surely 'tis not as bad as all that. Here, tell Edith all about it, and you will feel better."

Gillian's embarrassment faded under the warmth in the stranger's gentle brown eyes. No one had comforted her, really, since her mother had passed on, and when Gillian found herself buried against the Edith's ample bosom, she let out her woe in a long wail. "I am a big, gawky, ugly thing, and he hates me!"

"Tsk, tsk... That is not so, my girl," Edith said. "You are tall, true enough, but you are neither fat nor ungainly. Here, let me take a look at you."

Sniffing loudly, Gillian stood up and waited while the woman assessed her, turning her this way and that under a discerning gaze. "Well, you have not the coloring of my Aisley, but that does not mean you are not lovely. Why, just look at your eyes, rare as emeralds, and such thick lashes!

And the color of your hair, bright as a flame, and enough to heat any man's passions, I'll warrant.''

Gillian blushed, unaccustomed to such plain speaking, or, indeed, flattery of any sort. "Aye, you would please any knight with that figure of yours, and many a lady would kill for your curves.''

Startled, Gillian looked down at her body in wonder. She had never received compliments before, and although she suspected that much of what the woman said was designed to comfort, still, she suddenly saw herself from a different perspective—no longer too big and too boldly colored, but unusual. Maybe even special.

"Now, who is the great fool who would make you feel other than the beautiful woman you are?'' Edith asked, clucking in disapproval.

Before Gillian could answer, the chamber door was thrown back on its hinges with a loud bang, and Nicholas filled the doorway.

He was dripping-wet and naked, but for a dampened linen cloth around his waist that did little to hide his magnificent body, and with a low gasp, Gillian took in the whole of him, beautiful and deadly and larger than life.

Strength was there, riding beneath his skin, not in great, lumpy bulges, but in smooth, well-delineated muscle in his arms and across his shoulders. And his chest! Gillian had never seen anything like it. All too well she remembered the feel of it beneath her fingers, smooth and hard and thick with curly dark hair that made something jump and quicken inside her. And below, what she had taken great pains to avoid looking at in his bath now was boldly outlined under the thin material.

Gillian stared. Although in repose, it did not resemble Master Freemantle's wick in the slightest, but rather more a stallion's nether parts. Abruptly Gillian glanced away, her face red, her breath coming quickly at the frightening size of him.

The deafening quiet that had descended upon the women at Nicholas's entrance was broken by Edith, who stepped in front of Gillian, as if to protect the younger, taller woman from the man who stood before them, glaring ferociously. "My lord Nicholas! What are you about, racing around without your clothes?"

Ignoring the older woman, Nicholas pinned Gillian with his glittering, hateful eyes. "Get to your chamber, wife!" he said. His tone, though low and even, was laced with threat, but Gillian was too outraged to beware.

"You just bellowed at me to get out!"

"Do not raise your voice to me, vixen!"

"My lord Nicholas, what has gotten into you?" scolded Edith, still poised protectively before Gillian.

"Do not overstep your bounds, Edith," Nicholas snarled.

"It is all right," Gillian said, moving out from behind the older woman. "His quarrel is with me, as always."

"As I live and breathe, I never thought to see such a sight," Edith continued, as if her lord had not reprimanded her. Indeed, she seemed not to fear his wrath, for she put her hands on her hips and glared right back at him. "You should be the one to hie to your chamber, before you catch your death! And the lady can stay here with me."

"This is Aisley's room," Nicholas snapped.

"And since Aisley has her own home now, I am sure she will not mind the lady's presence here."

Although he looked as if he would fain kill them both, Nicholas made no move. "Very well," he snapped. "But I hold you responsible, Edith. She is your charge—for now." Flicking a contemptuous gray glance over Gillian, he added, "And for God's sake, contrive some decent clothes for her!"

When he left the room, still clutching his makeshift covering, Edith snorted and shut the door behind him.

"Are you not afraid of him?" Gillian asked. Nicholas was taller than she, but he fairly towered over the older woman, and his malice was greater even than his size.

"Nicholas?" Edith asked, dismissing the fierce lord with a shake of her head. "Nay, I am not frightened by him. Why, I have known the boy since he was but a mewling babe. And there is little that scares me anymore, after Dunmurrow!" She shivered, as if the very name chilled her.

"Dunmurrow?"

"Shh . . . you just sit down here by the fire, my lady," she said, coaxing Gillian onto a beautifully carved settle. Though it was a warm day, Edith threw a soft fur over her shoulders and another over her bare feet, until she felt cozy and pampered. It was easy to relax under the older woman's ministrations, especially after the harsh routine of the convent and the tense days since her marriage. Gillian rested her head against the smooth wood and closed her eyes.

"There now, that is better! Where shall I begin? Well, I am Edith, and I have served at Belvry since I was a young girl myself. I attended the lady of the castle, God rest her soul, and after she died, I took care of her daughter Aisley."

Gillian lifted her lashes in surprise. "Aisley is Nicholas's sister? I had thought . . ." She lifted her chin, uncertainty making her grim. "I have heard that a lord is wont to keep a leman."

"Nicholas?" Edith snorted. "Nay, the man is virile enough, but where he spends it all is beyond me. Probably churns it all back into the bile that makes him so fierce."

Gillian could not help smiling at Edith's words, though she was still amazed by the woman's plain speaking. So, Nicholas did not have a female installed at Belvry! Gillian ignored the tiny leap of pleasure that shot through her at the news, and told herself she was relieved to have one fewer enemy.

And yet, Nicholas had a sister. Gillian found it hard to picture such a female. Was she as cold and heartless as her brother? "Perhaps I should not be in the Lady Aisley's chamber," she said, voicing her fears aloud.

"Nonsense, child, she is grown and gone now, and lady of her own keep. Though 'tis not as fine as Belvry, she prefers to live there," Edith said, as if she did not quite approve of the choice.

Personally, Gillian was not surprised that Nicholas's sister should choose to stay away. She could not imagine anyone seeking the company of the soulless creature she had married. "Perhaps she fears him, as I do."

Edith scoffed. "Aisley is frightened of nothing," she said, her tone revealing mixed emotions about that fact. "After marrying the Red Knight, she can handle her brother easily enough." The older woman blew out a long sigh.

"Nicholas is not such a bad sort, my lady. He was but a young man when he went with Prince Edward, now our good king, to fight in the Holy Land. I know not what happened to him there, but we were told by that villainous neighbor of ours, may he rot in hell, that Nicholas had been killed. Of course, his poor father was heartbroken, though you would not have known it to look at him."

She eyed Gillian sharply. "Listen up, my lady, for you might as well know that the de Lacis are a cold lot, my little Aisley excepted, of course. They are not much for affection, and keep a tight control on themselves. Although they do not shout and scream when in a temper, like someone else I could name, neither will they touch another willingly, nor give in to the gentler emotions."

She shook her head sadly. "But they feel pain as keen as the rest of it, and after losing all his sons to illness and battle, the old lord sickened and passed on himself. That is when Aisley took over the demesne, and ran it very well, thank you, until she married Baron Montmorency."

The name seemed to affect the older woman deeply, and Gillian lifted her brows in an unspoken question. "Make no mistake, he turned out to be a fine man, but Belvry is my home, and after the wee one was born, I came back here with a new husband of my own." She gave Gillian a broad wink and a smile.

"But I am getting ahead of myself! 'Twas only when the castle was under attack, and Aisley's husband fighting bravely, that Nicholas returned. Just in time, they all say, to save us from our villainous neighbor, Baron Hexham. The people were well pleased to have a de Laci take his rightful heritage, and I am not the only one who hoped that he would marry soon and continue the line. But he had changed, coming back from the East a harder man, and after that business with Hexham... Well, he seemed but a shell of himself."

Edith brightened then, and grinned. "I must admit that I was surprised to hear him call you wife, but after meeting you, I am sure you are just the one to put everything to rights. Why, just look at the difference in the man already," the older woman noted. "Never in all my days did I expect to see Nicholas de Laci chasing after a woman, and him half-naked besides!"

She laughed softly, as if the memory were a pleasant one, but Gillian could hardly join her. She remembered too well the glitter of hatred in her husband's eyes. And, though she was grateful for Edith's chatter, she was dismayed to learn that the older woman, and perhaps other members of the household, expected her to have some influence over their lord.

Ha! They might as well wish for the moon, for it would be more likely to do their bidding than Nicholas, Gillian thought, doubly angry with him now.

She looked up to see Edith's brown eyes, eager with curiosity, upon her. "So tell me, my lady, how did you manage to get his attention?" the older woman said with a grin.

"In truth, I did nothing but be born," Gillian answered after a long silence. "You see, I am Hexham's niece."

Nicholas was surly at supper, and so inattentive to the steward who tried to report upon his holdings that the man gaped at him in astonishment. The food seemed to sit like a hot stone in his belly, and he soon pushed away his trencher, though he knew that if he did not eat, he would regret it later. The promised pain meant little, for he had lived with it for years. Instead, his thoughts traveled to the upper chamber where his wife was taking her repast alone.

It was only natural, Nicholas told himself, to wish to keep the object of his revenge within view. Although he had sent a soldier up to guard her door, he trusted no one, least of all Edith, to watch over his wife. The foolish old servant did not know, nor could anyone guess, that the little nun was really a vixen who might leap out a window at the slightest provocation.

The thought of her escape attempt made Nicholas rise halfway from his seat, and he would have gone up to check on her, but for the startled gaze of his steward. He shifted slightly, nodding to the man, then stared at his cup. Had the meals at Belvry always been so interminable? Was there no way to hasten the serving and eating of food?

He looked at the members of his household, seated side by side along the trestles that lined the tables of the great hall, and realized that they had become soft, taking their ease at length. He ought to send them scurrying to their pallets, and then . . .

"I am glad to see that you abandoned your previous attire for something more suitable." The sound of the low voice, suddenly so close to him, startled Nicholas, and he cursed himself for the lapse in his alertness. His eyes narrowed as he assessed the Syrian, who leaned near.

"What are you talking about?"

Darius lifted his dark brows in an enigmatic expression that made him look all the more exotic and foreign. "I had heard you were running around the castle wearing nothing but a scrap of linen to cover your modesty."

For the first time in years, Nicholas felt heat rise in his cheeks, at the reminder of his headlong rush after his wife. He picked up a bare bone and rolled it absently between his fingers. "'Twould be a bit chilly for continual wear," he said coolly.

Darius smiled slowly. "At first, I thought you were but donning your emir's robes, but from what I gather, your costume was even less substantial."

Nicholas did not comment. He had no intention of explaining himself to the Syrian, or of dwelling upon an incident best forgotten. If Darius's object was to inform him of the gossip, then he had done so. He had no wish to discuss it further.

"They say you charged after her like a bear—"

"Enough!" Nicholas said. Immediately he regretted his response. Was the Syrian trying to goad him? Nicholas assessed his companion with narrowed eyes. Although his expression revealed nothing, Nicholas had the distinct impression that the Syrian was amused. And he did not like it.

The bone in his hand snapped abruptly.

"Do you find something humorous, Darius?" Nicholas asked. The Syrian shook his head, his dark face impassive, his black eyes cloaked. But Nicholas persisted, staring hard at his companion until he realized that he would welcome a fight to ease his frustrations. Finally, he looked away, angered by his own lack of discipline.

"I will see to the sentries," the Syrian said. Nicholas nodded, and was grateful for a respite from that knowing gaze when Darius left his seat. It was getting late. He ought to seek his rest and attend to his wife.

Gillian. Nicholas's heart seemed to pound faster and harder as he pondered her fate, come the night. After what had happened in the bath, he was leery of sleeping with her. Nun or novice she was not unfamiliar with womanly wiles. Aye, innocent as she might seem, she could entice as well as the sultriest of harem dwellers. And he had no intention of becoming a slave to her body, when it was she who was at his mercy.

In truth, he ought to make her lie on the floor at the foot of his bed, like the meanest of servants. And yet her skin was so creamy and fine, Nicholas wondered if such a hard berth might not mar it. Perhaps he should just let her stay in Aisley's room.

Daunted by his indecision, Nicholas took a deep breath to clear his head. Usually his judgment was swift and sure, and he liked not this continued dithering. With a frown of annoyance, he resolved to keep his wife within his sight. She was a clever, bold thing, and he would be wise to keep an eye on her, lest he find himself deprived of his vengeance come morning.

His vengeance. Nicholas's blood quickened as he contemplated his course. Already he had discovered her deepest fear and how effortlessly he could torment her with it. He would let the vixen sleep on a thick pallet, so that she would suffer no bruises, but he would keep her within reach . . . at the foot of his bed.

For the first time this evening, Nicholas's lips curled into a ghost of a smile. Absently he stroked the curve of his cup with his thumb, again and again, while he pictured Hexham's niece on her knees before him. Aye, he would taunt her easily enough—with his sex.

Chapter Five

Gillian sat back, a bit uncomfortable under Edith's constant attention. Being waited upon took some getting used to, and the habits of the nunnery died hard. Still, the older woman seemed offended by Gillian's offers of help, so she played at the role of lady, and wondered just how long this treatment would last.

Somehow, she did not think Nicholas would approve.

"Well, you certainly have a healthy appetite," Edith commented. As the servant cleaned away the remains of the meal, she eyed Gillian closely. "Could it be that he has got you with child already?"

Gillian blanched. "Certainly not," she answered sharply. Then, feeling guilty for attacking her only friend here at Belvry, she took a deep breath and tried to find the words to explain. "'Tis an old habit," she said. "There was a time when I...when I did not have enough to eat...and since then I have filled myself whenever I can."

"Oh, my poor child," Edith said. Gillian turned away, too proud to see the pity she knew would be in the old servant's eyes, but to her relief, Edith did not belabor the subject. The woman simply made a brisk sound in her throat and moved on.

"Well, you look fine and healthy, so I am sure that a baby will be not long in coming, especially since Lord Nicholas wants you to attend him in his chamber this night," she said, giving Gillian a broad wink.

Gillian was horrified. The good food and friendly company of the older woman had relaxed her, but that easy mood fled at such news. She sat up straighter, so as to take slow, simple breaths, and stared, wide-eyed, at the door that had kept her closed away—and safe—from *him*.

"See, my lady, he cannot hate you as much as you say, or else he would not take his pleasure with you," Edith rambled on. Suddenly the woman's chatter seemed irritating, and Gillian would stop it before it embarrassed her further.

"The only pleasure he will take is in abusing me."

"My lady!" Edith said, with a gasp of surprise. "I admit that Lord Nicholas is not the gentlest of men, but you cannot mean to say he has hurt you?"

"Not yet, for he has not had the opportunity to...to consummate the marriage," Gillian said baldly.

"Oh!" Edith put a hand to her bosom, as if heartily relieved. "'Tis your fears that are speaking, my lady. Lord Nicholas is a fine figure of a man, tall and strong and well made. Why, he is the most handsome man I have ever seen, excepting my own dear Willie, of course."

"Yes, he is beautiful. Beautiful and terrible," Gillian muttered.

"Nonsense," Edith said. "He has been to the East, where men are said to acquire an expertise in the arts of love. You cannot tell me that Lord Nicholas does not know his way about a bedchamber."

Gillian blushed and ducked her head, unprepared for this frank discussion of what transpired between a man and a woman. Not since her days in Master Freemantle's household had she heard such bold speech, and the memory of the burgher's foul breath and loathsome touch made her shudder.

"Have no fear, my lady," Edith said. "There are ways and there are ways, and if Lord Nicholas does not please you as he ought, you can take things into your own hands, so to speak," she said with a loud chuckle.

"What?"

"I am only saying that there are some who do not respond to kind words and sweet smiles, but most men are swayed easily enough by a woman's attentions under the covers."

Stunned, Gillian stared, openmouthed, at the older woman.

"Aye, my lady," Edith said conspiratorially. "I have marked the way Lord Nicholas looks at you, and to my mind, you could have him at your feet easily enough, should you but make a bit of effort."

Gillian felt dizzy at the thought. She was distrustful of men and fearful of their lusts, and yet, when she bathed Nicholas de Laci, she had felt only a strange excitement. His body was so compelling that she had found her hands lingering at their task, her fingers exploring the broad pelt of dark hair that covered his hard chest. Trying to maintain a modicum of privacy, she had averted her eyes from the water's hidden depths, but she had found out later that everything about Nicholas de Laci was larger than life.

Gillian's heart started beating wildly as she remembered Nicholas de Laci as he had stood in the doorway, naked but for a scrap of linen. She pictured him leaning close, touching her, doing things to her that Master Freemantle had whispered in her ear. The images held a certain forbidden allure that Gillian would never have thought herself capable of feeling, and she closed her eyes, as if to block them from her sight.

When she did, her husband's face swam before her, handsome enough to turn any girl's knees to water, yet his expression showed not ecstasy but triumph, and his silver eyes glittered with malice. With a gasp, Gillian lifted her lashes, knowing that she could never turn him away from his twisted course of vengeance.

"Here now, calm yourself, my lady," Edith said, bending over Gillian, concern in her gaze. "I did not mean to upset you. 'Twas just a thought, and should you change your mind, you just ask old Edith for some advice. We will have haughty old Nick begging for your favors like a trained pup!"

Gillian smiled bitterly at the woman's words, for she knew just how impossible it would be to accomplish that feat. Edith was gentle and kind, but she saw what she wanted to see, and she had never faced Nicholas de Laci's dagger eyes, empty of all but his hatred.

"Well, now, you had better come along, and remember what I said, child," Edith added.

Gillian stood and nodded, but when the older woman turned, she made sure that her eating knife was secreted upon her person. Although not much of a weapon, she would use it, if endangered. By rights, her body belonged to her husband, but before God, she would not let him harm her.

Grimly she followed the servant toward the great chamber, where *he* was waiting. Fighting against the same sensations that must have assailed Daniel upon entering the lions' den, Gillian went in with head held high. She heard her husband's sharp dismissal of Edith and the ominous thud of the door closing behind the servant, but still she refused to look at him.

Silence settled around her, thick and ominous, and Gillian decided there was something horribly close about the bedchamber, although it was the biggest one she had ever seen. Large, warm and luxurious, it was typical of Belvry, this fantastic home of the de Lacis.

A huge bed with heavy hangings stood against one wall, across from a clean hearth surrounded by coffers and settles soft with thick pillows. Eyeing a fat woven cloth with exotic designs that must have been made in the East, Gillian realized that she had never dreamed of such a place. Truly, it must resemble paradise.

There was only one problem: *He* was in it.

He had never shared her tent while on the road. In fact, they had been alone only once, right here, when she attended his bath, running her hands over his sleek, wet skin and discovering the hard muscle that ran beneath it. Shivering at the memory that beckoned to her, Gillian forced herself to look at him.

All her longings disappeared in a rush. He stood before her now, so arrogant and cruel that she could hardly believe him to be the same man who had relaxed under her touch, or that she had felt anything other than revulsion toward him.

"You will stay here tonight, wife," he said, and she drew in a sharp breath. His mouth curved wickedly, as if promising myriad horrors, and without volition, Gillian's gaze dropped to his groin. He whirled away suddenly, pointing to a thick straw pallet at the foot of the bed. "There is where you shall sleep," he snapped, as though angered anew.

The floor was traditionally the repose of servants and squires, but Gillian did not protest. Although the bed was big enough to hold six people, she was relieved that she did not have to share it with him. Better to feel the hard tiles beneath her than his body against hers . . . naked. She trembled.

As if sensing her dismay, he turned on her again, leering spitefully. "I have been lenient with you, vixen, but our trip is over, and now you will be expected to pay the price for your uncle's treachery."

He walked slowly around her, like a cat stalking a mouse, but Gillian lifted her chin, refusing to be intimidated by his threats. "I have thought long and well on my revenge," he added, his eyes glittering as they always did when he spoke of his one true passion.

"Of course, it would have been better, if Hexham's brother had sired a son. Then, I could have killed him out-right, but since you are a woman, and at the king's behest my wife, I shall have to devise other methods of enacting my revenge."

His sharp gaze raked her slowly, and Gillian struggled to maintain her composure under his sly insinuations. "There are many ways to torture a man, but a woman—?" He left the question dangling in the silence, and Gillian's breath grew short. His lips curled, as if her fright pleased him mightily.

"Get to your pallet, wife, and await me at my leisure," he ordered, but Gillian could not move. Too busy trying to fill her lungs to heed his command, she could only gasp, and she kept on gasping until the scowl left his face and he eyed her with alarm.

"What the devil?" Stepping toward her, he took her by the shoulders and shook her slightly. His attentions only agitated her further, and Gillian could do naught but stare at him wide-eyed. His face swam before her, hard and beautiful, before dizziness engulfed her. He must have felt her sway, for the next thing she knew she was scooped up in strong arms and laid upon a soft fur on the great bed.

"By all the saints, 'tis no wonder you cannot breathe in this gown," he snapped, and, turning her, he began to loosen the ties. Gillian felt his hand, warm even through her shift as he rubbed his palm across her back, and despite all his warnings and her own wariness, it was not unpleasant.

Although his was not the gentlest of touches, neither was it threatening, and Gillian felt her terror ease at the rhythmic pressure. Indeed, to her surprise, she found the sound of his breathing, low and quick, and the sensation of his heavy hand against her, oddly soothing—until his callused fingers slid onto the bare skin above her shift.

Abruptly her comfort fled, for his fingertips seemed to sear her flesh with their heat and incite in her an unwelcome excitement. Starting, she gasped again, and he moved away, muttering imprecations.

When he returned, he pressed a cup of ale upon her, apparently from a flask he kept in the chamber. "Here, sit up and drink," he said. Although gruff, his voice seemed different to her ears, as if stripped of its usual cool distance. Though conscious of her gown gaping behind her, Gillian let him help her up against the pillows and took a sip.

"Are you all right?" he asked. Gillian nodded, acutely aware of how close he sat beside her, warm and solid and no longer fearsome. "Are you prone to these fits?" he asked, his tone harsher.

"No," Gillian answered softly. "Only when I am... Only rarely," she said, catching herself just in time. She would not let him know how well he had terrorized her—or did he gloat in triumph already? Gillian stiffened and glanced up at him, but he avoided her gaze, surging to his feet, with his back toward her.

"Good! Then I shall expect never to see you possessed by such demons again," he snapped. As Gillian watched, he leaned forward and pressed a hand against his stomach before straightening swiftly to his full, impressive height. The movement was so subtle that she would not have noticed, had she not been eying him so closely. Did her invincible husband suffer some ailment?

Gillian's concern fled when he whirled back toward her, his handsome face once more composed and cruel. "Rest yourself," he advised coldly, "for I will not have you die on me, as your traitorous uncle did. I will have my revenge!"

He stalked to the door and slammed it behind him, the loud bang of the wood echoing into silence, and Gillian was aware of a sharp pain in her chest that had nothing to do with her loss of breath.

Slowly she set the cup down upon a coffer and climbed from the bed. Easing the rest of the way from her outer garment, she folded it neatly and set it aside. Then she settled onto her pallet, still clad in her shift, and pulled a fur over herself. Accustomed to sleeping with a roomful of other women, Gillian found the quiet of the empty chamber strange.

The fire glittered nearby, making Gillian realize that this nest was far softer and warmer than her cot at the convent had ever been. And she would not have to rise again at midnight to kneel upon cold stone for lengthy prayers.

But Belvry held dangers that the nunnery did not. Perhaps this evening her husband would leave her alone and she might snatch some badly needed sleep, yet she could not count upon this respite. There were many long nights ahead, and Gillian knew the mysterious Syrian would no longer whisper to her of safety.

Suddenly, Gillian recalled the brush of warm fingers across her back, rhythmic and comforting and something more. An odd sensation that she had never known before had taken hold of her....

With a huff, Gillian turned over and cursed her weakness. Surely she was not succumbing to the charms of her husband's touch any more than she would to his handsome face? Better that she remember the demon that dwelled inside him! Nicholas de Laci might have treated her kindly for the briefest of moments, but Gillian knew the passion that drove him; she had seen it in his eyes and heard it on his lips.

Nicholas de Laci's only concern was for his vengeance.

Dawn was stealing in through the shutters when Nicholas rose from his bed and stood over his wife. She was curled up on the pallet, one fist tightly grasping her pillow, like a child, and, indeed, she seemed very young in sleep. Her face, so often tight with fury or pride, was serene in repose, her skin almost luminescent, while the light dusting of freckles made her seem real—and reachable.

Nicholas stepped back, as if she had burned him, but he did not turn away. Rarely had he the chance to study her unobserved, and, suddenly, it seemed very important that he do so. She was fine, like some rare wine perfected from costly grapes and seasoned with special herbs. The women of the East had been mysterious and exotic under their veils, and the Frankish women mundane in comparison, but Gillian... She sparkled like a ruby among lesser gems, more intoxicating than the sultriest resident of the harem and more alive than any of her pale sisters in Britain.

Years spent in detached observation compelled Nicholas to admit such things, even as he told himself that they did not matter. More important to discover were his enemy's weaknesses, and he would know them all. His eyes slid over her deliberately, lighting upon one pale shoulder that peeped out from under her fur. It was neither bony nor fat, but gently curved, and appeared smooth to the touch, and the dash of freckles he saw there struck Nicholas strangely, warming his blood.

He tore his gaze away, only to find that thick locks of silky-looking hair had escaped from her braid, to curl around her face and her slender throat. His heart pounding at the sight of the bright strands, Nicholas felt like cursing them aloud. The damned fiery stuff seemed to call to him.

He refused to answer. Turning his back on her, Nicholas concentrated on his hatred, long nurtured, and what he might do now that vengeance was within his grasp. Although he had never formulated a plan, taking part of his pleasure in the vague promise of his imaginings, now she was here and she was his, and he could do anything he wanted with her.

Originally Nicholas had thought to imprison her, perhaps in the tower of her uncle's manor, where Hexham had shut his own wife away from the world until her death. It had seemed a fitting enough fate for Hexham's heir. But sometime during the trip to the nunnery and back, Nicholas had abandoned that scheme. Gillian was too bold, too clever, to be trusted away from his sight, too prideful to be broken by simple confinement. He must needs find some other course for his revenge.

As if by another's will, Nicholas's eyes strayed to the huge bed, still rumpled from his residence. Upon his return last night, he had been surprised to find that she had moved to the floor. He had stood in the middle of the room for a long time, suffering a strange series of sensations, like blows to the body. He, who had been so empty not so long ago, had been inundated by unfamiliar emotions: relief, anger, temptation....

Abruptly Nicholas turned from the scene, unwilling to allow such an invasion. It had been but a trick of the night, a sleight of hand of shadow and light, a spell woven by a woman's perfume ... And he would have none of it!

Whirling away, Nicholas strode from the chamber and did not look back. He had lands to survey, and a sudden, urgent need to put some distance between himself and the flame-haired vixen who was his wife.

Gillian awoke to a gentle rapping. Had she overslept? The nuns would be waiting, and the abbess would be angry if she lay abed, but it was so warm, so soft, here....

"My lady? Are you in there?"

Gillian sat straight up, pushing some stray hairs back from her face as she surveyed her surroundings. *His* chamber. To her relief, the huge bed was empty, but she did not like knowing that he had been up and about while she slept, mindlessly vulnerable. Shivering slightly, Gillian called for Edith to enter, and the sight of the cheerful servant chased away her grim mood.

"Here, I have brought you some spiced wine, my lady," Edith said. She spared a contemptuous glance for Gillian's pallet and clicked her tongue. "Now, what are you doing on the floor? By faith, I am beginning to wonder about Lord Nicholas. He must be a fair caskethead!"

And so the day began, much later than usual for the former novice, and it continued at an easy pace that made Gillian feel like the most indolent of women. Although Edith had snared a young girl to help, Gillian insisted upon sewing right along with them as they hurriedly pieced together a better-fitting gown from some of Aisley's old garments.

They were ensconced in another of the castle's fantastic rooms, this one called the solar. It was full of light from many windows and littered with furniture and bright pillows and tapestries that even draped onto the floor. Gillian was hard-pressed to keep her attention on the task at hand, so lovely were her surroundings.

At last they finished, however, and Gillian slipped into the new creation. The heavy linen fell smoothly to her slippers, and Gillian stroked the fine material in amazement, never having worn such finery. Edith smiled and nodded, as though reading her mind. "And wait until you see the cloth he brought back from the East! You shall be richly garbed, my lady, and that is a fact. There are some advantages to marrying the lord, eh?"

Gillian blushed, but said nothing, for a few beautiful clothes seemed little recompense for suffering *his* vengeance. She frowned, for she had been so busy this day that she had put all thoughts of him aside. And yet, he would ever be there, like a spider, weaving his traps about her. . . .

Her dark musings were interrupted by the appearance of Osborn, the servant who had been so kind to her the day before. "Ah, my lady!" he said, smiling in such warm greeting that Gillian grew flustered, unsure of her place in this household.

"I would beg but a few moments of your time," Osborn said, so humbly that Gillian was tempted to laugh. *He was begging her?* Gillian shook her head in amazement. Although her husband had made it plain that he considered her less than the meanest peasant, his people seemed determined to show her every courtesy. In truth, she knew not how to behave.

"The cook sent me, my lady, to learn if there is anything special you would like prepared for the feast tonight."

Feast? Gillian wondered if she had forgotten some holy day.

Edith broke in. "My lady has been too busy to think of such pleasures. But she will attend to it now. Shall you go see what dishes they are preparing?" she asked Gillian.

Gillian nodded dazedly, letting Osborn sweep her off before him to the large, airy kitchens off the great hall. There she met Tancred, the cook, a capable fellow who oversaw the enormous number of activities in his dominion. Gillian, who had never seen such a huge operation in her life, was awestruck.

Planned for the meal was an amazing assortment of food: venison and hare and lamprey, pork and pigeons and peas, breads and wafers and desserts thick with fruit.

"And for my lord, I have a special frumenty pudding. He does not like his food to be too highly seasoned," Tancred explained. Gillian thought it odd for a man newly returned from the East to have such tastes, but her musings were interrupted by a burst of coughing. When she turned, she saw a young boy hacking loudly as he fueled one of the large fires.

Gillian stepped toward him, waiting until he could catch his breath before she spoke. How she could sympathize with that difficulty! "Have you been plagued long with this cough?" she asked.

"Nay, my lady, but 'tis making my chest hurt," the boy answered her solemnly.

"I would think so," Gillian said. She turned to Osborn. "Who tends to healing here?"

"Why, no one, really, since Lady Aisley left. Have you training in the arts?" the servant asked, barely able to contain his excitement.

Gillian smiled. "A little," she answered, for maintenance of the herb garden and medicines had been part of her duties at the convent.

"Oh, this is wonderful news, my lady. We are sorely in need of your skills!" As Osborn marveled, Gillian wondered if there was aught she could do to displease him. With his assistance, she prepared a drink for the boy, but she soon discovered that the supplies needed to be replenished and replaced.

"I think I shall have a look at the herb plot," she said. Happily Osborn led her to a low doorway and left her there, called back to the hall upon some urgent errand.

Rather relieved to be left alone, Gillian drew in a deep breath and surveyed the kitchen garden. It was in a large walled area separate from the rest of the bailey, and obviously had been well tended in the past. Unfortunately, now it looked as though the plants not used for seasoning had been abandoned, undoubtedly because no one knew their worth.

The afternoon sky was bright overhead, the breeze gentle and warm, and the smell of earth and greenery welcoming. Gillian felt a rare serenity descend as she walked among the shoots and tangles of living things, struggling to grow. Then, with a smile, she pushed up her sleeves and settled in to work.

Enjoying her unaccustomed privacy and firmly centered upon her task, Gillian lost all track of time. Not until the sun dipped low over the surrounding stones was she startled from her reverie by the sound of a frightful shout from inside the castle, behind her.

"Where?" The one word, fierce and demanding, roused Gillian from her thoughts, and she lifted her head, turning slightly toward the small doorway that led to the garden. In an instant, *he* filled it, tall and angry as some avenging angel. Only more handsome.

Gillian refused to be flustered. Without a word, she continued working, not even acknowledging the arrival of her husband and the red-faced soldier who trailed behind him. "Why did you let her out? Did I not set you to guard her?" Nicholas asked, his voice sharp and deadly as a blade.

"But that was yesterday, my lord!" Gillian heard the poor man protest. "You said naught of last evening or today!"

"Get back to your duties!" Nicholas snarled, obviously refusing to admit to his own mistake. Typical of the arrogant creature, Gillian noted. She yanked out a thick weed with more force than necessary.

"What do you think you are doing?" He was speaking to her now, she could tell, and though his tone was cooler, it was no less threatening.

"I am working. Go away," Gillian answered.

"What?" The shout rang in her ears, but she did not flinch.

"You heard me. I am working. Begone," Gillian said.

"What?" His bellow echoed upon the stone walls, and Gillian's own temper flared. Finally, she rose and turned toward him. His face was flushed, as if he were truly enraged, but Gillian could not imagine any reason for such a reaction, except his own foul humors.

"I am gardening!" she yelled back at him. "Are you blind, as well as deaf?" she asked, waving her arm across the area she had neatly cleared.

For a moment, Gillian thought he would surely strike her, but he remained still, his lips curled contemptuously. "Nay, I hear you well enough, but I would have you listen to me, and heed me well! You have no leave to garden, to heal the sick or to foul my kitchens with your presence. Is that plain enough for you, lady wife?"

Gillian opened her mouth to protest, but he lunged at her then, and she was forced to duck just out of his reach. She would have fled past him, too, if not for a troublesome vine that caught her foot and sent her sprawling upon her back amid the ivy.

Neatly trapped, she could only stare up at him, wide-eyed, as he loomed over her, his breathing harsh. Had she once thought him a popinjay? Underneath the cool surface, his blood burned with the force of his hatred—for her.

Gillian steeled herself for a blow or another outburst, but he just raked her with his terrible gaze, which came to rest on her bare calves. Feeling suddenly awkward, she reached down to tug the hem back into place, and he flinched, as if startled by the movement.

"Get up to your chamber at once," he snarled, whirling away from her without deigning to help her. Pushing herself up from the ground, Gillian dusted off her hands and marched obediently forward, then right past him. Although her knees shook and her once fine gown was soiled, she managed to keep her back straight and her chin held high.

Inside, she found the cook and his staff gaping like fish, their mouths hanging slack in astonishment. Another man, more richly garbed, nodded at her with some alarm before approaching her husband. Gillian refused to be embarrassed.

"But—but what of the feast tonight, my lord?" he asked.

Although Gillian tried to dart away, Nicholas snared her arm in a swift grip before halting to attend to the fellow. Biting back a pained yelp, she glared at her husband. "Feast? What feast?" he snapped, turning on the poor man like some frightful demon.

"Why, the feast to celebrate your... marriage."

Chapter Six

Nicholas sat at the head of the high table, poking at some frumenty pudding with one finger and ignoring the gaiety around him. In the end, he had allowed the special meal. Although he cared nothing for the opinions of the members of his household, he saw no reason to punish them for his wife's transgressions.

After this night, however, he would make it clear that Gillian was not to be revered or coddled by anyone, including that meddlesome Edith. Faith, he had taken his fill of her tart tongue. He would send her packing, her years of service to Belvry be damned, if she tried to come between him and his revenge!

Gillian! When he returned to find her missing, Nicholas had become frenzied, tearing through the castle like someone possessed, while his people stared at him stupidly, as if struck dumb by his fits. Faith, he could almost hear his father's remonstrance: A de Laci never raises his voice.

And yet his son and heir had shouted the place down, searching for his wife. Piecing together each bit of information on her movements, Nicholas had learned that she had left Aisley's chamber for the kitchens, where she had concocted a treatment for some servant boy's cough, then apparently strolled off to the herb garden without any attendant whatsoever.

When Nicholas finally found her, the impact of her presence had hit him like a blow to the chest, stunning him to silence, and it had taken him a good minute to recover himself. He was relieved, pleased even, that the object of his revenge was still well within his grasp, yet mixed in with that relief were other things: anger, a strange, tingling delight, and mounting frustration.

It had annoyed him to see her kneeling in the dirt like one of his villeins. He had not given her leave to wander about, mingling with the sick and ruining her hands. Then she had japed at him, and the temper he had not known himself to possess had snapped beneath the strain. Before Nicholas knew he had moved, she had been flat on her back before him, her gown hiked up to show her shapely calves, spread wide.

He had wanted to touch them, to fall upon her and lick the smudges from her face.

The memory sickened him. He felt light-headed, unbalanced, out of control. And *she* was the cause of it all. Though he had welcomed the existence of Hexham's niece, Gillian was not at all the weak-willed, cowardly convent-bred creature he had expected. She was neither old or ugly. And she was certainly not malleable, he thought, as she met his glare unflinchingly. With a boldness that made his blood run faster, she lifted her cup in a mock toast and drank it down.

Nicholas's gaze flicked to the empty vessel, and he wondered how much wine she had consumed tonight. Her green gaze held a recklessness that went beyond her usual defiance. The thought of the little nun giddy from drink made his pulse quicken, though he could not have said why.

He kept a wary eye upon her, although he did not expect her to do anything unseemly in front of the crowd. In truth, she acted as though she had been born to be chatelaine, for she faced his people fearlessly, undaunted by their expectations. All who greeted her were treated with kindness and courtesy, and yet she remained untouchable, as if she were above their reach.

Only her gown was less than worthy, for it looked pieced together, and still bore smudges attesting to her work in the garden. Nicholas frowned. What kind of woman dug in the garden without regard to her clothing? A nun—or a novice—who need not fuss over her plain black garb, he thought, feeling irrationally annoyed.

He liked not the memory. Instead, Nicholas pictured her in eastern silks of brightly hued blues and greens. Aye, greens that shimmered and shone like her eyes. And emeralds. The jewels were rare, but how well she would look in a girdle fashioned from them, or with them sprinkled amid the golden netting that covered her fiery hair.

Nicholas had told Edith not to put a wimple upon her head, so they had coiled it beneath a sparkling caul. In the East, the sight of a woman's hair was reserved for her husband alone, and Nicholas now found himself appreciative of the custom. Suddenly he was impatient to view Gillian's unbound, loose and flowing.... Surprised by his own longing, he glanced away from her, uncertain, unbalanced.

For years, he had concentrated everything on one goal, but now that it was finally within reach, his plans were becoming muddled by the very instrument of his revenge. Distractions. Nicholas thought he had mastered them long ago, but his discipline was faltering, worn away by Hexham's heir and the gnawing ache in his belly. Although plagued for a long time by stomach pain, he felt it now more keenly, as if it sought to lay him low.

But it would not, Nicholas vowed, his mouth grim. Nor would his wife. Glancing toward her, he found her gaze upon him in silent question, and for a moment he wondered whether she knew his thoughts. As he stared, caught up by her beauty, the people around him seemed to fade, their noisy celebrations receding into the distance. The air itself seemed to still, and smoky vapors part, to reveal only Gillian, at the center of the calm, at the heart of the world.

Emerald eyes met his, warily at first, then softly, and he noticed the deeper green of the edges, the amazing color of her lashes, the delicate curve of her brows. He was focused so intently upon her that it seemed as if she waited at the end of a tunnel, and he had but to take one step toward her...

"What say you, my lord?" The sound of his steward's voice brought Nicholas out of his trance, and he shook his head slightly to clear it. When he did, his surroundings returned, crowded with people and trestle tables and noisy with laughter and speech. Gillian was not perched like a prize at journey's end, but sat within reach, a dazed query in the eyes that held his own.

"Well?" his steward asked with a grin, and Nicholas cursed his lack of attention. Obviously, the crowd was clamoring for something. More entertainment? Although he had no interest in carolers, Nicholas rarely interfered with his steward's effective running of the household, especially since he was so infrequently in residence. Apparently the singing was finished, for they were calling for a game. Hoodman Blind, was it?

Gillian looked puzzled, and Nicholas realized that she would have known little of such things in the nunnery. How astonishing that her bright eyes should turn to him in question, after all that had gone on between them! He leaned close, and her scent wafted up to him, nearly making him flinch away. "'Tis but a game. The player is hooded, and must try to find his fellows.''

"But they speak of a boon, a kiss," Gillian said.

"Do not worry, little nun," he whispered. "None shall touch you but me." Her eyes went wide at his promise, and his lips curved in satisfaction.

Lifting a hand to approve the revelry, Nicholas was startled when it was clasped by an old knight, who pulled him to his feet. "Shall our lord find his bride?" the man shouted, and the crowd cheered.

Too late, Nicholas knew the price of his own inattention. He would never have approved the sport, if he had known that he was to be the participant. Now, he must play the jape or look the tyrant for calling a halt to such foolishness. Already some women were urging Gillian from her seat and a hood was being thrust into his hands.

Still Nicholas might have refused, if he had not caught sight of Darius's dark brow, lifted in a taunting challenge. Scowling at the Syrian, Nicholas let the old knight lead him to the center of the hall, where a space had been cleared for the sport. He dropped the cloth over his eyes and even allowed himself to be turned round and round by the revelers.

To one whose wits were addled by wine, the circle might be dizzying, but Nicholas was not so easily disoriented. He righted himself quickly enough, much to the crowd's disappointment, and began his quest. Ignoring the giggling females they thrust toward him, he moved slowly among unwashed bodies heavy with onerous perfume, in search of a fresher scent.

Bathing was a habit Nicholas had brought back with him from the East, and he would see that his wife embraced the custom, too, for he liked not the odor of his own people. And that was how he found her, of course. The gentle waft of her essence reached him, making him think of wildflowers and freckles and fiery hair, and although another was pushed in front of him in her stead, Nicholas followed it until at last he caught her in his arms.

The crowd erupted into cheers of approval, and he yanked the hood from his head, impatient for the sight of her. It fell to the floor, revealing his choice: a tall, elegant maiden with creamy skin and soft curves. Her green eyes were dazed, whether with wine or from the game he could not tell, and they stared up at him, wide with surprise.

"The boon! A kiss, my lord!"

Nicholas had half a mind to ignore the shouts, for he liked not being told his business, and yet, standing there looking down at her, it suddenly seemed the most natural thing to do as they bade. Gillian's cheeks were flushed, and her lips parted, as if to receive his own. He lowered his head.

He brushed his mouth against her waiting one, never meaning more, but the contact was so heady, so intoxicating, that he lingered, increasing the pressure. Then she opened beneath him, and his tongue delved inside as he tasted her dewy sweetness.

Hot. Powerful. Nicholas pulled her against him roughly, and she made no protest, but slid her arms up around his neck. Fingers caught in his hair and firm breasts moved against his chest as Gillian touched her tongue to his. He plunged deeper, thrusting mindlessly, while his palms slid down her back, eager, impatient, wanting.... And all the while, his blood sang in his ears, louder and louder—until he started at the sound.

The dull roar echoing in his brain was the cumulative noise of his people, cheering wildly. Nicholas lifted his head. "Long live Lord and Lady de Laci!" the crowd chanted. "May their line forever prosper!"

Their *line?* Nicholas stepped back, dropping his hands away from Gillian's body as if it burned him. And, indeed, he felt like one who had walked through fire. Shaky and off balance, he sought his composure, while the voices shouted their approval.

He had let things go too far, but then, he was unaccustomed to such displays. Never before had the people rallied around him so strongly or so passionately. Why would he have expected them to embrace his bride so fiercely? His eyes narrowed as he surveyed the hall.

He must repudiate her, before it was too late! Now was the time to tell them that Hexham's blood flowed through her. Now was his chance to publicly vilify her, and take pleasure in her shame. He could spurn her, humiliate her, and make sure that no one ever spoke to her again.

But as Nicholas looked out at all those happy faces, proud and expectant, full of joy and hope, something gave way inside him. For the first time in his life, he considered someone before himself. For the first time since taking his father's place as lord of Belvry, he put his people first. And so he said nothing.

Instead, he grabbed Gillian's wrist and dragged her across the long hall to the stairs, amid the whoops and cheers of their audience. At first, they trailed after him, as if it were his wedding night, but he stopped on the steps and bade them hold. Then taunts and bold encouragement were all that followed him as he led his bride to the great chamber.

Not until they were safely inside, the door bolted behind them, did Nicholas release his hold upon her. When he did, she raised both hands to her cheeks and backed away from him with a horrified look. "I have had too much wine," she whispered.

"Aye," Nicholas snapped, eager to blame her for all that had occurred below. "A drunken nun—"

"I am *not* drunk!" she cried, indignant. "And I am *not* a nun."

"Novice, then," Nicholas said, advancing on her angrily. "Still, what a credit you are to the convent, with your besotted debauchery."

"Besotted? Debauchery? How dare you? 'Twas you who kissed me! I would not touch you if my life depended upon it!" she shouted, green eyes flashing.

"You gave a fair imitation below!"

"'Twas but for the benefit of the people!" she protested, but her cheeks were flushed, and she ducked her head.

"So you say," Nicholas snapped. Then, realizing that he sounded like a small boy arguing with his nurse, he turned away, grateful that his father could not see him now. "Get to your pallet, wench, before I make you sorry for your wiles."

So intent was he upon his bride that Nicholas did not hear the soft scratching at the door that normally would have alerted him to another's presence. But neither would he have suspected that anyone would dare defy his prohibition to follow.

Two of his people had done just that, however, and they stood outside the great chamber, feeling no qualms about disobeying their lord. One leaned close, pressing his ear to the wood, while the other tugged at his tunic impatiently.

"Well? Well?" Edith demanded.

Willie straightened and scratched his grizzled head, perplexed by the behavior of Belvry's lord and lady. "They are fighting again, like cats and dogs."

"No!" Edith protested. "Surely not after that kiss!"

"Hear for yourself," Willie said, moving aside, so that his wife could take his place. She wiggled her round body into position, and Willie was sorely tempted not to take one generous curve in his palm. He restrained himself, however, contenting himself with admiring her delightful form, until he heard her soft gasp.

"By all the saints, I never thought to hear Nicholas de Laci raise his voice," she whispered. "Quiet as a fish and twice as cold, I always said, but lately..."

Edith stood up and stepped away from the door, her brow wrinkled in thought. "Perhaps all this shouting is a good sign, after all."

Willie snorted in disbelief. "And how can that be?"

Deep in concentration, Edith did not answer at once, but, slowly, a smile broke out upon her face. "I think that our lord protests too much, Willie, my boy. If he did not care for her, he would treat her with the same cool distance he does everyone else. Instead, he has been in an uproar ever since bringing her home."

Willie shook his head, unable to understand such reasoning. "Seems to me that the lad needs a little help with his husbandly skills."

"Aye," Edith agreed with a wink. "Perhaps you could talk to him, Willie," she suggested as she took his arm familiarly. "Give him a few pointers."

"Ha! And get tossed in the dungeon for my pains," he complained.

Edith sighed. "Well, something needs to be done, or we shall never see her increasing. And since I cannot have Aisley's babe nearby to bounce upon my knee, I would have one of theirs."

Willie shook his head once more. "You'll never get them to stop arguing long enough to do the deed, I'll wager."

"Will you, Willie, my love?" Edith asked, smiling suddenly. "Then 'tis a bet."

They had taken only a few steps along the passageway when the door to the great chamber was flung open and then slammed shut with a violence that made them both start.

Willie pulled his wife into the protection of his arms, but the dark figure that emerged did not even notice them.

Nicholas de Laci stormed toward the stairs, and before Willie could catch her, Edith followed. Hurrying after her, Willie crept down the steps to see the lord of Belvry stalk across the great hall and out the tall doors into the pouring rain.

"I'll be damned," he whispered, leaning back on his heels. He had thought he had seen everything at Dunmurrow, but this brother of Lady Aisley's behaved like no one he had ever known. "What kind of man leaves a beautiful woman to go out in a storm?" he asked.

Oddly enough, Edith grinned. "A sorely uncomfortable man, Willie." She glanced up at him with a gleam in her eye. "Perhaps our lord craves a dousing with cold water right now, to cool his ardor!"

Nicholas stood outside the castle walls and let the rain wash over him. His stomach burned, but he refused to acknowledge it. Instead of bending double, he lifted his face to the sky, drinking in the water as it cleansed his mind and body. Cool, wet, invigorating, it seemed to clear his addled wits and chase away his fevered distress.

A few days ago, riding toward the nunnery, Nicholas had thought everything was within his grasp, but now, due to his own carelessness, his life was spinning wildly out of control. He had to regain possession of it—and himself. Control, or the lack of it, had laid him low once, and he had sworn that it never would again.

In the Holy Land, Hexham had cast him to the mercy of the elements, the kindness of strangers and his own weak body. By the faith, how he had despised those endless days of recuperation! Nicholas clenched his hands into fists at the memory. He had worked long and hard to recover his strength, his independence, his wealth and his lands. He was not about to relinquish anything to any bright-haired woman, even if his people adored her.

Time. For years Nicholas had fought his own impatience, and now he told himself, yet again, to wait. Right now Gillian was new to the residents of Belvry, the promise of a future shared, but when they came to know her and she did not produce the hoped-for heir, they would lose interest in her soon enough.

Nicholas still ruled her fate—and his own. And although he could do naught for the pain in his belly, he could do something about the gnawing ache lower down. Nicholas frowned in annoyance. He had been without a woman too long, and that was the only reason he had kissed *her*.

It would not happen again, he vowed. He kept no leman at Belvry, for he allowed no claims upon himself, but there was a woman a day's ride away. She knew him only as a knight who paid good coin for her services and held him to no promises.

Nicholas's body grew tight at the thought of pumping between her legs. Her hair was brown, not red, and she had not Gillian's curves, but she would do well enough to sate his lust. Perhaps he would stay the night, doing all the things with her that a man might do with his wife. At the thought, Nicholas drew in a ragged breath, but he did not look back toward the castle.

He would leave at once, and stay until the wench had drained him dry! That would take care of one of his problems, and perhaps, after spending his seed, he could regain his faltering wits, besides. His decision made, Nicholas chose several of the men of mixed blood he had brought back with him from the East, worth twice their number in Franks in a fight, to accompany him. And, barking orders, he strode toward the stables.

He found Darius there, tending the horses, as though expecting Nicholas's sudden arrival. The Syrian's behavior no longer surprised him. "I will be gone several days," Nicholas said as he mounted his destrier.

"And what drives you from your beautiful home on a night such as this?" Darius asked.

Nicholas paused. That dark, inscrutable gaze seemed to judge him, and he liked it not. "I fear neither the night nor the rain, as you well know," he snapped, offering no further explanation for his precipitate journey. "I leave my demesne in your hands."

Although the Syrian's face was unreadable, Nicholas sensed his disapproval. "And what of your wife?" Darius asked. "In whose hands shall you leave her?"

Nicholas felt as if his horse had made a misstep, launching him into the air. So intent had he been on his own departure that he had given no thought to the possibility of her escape. "She dares not flee," he muttered. But the vixen was wily, and Nicholas could not afford to take chances. She might use his people's acceptance to her advantage, and then where would he be, if she left him? Emptiness as vast and lonely as the desert stretched out before him. "Make sure she has a guard at all times."

Darius bowed his head slightly. "I will render this service gladly."

Something in Darius's manner brought Nicholas up short. His eyes narrowed as he searched the Syrian's face, but, as usual, the dark man's expression revealed nothing. Perhaps his addled wits were making him see taunts where there were none. With a sharp nod, Nicholas jerked on the reins and sent his destrier into the drizzling rain, toward a woman who could ease his body without disturbing his mind.

Driven by an urgency that he could not have named, Nicholas did not stop until dawn rose over his destination.

His eyes were bleary from lack of sleep, but he told himself that he would take his rest soon enough, perhaps in the woman's bed, after spending himself in her body.

She was a widow, and the small but once fine manor in which she lived had fallen into disrepair, the village itself long ago annexed to Belvry. Leaving his men at the copse that marked her property, Nicholas rode on alone through the wet tangle of weeds, until the sight of a horse tethered outside made him hesitate.

Urging his destrier under a thick yew, Nicholas saw a short, fat man leave the house, jerking up his braies as he went. While Nicholas watched, the fellow tugged down his tunic and mounted the waiting beast. When he spied Nicholas, he nodded and smiled, revealing a mouthful of rotted, crooked teeth.

"Good morn to you, sir! You shall be getting yourself a fine ride on that wench, make no mistake. And at a fair price, too!" he said before heading on down the path.

Nicholas remained where he was, staring after the greasy man in stunned silence. His belly burned, and his head ached from the long, wet night spent on his horse, but one part of his anatomy no longer pained him. Although the body that had been chaste for a month or more craved release, the thought of plowing the same field as that unwashed creature left him decidedly cold.

He could search for another, of course, but whores were not to his liking, and he had not the time nor the energy to woo a more discriminating wench. Damn! He should have paid the woman to serve him only, though he had never been bothered before by sharing a wench.

Indeed, what did it matter to him? Nicholas told himself that even if she serviced a host of others, the widow could still satisfy him. The memory of his greasy predecessor would fade once she spread her thighs, and there would be no others in her bed while he pumped between them. With an determined growl, Nicholas dismounted and strode to the door.

The old servant who answered it recognized him at once, and showed him into the hall quickly enough. A good beginning, Nicholas told himself, his loins tightening in anticipation. Perhaps it was just as well that this woman honed her skills in his absence. She knew tricks that no convent-bred girl would ever master, he thought smugly.

And then he saw her.

She was lounging before the fire, wrapped in a fur robe of some kind and apparently little else. She appeared rumpled, her hair tousled, but, sadly, the look was not appealing. She seemed old, suddenly. Old and tired. Although she smiled in greeting, it was a tight, hard smile. Had he never noticed before how short she was? How fleshy? Her hair was too brown, her eyes too dull.

And she had no freckles.

"Welcome, sir knight," she said, in a sultry voice that had always entranced him. Now, it merely sounded forced, and Nicholas bent his head before she could see his dismay.

"Hello, Idonea," he said.

She leaned backward, letting the robe slip to expose her legs to his view, but Nicholas felt nothing. "I was passing through, and I could not ride by without giving you good greeting," he said.

"Passing through? Surely you can linger awhile?" she whispered. Stretching out upon the pillows, she ran her fingers along the edges of the material, parting it, so that her thighs were bared and the juncture of them lay in shadow, a tempting sight for any man.

Nicholas knew he could be inside her in a moment. "I regret that I cannot stay, but duty presses me on," he said. Slowly, he stepped nearer, but he did not touch her. Instead, he carefully placed some coins on the coffer where her morning cup rested.

Her delight was plain. "Are you certain you cannot tarry even for a quick ... moment?" she purred, reaching her hands toward him, as if to pull him down atop her.

"I cannot," Nicholas answered as he straightened. Giving her a nod, he made his exit, saving them both the indignity of trying to rouse his now dormant passions.

Chapter Seven

Gillian woke gently to the soft tapping at her door, then sat up with a start. The sunlight streaming through the shutters meant it was well past dawn. Was she alone? Feeling a little ridiculous, she stretched upward to peek over the edge of the great bed. One look told her that it was empty, its coverings undisturbed. Obviously, Nicholas had never returned, and the hours she spent lying in dread of his reappearance had been wasted.

Frowning, Gillian leaned back on her heels, not sure whether she should be annoyed or relieved. Where had he slept? *And with whom?* The latter question made her bristle with a primitive emotion so forceful that it took her a moment to realize someone was still knocking.

"Come!" she shouted, knowing full well it could not be *him. He* would never be so courteous; *he* did not ask permission to enter. When she saw Edith bustle in, Gillian forced a smile of greeting for the old servant, who glanced at her nest on the floor and clucked in dismay.

"You will never win the lord, if you stay on that pallet."

Win him? *Win him for what—and from whom?* Gillian thought, with no little dismay. Did Edith know where he had spent the night, and how? Gillian's fingers ached, and she looked down, surprised to see that they were clutching the blankets like claws. Releasing her fierce grip on the fabric, she stood.

What difference did it make to her where he laid his head or stuck his wick? Gillian thought, her lips pressed tightly together. She should be celebrating the fact that he had found some other woman to torment! "I have no interest in your lord, Edith, and you know it," she replied.

Edith made a sound of disagreement. "You seemed more than interested last night, in the hall."

Last night. Abruptly the memory of the game flooded through her: Nicholas, wearing a hood, searching the crowd for her, unerringly. That had not surprised her, for she sensed that he stalked her like prey and would ever find her. What had stunned her was what followed. She had never been kissed before, had never dreamed that such a simple act could be so stimulating, so overwhelming.

It all came back to her now: the feel of his hard man's body, all solid strength; the hot pressure of his lips; the wonder of his tongue invading her mouth, stirring her in some strange way, making her lean into him.

He had stolen her breath away, but it was not fright that had taken it from her. Not for one moment had she feared him or his touch. She had twined her fingers in his hair, pressed herself against him, wanted...what? Surely not *him?*

Impossible! Dazedly, Gillian realized she was still standing in her shift, sucking in drafts of air, her heart pounding furiously, while Edith studied her with a knowing smile. Flushing, she denied it all. "'Twas but a boon, a show for the people," she protested, ducking her head.

"It looked real enough to me, my lady, and it just proves what I have been telling you. Lord Nicholas is attracted to you, and you could snare him easily enough, if you just put forth some effort. You can catch more flies with honey than with vinegar!''

Gillian let the servant help her into a gown, but scoffed at her advice. ''Who would want to catch either flies or Nicholas de Laci?'' she asked contemptuously.

Edith ignored the jibe. '''Twould make your life easier, my lady,'' she noted softly.

The simple statement made Gillian choke, as if she wanted to weep, but she furiously fought away the threat of tears. ''I will not play the whore!'' she cried. ''And he has plenty of other women who would welcome him. He wants me solely for his vengeance.'' The painful admission stuck in her throat.

Edith straightened Gillian's skirt and patted her gently. ''All will be well, my lady. You shall see. A man does not kiss a woman like that when all he feels for her is hatred.'' She waved away Gillian's automatic protest. ''Just think upon it, if you will, while he is gone.''

''He is gone?'' Gillian asked, feeling suddenly bereft. ''Where?''

Edith shook her head. ''No one knows. He left the castle as soon as he left this chamber. Charged out of here as if the devil himself were after him.''

Gillian knew an odd mixture of emotions at the news. At least he had not taken his ease with someone here at Belvry! Gillian told herself she was glad not to have to face that embarrassment. And he was away! She could breathe easier, without him to torment her at every turn. She ought to be overjoyed. Why was she not?

''Yes, our lord ran out into the rain, just as if he needed a cold shower to dampen his ardor!'' Edith said, winking broadly.

''What nonsense!'' Gillian snapped. Ashamed at the sudden leap her heart had taken at Edith's foolishness, she turned her mind firmly away from her husband and toward her plans for the day. "Since he is away, 'twould be a good time to change the rushes in the hall and scrub the tiles."

The older woman clicked her tongue in disapproval. "That is servant's work, my lady."

Gillian smiled. "Then perhaps you would aid me." Accustomed to toil, she could not lie idle. And since *he* forbade her the tasks she would have chosen, she must find something else to keep her busy.

Edith snorted as she opened the door. Then, to Gillian's astonishment, the servant fell back, shrieking loudly and nearly knocking her to the floor.

"What is it?" Gillian asked, stepping forward anxiously. Outside, the passage was empty, but for a tall, dark figure in the shadows. Gillian started before she recognized it. The Syrian.

He was not as tall as Nicholas, but he looked as strong. Although she had seen him wearing a strange cloaklike garment wrapped around his torso, today he was dressed in a simple tunic, black except for a gold edging. The stark garment accentuated his foreign coloring, a deep, rich gold that was strange, but oddly compelling.

Like Nicholas's, his face had an almost feminine beauty, but, unlike her husband's, it was not roughened by a harsh demeanor. Darius seemed very comfortable with himself and his own masculine appeal. And, indeed, there was no question of it, from the sultry curve of his wide mouth to the lazy sensuality of his deep-set eyes, black as midnight and just as mysterious.

Gillian shivered. Here was a man who knew women well, and she could not help remembering Edith's inane chatter about men from the East and their skills. Apparently the servant had forgotten her own adage. "Lord have mercy, 'tis that foreign devil!" she wailed behind Gillian.

"There is no reason to be frightened," Gillian said.

"Humph! The infidel pops out of the shadows apurpose to frighten an old woman," Edith muttered. Without one word to the man, she pushed past him to hurry toward the stair.

Gillian shook her head at the woman's rude behavior, for no matter that the Syrian was different, he was deserving of the same treatment as any other man. Suddenly shy, she smiled and ducked her head.

"I am called Darius, lady. I am to guard you," he said, and Gillian remembered the voice, deep and melodious, that had comforted her on the road. She ought to thank him, she realized, but when she lifted her gaze to his dark one, she could not. His eyes seemed to delve deep inside her, to search her very soul.

Swallowing hard, Gillian felt suddenly close, alone with him in front of her bedchamber door. "Have you eaten?" she asked. He shook his head, his lips curving slightly at her concern.

"Come, then," she said, a bit shakily. "Let us have some bread and ale. If I am allowed to roam free today, that is," she added, lifting her chin.

This time he did smile. It was a slow, amazing movement of his lips that made Gillian want to stare. "You are free, lady, until his return."

Free? Gillian bit back a retort, for she would never be free, unless... She glanced sharply at her companion. Again she was reminded of his whispered words while she lay quaking in her tent. She had known him not, and yet he had gone out of his way to ease her fears. Perhaps her exotic guard could be persuaded to help her more tangibly....

Gillian leaned back on her heels and wiped her forehead with the back of her hand. She blew out a breath as she surveyed her work. The tiles they had finished fairly glowed, but Belvry's great hall was many times larger than any of the rooms at the nunnery, and the job was taking longer than she thought. They had waited until the rain stopped and fresh rushes could be gathered today, and they must needs finish soon, before the trestle tables would be assembled for supper.

Gillian glanced past Edith to a dark figure standing tall and silent in the shadows of the curving stone. Although she could not see it, Gillian sensed a dark gaze upon her, and she suppressed a shiver. Despite her good intentions, she was unnerved by the foreigner. He was handsome and courteous and attentive, but there was something about him that disturbed her, something in his eyes.

After two days spent under his unsettling scrutiny, Gillian had abandoned her vague notions of enlisting his aid. There was nothing he could do to help her, anyway, unless he was willing to take her away from Belvry, far from her husband's reach. And even if he was, Gillian was not sure she would want to go. Would she be jumping from the pot into the fire?

Ironically, she felt more comfortable with her fiendish husband than with . . . this kind stranger. Her husband she knew all too well, while she had the feeling that it would take a lifetime to understand Darius.

And if they fled Belvry, just where would they hide? Somehow Gillian did not think that Nicholas would let her go easily. His revenge consumed him, leaving little room for aught else. He would surely follow them to the ends of the earth, and then . . . Gillian shuddered. Then she would be worse off by far.

Tearing her attention away from the foreigner, Gillian bent to her task. She had no time to dally, and besides, it was wrong of her to consider using the Syrian so coldly, when he had shown her nothing but courtesy. He was a decent man, and deserved more than that. If it were not for those eyes of his . . .

Gillian shuddered. Hours of enduring that dark regard made her husband's glittering gaze seem palatable.

Nicholas was not in a good mood. He had ridden hard through a night of rain to gain himself some ease, but after two days and nights, he had returned even more frustrated than before.

Damn! He had glowered at every female he saw along the road home, wondering if this one or that one might be worth a halt, but they had all been too old, too young, too dirty, too . . . *something*. He ground his teeth, refusing to believe that his wife was the only female who appealed to him.

London. There he would surely find what he sought with little trouble. The city teemed with women, many of noble blood, who would be more than willing to spread their thighs for a wealthy knight. And there he might find a woman of eastern descent, with dark eyes and undulating hips and no temper, a woman raised from birth to cater to a man's needs. By the faith, yes! Nicholas's blood quickened at the notion.

He would take Darius with him and leave immediately, he thought. Then his lips curled as he remembered Gillian. Before seeking out his pleasure, he must complete his business, and right now, his most pressing concern was his revenge. He must stop this dallying and make up his mind as to the disposition of his wife.

In the meantime, he would practice celibacy. It would be no hardship for a man of his discipline. He had gone without women before, and one freckle-faced vixen would not break his control! Determined, Nicholas strode into the hall, suddenly eager to face her again. He told himself it was the sweet promise of vengeance that drew him, and not the exhilarating clash of wills.

Nicholas did not even notice the bare tiles beneath his feet as he searched for her. Although his steward hurried forward, Gillian was nowhere to be seen, and his foul temper returned. Was it not a woman's place to greet her husband? By the faith, he would take her to task for her failure!

Another, more insidious thought followed close on the heels of her absence. Had she fled? Impossible! Not with Darius guarding her, Nicholas reasoned, and yet anxiety, irrational though it might be, trickled up his spine. He did not even answer his steward's greeting, but let his question erupt. "Where is she?"

"Who, my lord?" Matthew Brown asked, backing away with a fearful expression.

Nicholas did not bother to ease his steward's discomfort. "My wife!"

Matthew slanted a glance behind him, where some servants were scrubbing the floor, and Nicholas felt a surge of fierce, alien rage. By the faith, why did the man not answer? Did he not know Gillian's whereabouts? And what had happened to Darius? Alarm slammed through Nicholas, making his stomach burn and sending his better judgment fleeing.

"Where is she?" he snarled.

With a bewildered expression, the steward pointed, his finger shaking visibly. "My lord, your wife is right...there."

Nicholas looked. He saw one of the ubiquitous small boys who inhabited the castle sit back and stare at him, while two women beside the youth remained on their hands and knees, busy at their task. And past them, amid the shadows by the hearth, stood Darius, keeping watch.

Nicholas stepped closer. The older woman he recognized soon enough as that harridan Edith, while the younger one . . . A lock of flaming hair fell from her heavy caul, and Nicholas's eyes narrowed.

"Gillian!" His shout sent both the boy and the steward scurrying away. In fact, the cavernous room seemed suddenly deserted, except for Edith, who lifted her head to scowl at him reprovingly, and his wife, who paused to wipe her hands before turning to answer him.

"Yes?" she replied calmly. Her placid demeanor only made him angrier, and he pierced her with an iron gaze. She was dressed in one of those pieced-together gowns, her face dirty, her hands red and ruined. She was his wife, by God, and did not belong upon her knees!

"What the devil do you think you are doing?"

"I am cleaning before we lay fresh rushes," she answered reasonably.

"Get up." Nicholas could see people peeking out of archways at him in astonishment, but he did not care. "We have servants to do such jobs here."

She rose to her feet, a mulish look on her face and her eyes sparking with defiance. "And what am I to be allowed to do?" she asked, raising her voice. "I am not to heal. I am not to tend the sick or work in the herb garden. And now it seems that I am not to tend the hall!" She swept out an arm and frowned in bitter accusation. "Just what am I to do, husband?"

"You are to tend to me!" Nicholas snapped.

"You?" she shouted. "You disappear in the night without a word, without telling anyone where you are or when you will return!" The words tumbled from her lips before she gulped and glanced away, as if regretting them, and Nicholas felt strangely light-headed. Had she been concerned about him? Had she *missed* him? He shook himself, certain that he was imagining things. The vixen had no doubt danced in glee at his absence. With an effort, he recaptured his anger and flung it across the space toward her.

"Get yourself decently dressed, wife! 'Tis time for supper, and I will not sit down to eat with a grimy peasant!"

She gasped and opened her mouth as if she wanted to say more, and Nicholas forgot the allure of a willing eastern woman. His wife was alive and fresh, and she filled him with her fire. She was so passionate in her own defense, that for a moment Nicholas let himself consider that passion unleashed in other ways.

Forcibly he jerked his thoughts away, only to notice the streak of dirt on her cheek. He raised a hand and struggled with the urge to wipe it away with his thumb—or his tongue—before dropping his arm as if she would burn him.

Damn! He was tired, hungry and angry, and his discipline was already slipping. Bellowing orders at the servants who skulked behind the archways, Nicholas demanded supper, whether the floor was bare or not. Then he took a menacing step toward his wife, who had yet to move.

"Go!" he shouted, pointing toward the stair. And she went, but not without sending him one last hateful look. Then, lifting her chin high, she stalked across the hall, more regal than any queen, lovelier in her worn clothes than another in the finest of gowns.

Watching her, Nicholas smiled tightly, assured of his victory over this strong-willed wench. But, oddly enough, he felt no triumph, only a fierce ache in his belly that seemed to spread both upward and downward. It pulsed through him so painfully, that he did not even notice the shadow that was Darius drift across the hall to follow his wife.

Despite his fierce hunger, Nicholas picked at his food. Gillian had bathed and dressed in a dark blue gown that drew his gaze far too much for his liking, distracting him from the business of his revenge. His stomach churned, and he felt as if his insides were being torn in different directions, like a man he had once seen dragged apart by two horses.

It was time he did something with the sharp-tongued creature who was his wife, for she had a knack of seeking out trouble. She could not seem to remain idle, but would always find some activity designed to irritate him. No more! Hereafter, she would not shame him by playing at being a servant. Nicholas's vague plans to reduce her to such had been abandoned as soon as he saw her scrubbing the floor like a peasant.

She was a beautiful woman, worthy to be any man's bride, and he would not have her kneeling in the dirt. She would wear elegant gowns and jewels and keep her hands soft and unmarred, not for her sake, but for his own. Because he took pleasure in seeing her thus.

She wanted duties, so, by God, he would give her duties. She would tend to him, as a wife should, only more so. He wanted her more obedient, more attentive, more eager to do his bidding, than the most faithful bride. She would be at his beck and call, morning and night, like a squire, only more pleasing to the eye and enlivening to the spirit. Aye, that would be fit punishment for the headstrong wench, for it was what she was least inclined to do, he thought with a smile.

Nicholas's momentarily lightened mood was disrupted by the sight of Edith bustling toward him purposefully. Glowering, he warned her away with his eyes, but the old woman did not flinch. Indeed, she hurried forward with a pleased expression and plopped a large cup on the table before him. He already had his ale, so what the devil was this? All his household knew he refused wine.

"Welcome back, my lord! 'Tis a delight to have you home again, and to celebrate your return, I had a special drink made for you," the servant said.

"What is it?" he demanded suspiciously.

"Why, 'tis a tonic, my lord," she said, hands upon her ample hips.

"A tonic? I have no need of a tonic, woman. Take it away," Nicholas said, dismissing her with a turn of his head.

She did not leave, but hovered at his elbow. "Now, my lord, when I noticed the arrangements in the great chamber, I put my mind to helping set things to rights, and this is it!" she pronounced.

Obviously the old woman was being even more obtuse than usual, for Nicholas had not the faintest clue to what she was talking about. His eyes narrowed at the mention of his bedchamber, however, and he pinned her with a threatening gaze.

"Just try a sip, my lord," she urged. "'Tis a wondrous drink that will make your blood flow more readily."

Normally Nicholas ignored the old woman's eccentricities, but he had been sorely tried of late. Struggling to keep his burgeoning temper in check, he said, very slowly, "My blood flows just fine."

Edith sighed and leaned closer, as if to impart some great secret to him. "Now, my lord, perhaps you do not get my meaning. I have it on the best authority that this will make your sap rise, often and long."

While Nicholas stared at her, stunned to silence, she winked broadly, and he felt his cheeks heat with an unwelcome flush. Rage rushed through him, and he turned on his wife, fixing her with a piercing glare that promised swift retribution. "Was this your idea?"

Green eyes wide, Gillian leaned back, away from him. "Of course not! She . . . she asked me for a recipe for a man who..." Gillian's creamy skin turned crimson. "But I thought it was for her husband!" she protested.

"I had no idea she would give it to *you!*" his wife continued with a horrified expression. "I do not want your sap," she said, pausing to flick a glance at his lap, "or anything else, to rise!"

Beside her, the Syrian burst out laughing, and soon all those at the high table who had not dared smile at his discomfiture were chuckling or hooting with glee. Unaccustomed to such merriment at his expense, Nicholas felt his anger rise and burst like a foreign thing. His brain knew restraint, but something else seized control of him, and he swung out an arm, toppling the offending cup. He watched its contents run along the table and drip to the floor as silence fell once more.

"Get you gone, Edith, before I send you back to Dunmurrow," he said, and the servant who had grown far too bold paled at the mention of Aisley's new home. She stepped back, mumbling apologies, and with her exit, silence fell. Everyone returned their attention to the food, while Nicholas tore off a piece of bread with a vicious swipe, though he wanted it not.

"Nicholas." His name filled the quiet, and he stilled at the sound of it on Gillian's lips, awareness singeing him so strongly that even his skin felt hot and prickly. She had never called him by name, had never even addressed him that he could remember, though she should have been using "my lord," as was his due. He ought to take her to task for that lapse in respect, but the sound of his name, spoken in that husky voice of hers, was too affecting, too compelling, for him to ever want anything else.

"She meant no harm," Gillian said, and for a moment, Nicholas was so dazed that he could not follow her words. "She is only an old woman, trying to do her best by you."

Edith? She would talk to him of Edith? Nicholas turned upon her again. "Do not take her part, unless you are eager to embrace the results of her folly! Or perhaps you are eager for the marriage bed, wife?" he taunted, watching her turn pale at his words.

"Believe me, wife, I need no tonic to raise my tarse. Shall we test it here and now?" Grasping her wrist, Nicholas pulled her arm toward him and pressed her palm flush against his groin.

It responded immediately, swelling and stiffening beneath the pressure until he was hard as stone and jutting up into her hand. His simple taunt became something more, as her touch rocked him to the core, sending heat flashing throughout his body, making his hips push toward her imprisoned fingers. His thighs trembled with aching want such as he had never known, and he bit back a groan. Only the presence of his household prevented him taking it further. Only the look of absolute terror on her face made him release his hold upon her.

The moment he did, she sprang away from him and up from her seat, nearly knocking it over in her haste to flee. He watched her go, too stunned by his reaction to call after her. When his brain finally began to function again, it told him that he ought to take some measure of satisfaction in her fright, but all he felt was hot, pulsing need.

Chapter Eight

Gillian ran, gasping, up the stairs, mindlessly seeking sanctuary where none existed. She realized the hopelessness of her search when she reached the door of the great chamber, for it was *his* room, filled with *his* bed. Resting her forehead against the wood, Gillian slumped against it, loath to enter.

As soon as she halted, the memory of what had happened below assailed her. Lord have mercy, she had thought him a stallion before, but beneath her hand his wick had become so huge, so horrifying, that her breathing had stopped. She was still trying to catch it, and she closed her eyes tightly, trying to concentrate on her flow of air and not upon *him*.

The fiend tormented her apurpose, of that Gillian had no doubt, and she welcomed the anger that came hard on the heels of her fear. How could he make her touch him, right there at the supper table, where people could see? Her cheeks burned, and she slammed a fist into the door, releasing her shame and frustration with the violent blow.

If only she could banish the recollection as easily. Her fingers tingled still where they had pressed against him, hot and hard and threatening. Gillian sucked in a deep, shaky draft, fighting her terror and revulsion.

But that was not all she felt. Underneath the more familiar emotions seethed something new and different and even more frightening: a strange quickening that centered deep inside her. Loosing a long, ragged sigh, Gillian realized that for an instant, when her palm held him, she had wanted to twine her other hand into his hair and put her mouth on his, losing herself to sensation. *Surrendering.*

Gillian blinked rapidly as anxiety swamped her. She could run from her husband, but how could she run from herself? There was no place to go, nowhere to hide.

Immersed in her misery, Gillian did not notice the small sound behind her until something drifted out of the shadows. Then she started, gulping back a cry as the form took shape. The Syrian. Lifting her head from the door, Gillian straightened, sniffing slightly.

"Do not fear him, lady. He will not hurt you," the foreigner said, with a vehemence that made her uncomfortable. She did not want anyone to see her in this vulnerable state, especially not this stranger.

Turning to face him, Gillian did not dispute his words, for she knew he meant well. She nodded, eager to be rid of his prying eyes, but he was not yet finished. To her surprise, he took both her hands in his, clasping them lightly in a reassuring grasp. "Have faith, lady. And remember that you have friends here," he said. His kindness made her want to weep—until he spoke again in defense of her husband. "Your lord has been filled with hate so long that he is afraid to feel anything else," he whispered.

"Afraid?" Gillian scoffed. "He fears nothing."

Darius shrugged, as if unwilling to argue with her, and a long silence followed that Gillian suspected was rich with hidden meaning. If only she were clever enough to decipher it. Nicholas she understood, for all her mixed emotions about him, but this mysterious man was beyond her comprehension. She stared up into his face, half hidden by the shadows of the passage, seeking answers, but the only reply was the sound of a deep, smooth voice, so laced with menace that it sent shivers up her spine.

"Take . . . your . . . hands . . . from . . . my . . . wife." Nicholas pronounced each word as if he might explode at any moment, and Gillian saw him then, standing behind the Syrian, his face utterly cold and still. He did not raise his voice, and yet the icy tone was more threatening than his loudest shout.

Although Gillian quivered, Darius apparently felt no fear, for he squeezed her fingers lightly before releasing them and turning to face his friend. Or his enemy. At this point, Gillian could not tell what Nicholas had become. She backed up against the door.

"What do you here, Darius, alone with my wife before her bedchamber?" Nicholas asked. Gillian saw his hand drift to the dagger at his waist, and she bit back a cry. Surely he would not take the knife to his companion! "Well?" he taunted softly.

The Syrian showed no concern, nor did he touch his weapon, a large, curved blade so deadly-looking that Gillian's anxiety shifted toward her husband. "I am guarding her, as you requested," Darius replied evenly.

"You are relieved of that duty," Nicholas said slowly. "And if you ever touch her again, I will kill you."

The Syrian nodded, leaning forward slightly in a bow of sorts, and left without another word. Lord have mercy, the man acted as if a threat to his life were as nothing! Gillian collapsed against the door, relieved that no blood had been shed, but then her husband's attention focused on her, and she stiffened under the sharp edge of his rage.

"Inside," he said, and Gillian pushed at the wood with shaking fingers, never taking an eye off the predator who loomed over her. Once away from the closeness of the passage, she felt better, and she moved to the middle of the room, head held high, refusing to cower as she turned to face the beast he had become.

Like a fallen angel, he stood before her, too beautiful to be real, too terrible to be trusted. Heat seemed to pour from him in waves, a combination of fierce anger that repelled her and hot masculinity that drew her against her will. Gillian swallowed hard. She could almost imagine the fires of hell lapping at his heels.

"If he has done more than hold your hand, I will kill you both," he promised, his voice a guttural bark.

What? The insult astonished Gillian, and she stared at him blankly. Surely he did not really think that she and the Syrian—?

His gaze never left her, bright and probing and denying her innocence. "Perhaps you did not realize, little nun, that 'tis not wise to be alone with a man!" He spat the words out, as if the very taste of them was foul upon his tongue.

"We were talking, nothing more!" Gillian protested, alarmed by the look in the glittering depths of his eyes. "Trust you not your own guard?"

"Nay! I trust no one when it comes to you!" Nicholas growled, taking a step toward her.

Comprehension dawned slowly, laced with so much disbelief that Gillian shook her head, as if dazed. Regarding him with wide-eyed wonder, she whispered the truth. "You are jealous."

He flinched, but did not deny it. "You are mine, body and soul, and you had best remember it!" he warned her. "I do not want to see you speaking to the Syrian again. Aye, or even looking his way!"

He was jealous! Gillian felt an odd tingling in her chest that was not a loss of breath. "Oh, for the love of Saint

Paul! The foreigner is nothing to me! What would he want with a big, gawky red-haired girl? He has shown me kindness, that is all. Truth to tell, he unnerves me, with those eyes of his," Gillian said, pausing to shudder at the memory of them looking into her soul.

When she glanced up, Nicholas seemed calmer. Perhaps his temper was spent. And he accused *her* of having fits? The man acted like a raving lunatic at times. Gillian watched him lift a palm to his belly, and she knew that all this angry shouting aggravated his condition.

"I can give you something that will help." The words were out of her mouth before she considered them, and Gillian immediately regretted her speech, for he jerked his hand away as if his own flesh had burned him.

"What?"

The icy-smooth tenor of his voice did not bode well for her efforts, but Gillian persevered. "Ground ivy will ease the pain in your stomach. I can easily prepare it for you."

"I want nothing from you!" he snarled.

"Be sensible!"

"Be quiet!" Nicholas snapped, moving away from her. "No doubt you would like the chance to poison me, but I will take nothing from your hand, heir of Hexham. Your blood is tainted!"

Gillian fell back, as if he had struck her, so forcibly had he reminded her of her place within his world. Ever it would come down to this: She meant naught to him but a chance for vengeance.

And to think she had actually accused him of being jealous! Nicholas de Laci was not capable of such a reaction; there was no room in him for anything but hatred. His anger had been precipitated solely by possessiveness. He would let no other covet—or even comfort—the object of his revenge.

The knowledge sank through Gillian's body like a stone, dragging at her spirits, deadening her heart. Suddenly chilled, she wrapped her arms about her chest, hugging herself close.

"Listen to me, *wife,* for I would make clear to you your position in this household. You will no longer take upon yourself the duties of a chatelaine or even a servant. You will respond only to my orders, attend solely to me, speak only to me, look only at me. Have you had a bath?"

Gillian's mouth dropped open at his abrupt query, following so closely upon his startling mandates. "No, I—" she began, but he held up a hand, forestalling her words. She snapped shut her lips, unsure what he was about. Why was he so obsessed with cleanliness? Although they were hardly filthy, the nuns had been more occupied with matters of the spirit than with those of the flesh, and Gillian was unaccustomed to such concerns.

"As my wife, you shall bathe daily," Nicholas ordered. Striding to the door, he stuck his head out and called for Osborn to fetch hot water. Gillian gasped at his audacity. His manner alone was bad enough, with his constant shouts and commands; did he think to control even her most personal habits? Gillian dropped her arms to her side and glared at him. The man was outrageous!

He whirled back toward her, his face implacable. "As I said, your sole task is to attend me. You will be at my beck and call, day and night. Whatever I want, you shall fetch for me personally. You will bring me my morning cup and make sure that I am bedded down comfortably every evening."

Gillian blanched at the mention of his bed, but was too angry to lose her breath over it. What kind of tasks were these? At the convent, everyone did for themselves, with only a few outsiders to help. And when she served in Freemantle's household, she had cleaned the hearth and scrubbed the floor and worked hard. What did this man want of her?

"And you will go about your work willingly. I would have you strive to behave more like an eastern woman, for they not only know how to please, but are submissive and obedient, anticipating a man's every need," he said, his lips curving wickedly. "In effect, Gillian, you shall be as a slave. *My* slave."

"Slave?" Gillian protested, choking on the word. "You are barbaric! There are no slaves in Britain. Go back to the East, and find yourself some godless infidel to dance upon your whims!"

Ignoring her outburst, he circled her in a way that might have been calculated to dismay her. "Do not make the mistake of condemning a culture you do not understand. There are many fine things to be learned in the East. There, a wife lets down her hair only for her husband."

He turned suddenly, and for once, his silver eyes did not glitter with malice. Instead, they seemed to smolder with a hidden fire. Gillian took a step back, unsure whether the change was an improvement. "I would like you to adopt that custom. In fact, I would like to see it now."

"What?" Gillian gaped, uncertain just what he was asking of her.

"Let down your hair. I wish to see it," he whispered. His voice had gone all liquid and strange, and Gillian's heart threatened to pop out of her chest. "Then you may bathe."

"What?" she whispered, unable to believe her ears. He expected her to get into that tub, without her clothing, while he stood by and watched? Something oddly akin to excitement sizzled along the surface of her skin and shot through to her innermost parts. But along with that strange awareness came fear, and Gillian felt the old, familiar constriction in her throat. She gasped, staring at him in panic.

Gillian did not know what she expected—certainly not sympathy—and yet she looked to him for aid. He was the only one who could help her, and a few nights ago he had. Now, however, he assessed her with narrowed eyes, obviously angered by her distress. "Have you been raped?" he asked bluntly.

Startled by the question, Gillian sucked in a deep draft of needed air. "No, of course not! Why would you ask such a thing?"

"Because you have an unnatural fear of intimacy."

Gillian spluttered, astonished by such open speech. Of course she was afraid, as would any woman be when faced with a husband who despised her. "And why should I not? You are a brute, who would abuse me for your own sport!"

"Have I ever raised a hand to you?" he snapped. "Have I ever hurt you? By my faith, I could kill you, and none would stop me, but when I ask you to unbind your hair, you look as if you would faint!"

He whirled away in disgust, and Gillian stared at his broad back. Yes, he had hurt her many times with his sharp tongue and dagger eyes, but never with his fists. In truth, he had done little, physically, to her, and certainly nothing terrible, she thought, remembering the way he had pressed her palm to him.

Gillian swallowed hard. "I was a servant once before," she said softly. "It was a hard life, but the worst part was when my master would...fondle me." She heard Nicholas's swift turn, but could not look at him.

"He never raped me," she hastened to add, "but he would back me into a corner and...squeeze and pinch me and talk foully." Gillian blew out a long breath at this telling, for she had never spoken to a soul of that shameful part of her life. Indeed, she had never even confessed her sins to the convent priest.

Yet the words grew easier, as if she unburdened herself of the past by sharing it. "He would drop his braies, pull out his ugly little wick and wave it at me—"

Before she could utter another sound, Gillian found herself pushed, none too gently, back against the wall. It was Nicholas who pressed her, who took her chin in his hand and forced her to look at him. Unwilling to face his revulsion, Gillian wanted to close her eyes, but he made her open them, and to her surprise, she saw neither shame nor horror on his handsome features.

He was angry. His eyes glittered, more fiercely than ever, and Gillian drew in a startled breath.

"His name!" Nicholas demanded hoarsely.

"Who?" Gillian asked, her head spinning at both his nearness and his rage.

"The bastard who did this to you!"

"A-Abel F-Freemantle of Renfred," Gillian stammered, puzzled by his sudden savagery. He dropped his arm and whirled away, crossing the room in great strides to grab his traveling pack.

Leaning against the wall where he had left her, Gillian watched in astonishment. "What are you doing? Are you leaving? You just returned today," she protested. "Where are you going now?"

Over his shoulder, Nicholas looked at her as if she were witless. "I go to kill him, of course."

"Who? *Abel?*" Gillian asked, her voice rising in panic. "Nicholas! You cannot mean it! Do not!"

He halted abruptly to pin her with that frightening gray gaze. "You have some affection for the bastard?" he asked, his tone silky with menace.

"No, but neither do I wish to have his death on my head!" Gillian said. "For the love of Saint Paul, why must everything always be black and white with you? All or nothing? Hate or indifference, and naught in between?''

He did not answer, but stalked toward her, all cold fury. Anyone with sense would have backed down and been quiet, but Gillian had never been known for her restraint. She lifted her chin. ''Yes, the man frightened me, and I did not like what he did, but he had some good in him. He took me into his household when I had nowhere else to go. I might have died, had it not been for him.''

Nicholas stood in front of her now, a tall, angry knight who could crush her in an instant, and Gillian knew she must turn him from his blood lust. Unable to think of the words to persuade him, she reached out to lay a restraining hand upon his arm. It was a simple enough gesture, intended to both calm and entreat her husband, and yet it turned out to be so much more than she expected.

The minute she made contact, Gillian felt as if she had stuck her hand into the fire. Her palm sizzled, sending bright sensation through her, and she looked up at him, startled. Their eyes met, hers dazed, his smoldering, and then he slowly let his gaze fall to her fingers, where they rested on his sleeve.

Suddenly Gillian realized that this was the first time she had ever really touched him of her own will. For a long moment, she, too, stared stupidly down at where they were joined, and then, just as swiftly as before, she was pinned against the wall. Again Nicholas took her chin in his hand, but this time he lifted her face to meet his own. His intention dawned on her only a second before his mouth came down upon hers.

No Hoodman Blind boon was this, but a claiming as fierce as Nicholas himself. Almost immediately, he thrust his tongue deep, and Gillian shuddered with the force of it. As if of its own accord, her hand slid up his arm to curl around his neck, beneath his dark hair. He pressed against her, tall and hard, and she reveled in the feel of his male body, so unlike anything she had ever known.

His knee pushed between her thighs, nudging at the very center of her, and Gillian gasped, though she was unafraid. Never in her darkest dreams had she imagined such excitement, such frantic, hot delight. Boldly she ran a palm up the front of Nicholas's broad chest, then grasped his tunic tightly, as if to anchor herself against the passion that buffeted her very being.

Opening her mouth wider, Gillian returned his kiss, sending her tongue swirling to meet his, and Nicholas grunted in approval. His hands moved over her shoulders and arms and along her waist, as if he would mark her as his own.

"Where did he touch you?" Nicholas rasped against her lips. Struggling to understand the question, Gillian opened her eyes to meet smoky ones simmering with heat. Listening to his shuddering breaths, she realized, with a sense of heady power, that now it was Nicholas who struggled for air.

"Where?" he demanded. Emboldened, Gillian did not falter, but took his hand and dragged it to her bodice. Their gazes locked, her chest heaved, and slowly, so very slowly, Nicholas caressed her breast. Gillian gasped as bright, hot sensation leapt through her. Closing her eyes, she let her head fall back, and he took her mouth again, fiercely, even as his hand closed around her, his thumb stroking her nipple into a hard peak.

It was heaven, but fiery as hell, in the embrace of this beautiful, terrible creature, and Gillian felt herself falling from grace. What might have happened next, she would never know, for suddenly the door opened and Osborn bustled in with more hot water. Although Gillian clung, heedless, to the arms that held her, Nicholas stepped back, breaking away as if they were guilty lovers. Which, of course, they were not.

"Your water is here," he whispered hoarsely. Then, without a backward glance, he retrieved his pack and strode out of the chamber, leaving Gillian sagging against the wall, her heart pounding desperately.

She stood where she was for a long while, ignoring Osborn's cheery chatter until the servant left her alone with the tub. She wanted no one to attend her, for she felt strange, as foreign to herself as Darius, because of her swollen lips and heated skin.

With trembling fingers, Gillian removed her gown, and when it fell to the floor she felt more naked than ever before, as if something besides her flesh had been bared. For the first time in her life, she looked down at herself. The body she had always thought too tall and gawky suddenly seemed lush and vital, her breasts heavy, her nipples hard, her thighs hot and moist where they had closed around Nicholas's hard, muscular leg....

Flushing, Gillian stepped into the water and sank down to her chin, but she could not relax. Her entire being felt warm and alive and wanting.... Angrily Gillian scrubbed herself clean, as if to erase all traces of him, and as soon as she was finished, she climbed out, dried herself and dressed quickly in a fresh shift. Settling into her cozy nest at the end of the bed, she closed her eyes, but sleep would not come. The large chamber suddenly seemed especially quiet—and empty.

It had nothing to do with Nicholas.

Well, in all honesty, Gillian had to admit that her husband was so much larger than life that he filled any space, even this enormous room, with his fierce personality. And now that he was gone, it seemed particularly toom.

That was all, Gillian told herself. Her restlessness had naught to do with what had passed between them, with the kiss, or whatever one would call what had happened up against that wall. Gillian's eyes flickered to the spot, as if seeking some sign of what had occurred there, but no mark of the momentous event that had so affected her remained.

Gillian tried push the memory to the back of her mind and concentrate, instead, on the conversation that had gone before, in which her husband had demanded that she act the part of some infidel slave girl. Or, worse yet, when she had offered to fix him something to help his stomach and he had turned on her like a wild beast.

Any fool could see that Nicholas's stomach pained him, if he observed him closely. Although he tried to hide it, Gillian had noticed the telltale movement of his hand to his belly and how his entire body tensed with the worst of it. Was he too proud to seek aid?

Perhaps it was only her help that he refused, for Gillian remembered how the cook provided him with bland foods when everyone else was clamoring for exotic spices. Gillian stiffened, her chin automatically lifting at his rejection. Let him suffer, then, the stubborn wretch!

Poison indeed, she fumed, recalling his accusation. She ought to take him up on his suggestion. A sprinkle of nightshade, and then she would be free of his bullying ways forever! Gillian savored the idea for a moment before the ramifications set in. Even if she could bring herself to do murder, she would not be her own master. As a rich widow, she would be prime game for Edward to marry off again, and Gillian shuddered at the thought of living with someone else.

If she ceded Belvry to the king, maybe she could return to the convent, but Gillian did not find the notion as comforting as she ought to. Too vividly, she remembered the feel of the cold stone floor under her knees after hours of prayer, and the disorientation of being roused at midnight to chant before catching snatches of sleep and rising again at dawn.

Crossing herself quickly, Gillian was ashamed of her own failings, but now that she had been to Belvry, with its beautiful lands, friendly people, fine food, soft pillows and private chambers ... She realized with a sudden start that she would rather brave her fiendish husband than go back to the nunnery.

Of course, her choice had nothing to do with *him*. If she was sent away, she would miss Edith and all those who had been kind and welcoming to her, even Darius, with his strange, watchful eyes. She would certainly not yearn for her husband, with his hateful gaze and fits of temper and hard body and hot mouth....

Gillian raised trembling fingers to her cheek, where he had touched her, and let them slide lower down, over her breast. Her heart pounded wildly, as if it might burst from her body, just at the memory of what he had done to her. Nicholas's rough hands had felt nothing like Freemantle's clumsy groping. Indeed, she could now barely recall her old master, for Nicholas had made her forget all else but him, as if in those few, fevered moments, he had marked her as his own.

And perhaps he had. Try as she might, Gillian knew she could no longer lie to herself. She wanted Nicholas to do it all again—wanted him as fiercely as she had once despised him.

Alone in the vast room, she gasped for breath, for the knowledge of her weakness was as frightening as it was heady. And, ultimately, disastrous. For as much as she yearned for her husband, she could never surrender herself to him.

Chapter Nine

Nicholas did not try to tamp down the eagerness that ran through him as he approached Belvry. He told himself that it was natural to enjoy returning to his own lands and that it had nothing to do with Gillian.

Still, she sprang to mind, strong and tall and fiery, a mate worthy of any man. And she was *his*. This time he would not find her engaged with the servants in some lowly task, nor would he discover her in some private conversation with Darius. The Syrian would keep his distance from Gillian.

As would Abel Freemantle.

Nicholas's lips curled. All the pleasure he had thought to feel when tormenting his bride had come to him in the form of Abel Freemantle. He had descended upon the burgher's home like an avenging angel, dragging the bastard out in front of his entire household. Nicholas had cataloged his crimes until he was on his knees, begging for his life, while his wife and children wept and pleaded, too.

Even then, Nicholas had wanted to run the man through, and only the memory of Gillian's remonstrations had stayed his sword arm. Exacting a promise from the quaking burgher that he would touch no one but his wife ever again, Nicholas had let him live. The man had agreed most willingly, especially after Nicholas threatened to come back and castrate him if he broke his word.

Assured that the burgher's perverted games were over, Nicholas had left, without ever giving his name or revealing the source of his information. Gillian should be pleased, he thought, not bothering to wonder why her opinion should concern him.

But it did. Nicholas looked forward to her reaction. Aye, when she learned of his deed, she would be most grateful—indebted to him, even. Anticipation heated his blood, and he strode into the great hall swiftly, his eyes searching for her.

Almost immediately, they found her, and he smiled in satisfaction. At last, she had heeded his words well and would attend him as she should! For the first time since their marriage, she was waiting for him upon his return, dressed appropriately in a gown green as her eyes, her cheeks flushed becomingly as she moved forward to greet him.

For a moment, Nicholas considered catching her up in his arms, but he swiftly discarded the notion, startled by the odd turn of this thoughts. He did not want her to think he was actually glad to see her, because he was not. Was he?

Scowling at his own weakness, Nicholas noticed his steward approaching, but his attention was upon Gillian. He forced himself to stop and let her come to him. It felt heady, this first glimpse of her as his personal slave. When she was but a few feet from him, she stopped, and he wondered if she would reach for him.

She did not. Instead, she curled her fingers into fists and glared at him. "How could you? What of his widow and children? Who will provide for them, now that you have murdered their father in cold blood?"

Out of the corner of his eye, Nicholas saw his steward quickly change direction, and it was just as well. He had a few things to say to the woman who was shouting at him, her eyes flashing fire. "What the devil are you ranting about?" he snapped.

"Master Freemantle! What have you done to him?"

"'Tis none of your business, or have you so forgotten your place in this household?" Nicholas yelled back.

"I will be no man's slave!" she shrieked, and to his astonishment, she grabbed a forgotten cup from the table and threw it at his head.

It missed him by a bare inch. "Halt, vixen, or you will rue your actions, I promise you!" Nicholas warned, descending upon her. He was not quite sure what he intended, for when she riled him like this he could not think. He only knew he had to get his hands on her. Paying no attention to the gasps of the bystanders who turned and fled from the hall, Nicholas stepped forward just as Gillian let fly with another missile.

Nicholas dodged it and lunged for her, but she leapt onto the table. He watched in amazement as she lifted her skirts, giving him a tantalizing glimpse of her shapely calves as she moved, fleet of foot, toward the other end.

"Gillian!" he shouted, his patience waning. *"Get down, or I will drag you down!"* When she ignored him, he gave chase, racing to head her off. And when he caught her, he promised himself, she would regret her very life.

As Piers helped her down from her palfrey, Aisley gripped his muscular upper arms, gaining strength from him, as she always did. In truth, she had mixed feelings about descending, without warning, upon her brother. At the best of times, Nicholas was not a man to appreciate family ties, and now, so soon after his marriage to Hexham's niece, would probably qualify as the worst of times.

Yet Aisley had been unable to stay away. After hearing about the poor girl who was to be torn from her life in the convent and sacrificed to her uncle's enemy, Aisley had to intervene. Although she doubted that Nicholas would listen to her pleas, she could hardly stand by and let him take revenge upon a helpless nun.

So she had convinced Piers to bring her, hoping that their presence would have a softening affect on the hard man her brother had become. Glancing around uneasily, Aisley was surprised that he had not come out to greet them, for he kept a wary eye on everything and everyone.

What if he refused to see them? Aisley worried her lip and told herself that Nicholas could not be that churlish. His lack of welcome could easily be ascribed to thoughtlessness, for he rarely considered anyone but himself. Thus assured, Aisley joined Piers at the entrance to the great hall, only to stop short, startled by shouting in the usually peaceful environs of Belvry.

"What is that?" she asked, turning to Piers. Alert for danger, he rested a hand on his sword hilt, while Aisley peered into the hall in confusion. But for brief skirmishes with their now deceased neighbor, the residents of Belvry had enjoyed harmony and prosperity for many years.

Aisley watched her husband cock his head to take advantage of the hearing that had sharpened during his blindness. "It sounds like your brother," he said, with a puzzled expression.

"Nicholas? He has never raised his voice in his life," Aisley said. Whoever was yelling sounded more like Piers in the throes of one of his tempers than her cool and detached brother. So where was Nicholas, and why did he allow such a clamor?

Determined to find out just what was going on, Aisley stepped into the hall where she had once reigned, only to stare, left dumbfounded by the sight that met her eyes. Uncertain, she walked closer, but there was no mistaking the dark hair and tall form of her brother.

Nicholas was chasing someone around the table—a female! As far as Aisley could recall, he had shown little but contempt for any woman, yet he was pursuing this one like a man possessed. While Aisley watched in astonishment, her stoic brother, who never raised a hand in anger or affection, picked up the woman and slung her over his shoulder like a sack of grain!

She and Piers had nearly reached him when he turned around, and Aisley was stunned to see his surprise—the first emotion besides hatred that had crossed his face in years. Indeed, their presence appeared to leave him speechless, and he stood gaping at them, while the woman hanging over his back tried to kick him and strike him with her fists.

"Stop that!" Nicholas called over his shoulder. He glanced back at them, and Aisley could have sworn he was embarrassed. Nicholas, who had once seemed to feel nothing? She had to bite her lip to keep from smiling.

"Aisley, Piers," he said, grunting when the woman's toe caught him in the gut. "What brings you here?" Upon hearing him speak, the female stopped rebelling and stilled, but Nicholas offered no explanation for her position or her struggle.

"Have you a recalcitrant servant there?" Piers asked finally, eyeing the comely bottom perched on Nicholas's chest with more amusement than Aisley dared.

"What? Ah, no," Nicholas said. His eyes darted to the derriere, and then back to his guests. "This is my wife."

Aisley stared in amazement as Nicholas slowly let down his burden. The woman slid along his tall body to stand upright upon her own two feet, but he kept a protective arm around her waist, as if he were afraid she might bolt. Would she? Aisley could hardly believe the wild creature who had dared fight against her brother was his novice bride. Although Aisley found all that kicking and squalling rather unseemly, when the girl turned, her face crimson, her eyes downcast, Aisley was disarmed.

She was pretty. Although very tall, she was not a big woman. Her body was blessed with womanly curves, yet she remained slender and held herself with dignity befitting a de Laci. A lock of red hair slipped from her caul, marking her as temperamental, but it was a lovely color, and under delicately arched brows, her eyes were an arresting emerald green.

This was Hexham's niece? She did not resemble that raven-haired bastard in the slightest, nor did her wary gaze reflect his treacherous wiles. Indeed, had she not known, Aisley would never have connected the two. But what of Nicholas? Could he see past his hatred to the lovely young woman at his side?

Aisley assessed the girl closely, surprised to see that she did not appear to be ill-used. On the contrary, she seemed to be in the bloom of health, and the way Nicholas anchored her to him was very interesting. It was not the embrace of an enemy.

Glancing back at her brother, Aisley decided that he was still tongue-tied, though she could hardly believe it. More astonishing yet, his usually impassive face seemed to flicker with a variety of emotions. Embarrassment? Pride? Protectiveness? Aisley would have studied him further, but for his lack of common courtesy.

"Hello. I am Nicholas's sister, Aisley, and this is my husband, Piers," she said, smiling in greeting. "You must be Gillian." Immediately the girl's face brightened, transforming her features, and Aisley nearly caught her breath.

Nicholas's bride was more than just pretty. She was a vital, beautiful woman.

A wail from behind her made Aisley turn toward the procession that followed and the nurse who carried the baby. Reaching out, she took the child, who quieted immediately. "And this noisy girl is Sybil," she said, cooing at the infant.

When she looked up at Gillian, the wonder and longing in the green eyes stunned her, and she automatically held out Sybil to her. "Say hello to your aunt Gillian," she urged softly.

Nicholas's wife took the baby with an expression of awe and held her gently. Sybil, to her credit, did not fuss, but gave her obviously doting audience a big grin. "She smiles at me!" Gillian exclaimed, making Piers chuckle. "I have never held a baby before."

The comment made Aisley glance at her brother, who was watching his wife intently. Nicholas had no love for Sybil, yet he did not seem to look right through her, as he so often had in the past. In fact, he appeared to see the child for the first time as he watched his wife with her.

Nicholas had changed. Everything Aisley had witnessed so far attested to it, and when he met her gaze, she discovered the most astonishing improvement of all. Her brother's eyes neither glittered with a hatred that threatened to consume him nor were empty and cold. Something was there, something new and different....

Aisley caught only a glimpse of it before his features hardened once more into cool detachment. "Have you not fostered the child out yet?" he asked.

She would have laughed at the question, had his voice not been so smooth and cruel. She had suffered the hurt of his indifference, but he would not visit it upon her daughter.

"No, Nicholas. She is just a baby, too young to be sent away from her mother."

"Aisley does not believe in fostering," Piers said, in his own strong way that brooked no argument. Bless him for agreeing with her that the practice of placing young children in another household, away from their parents, did little to promote a loving family life.

"My children will stay with me," Aisley affirmed, and all the power of her conviction rang in her words. Although she had become too valuable to her father to be spared, she had seen her brothers leave home, only to return as strangers, all of them cold and untouchable and so very different from her warm, loving husband.

Aisley glanced back at Sybil, her heart softening, and was surprised at the bright green glare that Nicholas's bride flashed his way. This red-haired woman braved much....

"As you wish." Nicholas acceded with a curt nod, and Aisley blinked in amazement. Obviously, more than simple revenge was taking place within the confines of her brother's marriage. Perhaps there was hope for Nicholas yet....

"You must be tired after your long journey," he said abruptly. "Osborn! Prepare the Lady Aisley's old room for her and her husband." Osborn came scurrying out of the shadows, just as though he had been hiding there, and Aisley took Sybil from Gillian, who relinquished the child with obvious reluctance.

With a final encouraging smile, she left Nicholas's wife to follow Osborn toward the stairs.

Hurrying along, she quickly reached the servant's side, and soon her former people began to welcome her, streaming out from under the archways as if they had not dared go out into their own hall. Aisley paused to greet them, and although she usually did not encourage gossip, she found herself eager to hear what they thought of their lord's new wife.

What Aisley discovered shocked her, and she said as much to her husband as they sat down to supper at the high table. Sliding a quick glance away from her sullen brother at the head of the dais, she leaned close to Piers. "The people of Belvry are afraid!" she whispered heatedly. "They run and hide when Nicholas comes within a stone's throw of his wife!"

"Why?" Piers asked, eyeing her with curiosity.

"Because he acts like a madman around her, screaming and shouting and chasing after her as if his wits had left him!"

Piers's lips curved in bemusement as he sliced their trencher in two. "Obviously, I did not stay here long enough for them to get to know me well. Else they would not fear a man's temper."

Aisley smiled in spite of herself, her heart softening as it always did around her husband. "'Tis not the same thing at all. Everyone knows of your passionate nature, and they no longer fear you."

"Really?" he asked, brows lifting in amusement.

"Well, most of them, anyway. But that is different! These people have known Nicholas since he was a child, and they are frightened by the sudden change in him."

Piers shrugged, obviously unconcerned. "Has he hurt anyone?"

"No, not as far as I know," Aisley answered. "Though they complain of his excessively foul humor. And they are wagering! The whole household is placing bets upon who shall be the victor in the battle between the lord and his lady!"

Aisley frowned in disapproval, until she saw the corners of Piers's mouth twitching. "Well, 'tis not right," she asserted. "I talked to Edith for only a moment, but I suspect her fine hand in this! You know how disrespectful she can be! What do you think?"

"I do not believe the Church looks very highly upon such gaming."

"Not about the wagering!" Aisley said. "About Nicholas and his wife!"

"I think you dragged me from my home for naught," Piers answered, in his dry way, "for that lady is no more abused than you are."

Beneath lowered lashes, Aisley studied the regal beauty who sat quietly beside Nicholas. "She does look good, much better than I expected, but do not underestimate my brother. He can cut to the quick with just a glance, and 'twould leave no marks."

"Surely the red-haired nun is a match for him," Piers said with an appreciative grin.

"I wonder..." Aisley mused. Nicholas's wife did not look abused, nor fearful, but she was stiff and silent, and had situated herself as far from her husband as possible, while Nicholas... Nicholas picked at his food and eyed everyone with the same hard expression.

Aisley bit her lip anxiously. Perhaps she had only imagined the changes in him this afternoon, for now he appeared as cold and unfeeling as ever. He kept his distance from his wife, and if there was any warmth between them, Aisley could not see it.

Gillian covertly watched Nicholas's sister and her husband, and for the first time in her life, she committed the sin of envy. The two seemed so happy together! Aisley was dainty and beautiful and confident, and Piers, for all his intimidating size, seemed kind and gentle. He treated his wife with a respect and affection that was apparent, and it made jealousy burn in Gillian's breast.

She would not deny them their happiness—far from it! But she coveted a small portion for herself: a husband who did not rage and insult her at every turn, who did not despise the very blood in her veins and charge off to kill as if he enjoyed it. And along with such a man, Gillian would wish for a child.

A baby of her own.

It was like a revelation, this sudden, fierce need, and it had appeared out of nowhere, for Gillian had long ago given up dreams of a family, her years at the nunnery leeching out any lingering hopes. In truth, she could not even remember the last time she had thought of children, but seeing Sybil had changed everything.

The moment she held the infant in her arms, Gillian had been rocked with a longing stronger than she had ever known. Never before in her life had she wanted anything beyond the rudimentary needs that had once been taken from her: food, shelter, and warmth. But now she wanted something else. She wanted a baby.

Gillian had thought of nothing else since the encounter, and she would be sitting with the infant right now, if she thought Nicholas would allow it. With a pensive frown, Gillian slid a glance at her husband, who was picking at his food again and glowering at his guests. She drew in a deep breath as she realized that if she would just gather her courage together, she could obtain what she so desired.

Shuddering, Gillian stifled an embarrassing gasp before she regained control of herself. Whatever went before would be worth the prize, she thought with a firm resolve. And just how bad could it be, this bedding?

Abruptly the memory of Nicholas pressing her against the wall, his knee thrust between her legs, his mouth hot and powerful on her own, came to her, vivid and startling in its intensity. Gillian glanced over at his hand, strong and lean and long-fingered, and she was overcome by the recollection of it cupping her breast. Her heart pounded, making her feel giddy and reckless. She could do it! She would! But then her gaze slid to his face, cold and unyielding and filled with hate, and she knew the answer to her own question.

It could be bad, really bad.

But what of Edith's promise that she could enslave her husband, if she but expended some effort? The old servant had tendered advice more than once, hinting at practices that made Gillian's cheeks burn crimson. Could she really do such things with Nicholas? Reaching for her cup, Gillian noticed that her hand was trembling, and she sloshed ale upon the table in a nervous grab for the vessel.

The mishap made Nicholas swivel to pin her with the full force of his chilly gray gaze, and Gillian faltered. Coward! she thought to herself, knowing she could never seduce this man, no matter what Edith said. Lifting her chin and taking a deep drink, she was reminded of Edith's folly with the spring tonic. Obviously, the old servant meant well, but was not always right.

And Edith had a high opinion of Nicholas de Laci that Gillian did not share. Perhaps the fiend had not murdered anyone that Edith knew, but Gillian had watched him rush off to kill Abel Freemantle like a madman. Gillian realized that she could do nothing with that painful knowledge still fresh in her mind.

An emptiness seemed to grow inside her at the thought, and Gillian turned her attention to her meal. The food was a comfort, as always, and she finished her own quickly. Then, without even thinking, she began picking untouched pieces from her husband's portion, as well. Listening absently to Aisley's soft voice, Gillian lifted her head when addressed, answering questions about her life at the convent as best she could.

Still hungry, Gillian was in the process of spearing a chunk of meat on her husband's trencher when Aisley made the blithe comment "But you were never made to be a nun. You were so good with Sybil that you must have children of your own."

Startled, Gillian dropped the morsel directly upon Nicholas's outstretched arm, and he roared to life like a slumbering beast. "Enough idle chatter! 'Tis late, and our guests must be tired," he said, glaring at his sister and her husband as if he would like to toss them outside. "Come, wife," he commanded her, and taking her arm in a grip that brooked no resistance, he practically dragged her up to their chamber.

He did not release her until the door was closed behind them, but this time Gillian was not frightened. She was too furious. She turned upon him like a cat, clawing at his face, until he held her away, stunned at her fierceness.

"How dare you treat me thusly in front of your kin?" Gillian shouted. "You murdering bastard!"

With a low oath, he tossed her away from him, and Gillian landed against the bed, suddenly eager to finish the fight between them. She raised up on her elbows, but he held up a hand, stopping her protest.

"Lest you mark me with your claws, vixen, I would have you know that I did not kill your burgher. I let the bastard live, with the promise that he would keep his filthy paws to himself."

For a moment, Gillian could only lie there, gaping at him, so stunned was she by his words. Nicholas de Laci showed mercy? Truly, the world was full of strange wonders! So amazed was she that it took her a while to find her tongue, but when she did, the words came easily. "Thank you," she whispered.

He stared at her long and hard, as if her speech had startled him, as well. Then he whirled away from her. "Now that we have finished with that business, I would remind you that a lady does not throw objects at her lord, or climb upon tables set for a meal, or attempt to scratch his eyes out!"

Gillian blew out a harsh breath. "Maybe if I were the lady of the castle, I would remember these strictures, but since I am not..."

"Neither does a slave attack her owner, vixen!"

"I will not be your slave!"

"Aye, you are, and you shall do your duties now! You are mine, and you shall do as I bid! Let down your hair!"

Gillian gulped, but her anger had been building for too long, disgrace upon disgrace, until it was too strong to give way to fear. "Oh, no," she said, shaking her head. "You will not terrorize me again. I am sick to death of your taunts!"

She remembered a long ago lesson her brother had taught her: The only way to handle a bully was to face up to him. And, taking a deep breath, Gillian did. She pushed off the mattress to rise straight and tall, and threw his taunt back at him.

"You want me? Then come and get me!" she said, lifting her chin in challenge. Once spoken aloud, the words were not so frightening, and Nicholas's stunned expression only made Gillian stronger. With determined fingers, she reached behind her and undid her gown, watching both the bodice and her husband's mouth gape open. Nicholas looked thunderstruck, for once seemingly speechless, and Gillian knew her own power.

"If you think that molesting me will bring you the triumph you seek, then go ahead, have at me!" she said, yanking off her gown and tossing it onto the floor. "But be warned that no matter what you do to me, I will never surrender to you."

Gillian stood before him in her shift, unashamed and unafraid, and glowing with a heady sense of freedom. While her husband stared, she lay back on the bed, her calves barred to his view. He remained motionless, but his eyes were burning into her now, and she could have sworn his hands were trembling. Or perhaps it was her own, as they touched the hem of her shift.

For a moment, time seemed suspended, as she reached for it, ready to draw it up, to take the final step. Then there would be no going back, no time to worry about her choice, only a headlong rush into the unknown. Yet Gillian already felt triumphant. She was no gasping wreck tonight. She was facing her own demon, and she could see moisture beading on his handsome brow. His fists were clenched at his side, as if only the force of his will restrained his body, and his gaze held no hatred, only a wild heat that set her heart racing and her body throbbing as it locked with hers.

And then he stepped back, away from her, shaking his head so that one thick lock of hair fell forward. "I would not have you if you were the only woman on earth," he whispered, his voice raw and hoarse. "I would rather get myself upon the lowest pox-ridden whore."

He turned on his heel and left, slamming the door behind him, and Gillian dropped back against the furs, feeling oddly as if he had kicked her in the chest.

Chapter Ten

Nicholas brooded into his cup, annoyed at having to play the host. Although his father would not have approved, he had drifted away from such niceties long ago. Sometimes he wondered if all the civilization had been leeched from him in the blazing desert, never to return in full, for he did not welcome his visitors. He resented them.

This morning, he had risen early, in hopes of avoiding his sister and her husband, but Piers had caught him, coaxing him into riding his lands. Nicholas had grudgingly agreed, even as he wondered about the kind of man who could give up all that was Belvry without a protest—for that was just what Piers had done.

The Red Knight had held this demesne for a time after his marriage to Aisley, yet when Nicholas returned, he had ceded it back without argument. He claimed to prefer his old keep to the newer, more luxurious castle at Belvry! What was wrong with the man, and with Aisley, too?

Both of them were mad! Or so Nicholas had always thought. Now he began to wonder if something was wrong with himself. Although he appreciated the beauty and wealth of his holdings, he had never felt as strongly as Piers and Aisley did about their home, Dunmurrow. He had never felt strongly about anything, except his vengeance. And even that was wearing thin, although he clung to it as if it were the only thing keeping him alive.

Nicholas's belly burned, and he shifted in his chair, his irritation growing. If not for the man beside him, he could be attending to his business. What was the meaning of this sudden visit? Although Nicholas had arrived without notice at Dunmurrow more than once, he had never expected to receive the same treatment from his sister and her husband. That was another situation entirely, he reasoned, for they must tote around that infant. The one Gillian had taken to so quickly.

The thought of his wife made Nicholas's body ache even more fiercely, although he had thought himself accustomed to the torment. His old stomach ailment attacked with renewed vigor, while the more recent affliction in his groin grew...worse. He felt as if he had been hard ever since Gillian had offered her body up to him last night.

When she lay back upon his bed in nothing but her shift, the creamy skin of her parted legs revealed to him and her hand poised at the edge of the material, time had stopped. Nicholas knew his own limits, and he had realized that if she managed to pull up the thin fabric that covered her, he was doomed. So he had spewed some lies at her and fled. *Run*, from his wife. The knowledge did not improve his mood.

"A bath might be in order for me this afternoon," his companion said, and Nicholas lifted his head to glare at the speaker. His evil look bounced off Piers, as seemingly did all else, and Nicholas spared a moment to despise the composure that he had possessed, too, until recently. The Red Knight was said to have a fearsome temper, but Nicholas had never seen it. Oh, the man was fiercely protective of Aisley, but rarely did he rouse himself to action. Fanciful tales, Nicholas thought sourly, as unfounded as the other gossip about the Red Knight.

While Nicholas watched him grimly, Piers leaned back and lifted his cup. "Perhaps your new bride—"

"My wife attends no one but me!" Nicholas caught himself shouting and lowered his voice. "Get Aisley to bathe you," he said, with hushed vehemence. His threatening manner did little to offend his guest, who had the audacity to grin at him.

"Something amuses you?" Nicholas demanded, suddenly eager for a fight. The gnawing ache in his groin had made him testy, and the unsettling encounter with Gillian had left him feeling oddly unmanned. Essentially, the vixen had challenged him, and he had backed away like a coward. Nicholas knew an urge to prove himself as his own master, and what better way than with his fists?

"Hell, yes," Piers said. "'Tis good to see you alive at last, Nicholas, and with something besides hatred."

"You speak nonsense."

"As you say. Yet I have noticed that your bride is no aged hag, nor is she even a pallid nun. Gillian is a vibrant woman, young and beautiful. 'Tis enough to turn any man's thoughts away from revenge," Piers said, not even bothering to hide that insufferable smile.

"Think you that I do not hate her?" Nicholas demanded, for the barb came too close to the truth for comfort.

The genial look faded from Pier's face. "You would be a fool to do so."

"How easily you slander me, brother!"

Piers's expression darkened. "Wake up before it is too late, Nicholas. 'Tis time to quit clinging to a long-dead feud. Make a family and a life for yourself, man! 'Tis a prize you have—a lovely wife to give you many sons."

"Ha! I would get nothing on the wench but vengeance!"
Nicholas snarled, though his threats had begun to sound
idle, even to his own ears.

Piers did not see through them, however, for he slammed
down his cup in righteous indignation. "If you were not
Aisley's brother, I would be tempted to knock some sense
into you."

"Why let that stop you?" Nicholas rose to his feet in
challenge. He was sick of the big knight's advice and superior attitude. Faith, he would not be lectured to in his own
hall by an uninvited guest!

"I believe a man should stand by his family, not seek to
divide it with petty squabbles, like some foolish and reckless young cub."

It had been a long time since anyone had called him a
child, and Nicholas's temper snapped at the implied insult.
With a shout of anger, he lunged across the table at Piers.
Wooden cups clattered against the wall and benches crashed
to the floor as he dived into his brother-in-law. Servants who
had returned to the hall after the visitors' arrival scattered,
fleeing to safety like mice.

Although Piers was bigger and taller, he was the elder by
a few years, and Nicholas had acquired a few tricks living in
the East that made him an even match for the Red Knight.
Grunting in triumph, Nicholas swung a fist at a nose that
had obviously been broken before, but Piers was too quick,
ducking away, swifter than most men his size. With a thunderous bellow that fairly shook the roof, he threw Nicholas
off.

Rolling amid the rushes, Nicholas barely had time to take
a breath before the huge knight was on him, trying to gain
a hold. Ignoring the screams from the archways, Nicholas
fought back with the fierceness of his own frustration—with
Piers, with Gillian, and with the revenge he had yet to sa-

vor. He heard a groan and knew the deep satisfaction of drawing blood before his own jaw connected with the tiles.

Aisley watched the old servant who had come to her chamber closely. If anyone knew the state of affairs between Nicholas and his wife, it would be Edith. Although it had been difficult to pry the older woman away from the nursery, Aisley had done so, in order to speak privately with her, and Sybil had been left in the care of her nurse and a sad-eyed Gillian.

Even Aisley had noticed the change in Nicholas's bride this morning. The woman she had thought so vibrantly alive was quiet and subdued now, the fight that had blazed so fiercely in her when they arrived seemingly gone. Aisley had no idea what had happened after Nicholas dragged his bride from the table last night, but obviously something had occurred to rob her of her spirit. She was afraid to imagine what, and worried that Gillian might end up as empty as Nicholas himself.

After listening to Edith carry on about Sybil for ages, Aisley could bear the suspense no longer. "What of Nicholas and his new wife?" she asked. She was not encouraged when Edith sighed heavily in answer.

"'Tis an odd arrangement, make no mistake. She sleeps at the foot of the bed on a pallet, and it seems that Nicholas has made no move to consummate his vows." Edith clucked her tongue in dismay. "The boy has not been the same since his return from the Holy Land, but this... Why, 'tis unnatural!"

Aisley smiled at the words, for not too long ago Edith had sworn the marriage bed was a frightful place. That had, of course, been before she wedded an old soldier and changed her tune. Now she was happily ensconced with him at Belvry, but she obviously longed for babies to spoil, and it looked as if she would get none from Nicholas.

Privately Aisley suspected that her brother kept away from Gillian for his own peace of mind. After all, how long could a man exact revenge from a woman with whom he was intimate? Even Nicholas could not be so hard-hearted. Indeed, in his erratic behavior yesterday Aisley had seen a tenderness she would never have thought possible. But last night . . . "Has he hurt her?"

"Well, of course not!" Edith said, indignant. "I have never known a de Laci to raise a hand to a woman—or, outside of battle, anyone else, for that matter."

As if summoned by their words, the object of their concern suddenly burst into the room. Her face was flushed and her chest rising and falling rapidly, and Aisley rose abruptly, fearful for Sybil. "What is it?"

"They are brawling below!" Gillian announced breathlessly.

"Who?"

"Nicholas and your husband, Piers!"

Snorting in disbelief, Edith charged off, with Aisley and Gillian behind her. Although there was no love lost between Piers and her brother, Aisley could not imagine the two actually coming to blows. Piers had a deep respect for family, which made the very idea absurd, and yet, even before they reached the hall, Aisley heard a familiar bellow.

"What is *that?*" Gillian asked, turning wide green eyes toward her.

Aisley sighed ruefully. "'Tis Piers. He has lost his temper. What could Nicholas have done to provoke him?"

Frowning grimly, Gillian rushed on. "It is hard to tell, but if there is one thing at which your brother excels, it is . . . provocation."

At the bottom of the steps, Aisley stopped still, unable to believe her eyes, for Piers and Nicholas were rolling about on the floor like a couple of wayward peasant boys. Appalled, she would have left them to their foolishness, if not for telltale signs of blood that told her that someone was already hurt.

"Piers! Nicholas!" she chided, stepping forward, but they ignored her.

"The red devil will surely kill Lord Nicholas!" Edith wailed, backing away from the melee.

"Piers! Nicholas!" Aisley raised her voice, but it was drowned out by her husband's roars and the crashing of benches that the two left in their wake.

While Edith shrieked and Aisley watched helplessly, Gillian ran forward, a bucket of water from the kitchens in each hand. Apparently oblivious of her own danger, she approached the thrashing duo, lifted an arm and tossed the contents of one and then the other over the two men, just as if they were a pair of wild dogs.

The fighting stopped immediately, the outraged combatants protesting their ill-treatment loudly before rising to their feet, coughing and spitting, both covered with water, dirt and bits of rushes from their roll upon the tiles. Piers shook his head, his long, golden mane sending droplets flying into the air, and Aisley could see a smear of blood along his mouth. Her brother looked no better. Nicholas swiped at his face with both hands, but a thin line of blood trickled from his nose.

"You both are a disgrace," Aisley declared in disgust. For the first time in her life, she was prepared to scold her brother, but he would not meet her eyes. Turning to Piers for an explanation, she saw only anger, barely suppressed, and her heart sank. Obviously, her husband's temper had not been assuaged in the battle.

"We leave within the hour," Piers said, daring her to dispute him. Aisley bit her lip. She knew his rage as well as she knew his passion, and in the face of it, she could do nothing but nod her agreement. Her hopes of intervening here were for naught. Slanting a glance at the tall, red-haired woman who stood defiantly over a pile of water-soaked rushes, Aisley sighed.

Nicholas's wife was on her own once more.

Edith had been sent to fetch some clothes she had made for the baby, and Gillian was relieved at the peace and quiet that descended over Aisley's chamber in the absence of the wailing woman. As much as Gillian liked the old servant, her loud crying had begun to irritate.

Tears had never changed a thing, as Gillian well knew, and they could certainly not undo Nicholas's latest folly, quarreling with his kinsman. Already the tale had spread throughout the castle, and the servants darted dark looks at their master. Although he had held Belvry but briefly, Piers had been well liked, and none cared to see him or their own Aisley depart so quickly.

Gillian, too, felt the loss, for she had immediately been comfortable with the light-haired lady, who appeared unreachable, but was not. Gillian had looked forward to befriending Aisley and her warrior husband during their stay. Now that they were leaving, she would never have that chance, and, worst of all, she would miss the babe who rested in her arms.

The knowledge added a new ache to the heaviness in her chest she had suffered since last night, a dull pressure that would not leave her. Holding the infant close, Gillian realized that Sybil was the first being she had hugged to her since her childhood, and the discovery was not comforting. When would she ever do it again?

Never. For she would have no children of her own. *He* had made that clear enough. Gillian could not even think his name, and had fled to the nursery rather than face him. She had no stomach for whatever demands he might make upon her now, with his bizarre plans for slavery and such.

She told herself that her sadness sprang from the loss of her dream, the hope for a family of her own. Like a shooting star, it had come upon her yesterday, bright and hopeful and stronger than anything she had known, only to disappear, destroyed by a force more powerful. Her husband.

He had been tormenting her, of course. The Hoodman Blind kiss, and that other kiss against the wall, and all those smoldering looks of barely controlled passion, were but a game, a taunt, another sharp facet of his revenge.

Gillian told herself that she was relieved to have found him out. No more would she have to suffer his sly insinuations and bold claims about bedding her. She should be celebrating the news. Instead, she felt insulted, demeaned somehow, and that unnamed, unnatural heaviness grew in her chest.

"I wish you could come visit us at Dunmurrow," Aisley said, drawing Gillian's attention to the fair-haired woman, who was packing a trunk that rested on the bed. "'Tis not as fine as Belvry, but I have come to love it more dearly."

Courtesy prevented Gillian snorting at the suggestion that Nicholas would ever allow her make a pleasure trip. Instead, she expressed her own regrets. "I wish you could stay."

Aisley glanced up at her with eyes so much like Nicholas's that Gillian paused in startlement. The same, and yet not so, she thought, for Aisley's were soft as a silvery moonbeam, not sharp and painfully bright as a dagger's blade.

"I wish so, too," Aisley said with a soft sigh, "but Piers can be very stubborn at times. He is a wonderful man who feels strongly in all things, including his temper, which is legendary." She smiled, as if at a fond memory, but Gillian could not join her.

"I can find nothing pleasing in Nicholas's terrible temper," she muttered.

Aisley looked at her in puzzlement. "Nicholas? Why, I never even heard him raise his voice until yesterday."

Gillian made a low sound of disbelief. "'Tis his way to fly into fits, raging like a madman."

"Nicholas?" Aisley asked again. She shook her head. "If you say so, it must be thus, but I can barely conceive of it. Then again, I would never have imagined him brawling like a peasant boy! He is much changed." Aisley paused, as if trying to decide what to say. "But 'tis not all to his detriment."

Taking a deep breath, like one who has made a momentous decision, she closed the chest and walked over to the settle by the fire. There she took a seat and motioned for Gillian to join her. "I had hoped that we would have many opportunities to talk during my stay, but since that is not to be, I would share with you a little that might help explain Nicholas to you, his wife."

Curious, Gillian carried Sybil, who was busily tugging at her caul, with her to a nearby coffer. There she sank down and listened attentively.

"Although my brother was never affectionate, like Piers, he was a good man," Aisley began. "He left to fight in the Holy Land a strong, handsome youth filled with promise. When we heard of his death, we grieved greatly, especially my father, who had lost other sons to illness." A shadow passed across the lovely lady's face, but she continued.

"We found out later that Nicholas was injured in battle. Unable to help himself, he waited for aid, and when his neighbor, Baron Hexham, arrived, he thought that his suffering was over." Aisley's small hands closed into fists. "But it had just begun. Instead of taking him to safety, Hexham dragged him behind some brush and left him for dead. I do not know how long Nicholas lay there, slowly bleeding, beneath the Syrian sun," Aisley said.

Despair, so heavy it nearly suffocated her, settled over Gillian. Although Edith had told her the tale, she had been spared such details, and the aching sound of Aisley's delivery. *No wonder he despises me!* Gillian felt as if every last drop of hope had been squeezed from her body.

"I only know, through what he told Piers, that a peasant woman finally found him and nursed him back to health," Aisley said, and the weight of Gillian's torpid anguish was broken by a fierce stab of jealousy. Whether she willed it or no, Gillian envied the woman who had comforted a weak and sick Nicholas, who had nursed him back to health, touching his body, and mayhap his heart, as well. Lowering her lashes, Gillian glanced down at Sybil, refusing to let Aisley see the course of her thoughts.

"Apparently he made some sort of life over there, raising money and gathering men for his return, but he did not come back until the news of our father's death reached him. By that time, Hexham was harrying Belvry, and Nicholas barely saved his heritage from his old enemy. Hexham escaped, but Nicholas gave chase, driving him to madness, finally, with unflagging pursuit. Hexham came to Dunmurrow and forced Piers to kill him, rather than face Nicholas."

Gillian shivered. All this talk of battles and murders was beyond anything in her experience, and she began to sense that Nicholas was beyond her, too. "The point is that from the moment Hexham betrayed him, my brother has lived for naught but revenge. When he was deprived of that, it was as if he had lost all purpose. Only when he heard of you did he regain any of his spirit, but, again, it was hatred that drove him.''

Gillian felt her breath catch once, twice, and then Aisley reached out to take her hand. The delicate fingers closed around her own gently. ''I did not tell you all this to discourage you, but to encourage you, Gillian. When I first heard of your marriage, I feared the worst, yet what I have seen here is far from what I expected. My brother is much changed. *You* have changed him.''

Gillian opened her mouth to argue, but Aisley stopped her with a raised hand. ''What is your plan?'' she asked abruptly, leaning forward eagerly.

''Plan?'' Gillian asked in puzzlement.

Aisley smiled. ''When I first married Piers, I schemed to have it dissolved by saying that we were related,'' she said, with a soft laugh that stunned Gillian. ''Surely you must have something up your sleeve.''

Gillian eyed her blankly, for she had not really plotted anything. She had considered and discarded the idea of asking the Syrian for help, and had failed in her attempt to seduce her husband into compliance. In truth, she had vowed nothing except that she would survive whatever Nicholas had in store for her.

''Well, whatever you are doing, it is obviously working,'' Aisley said. ''If anyone can bring Nicholas around, 'tis you, Gillian. You can do it. Help him, will you?''

Gillian was dumbstruck by the request. Help Nicholas? The idea was laughable. Although sometimes she found herself weakening toward him, she would never surrender herself into his keeping. And the one time she tried to assist him, he had thrown her gesture back in her face, along with the accusation that she would poison him! Unable to give Aisley the assurance she wanted, Gillian rose to her feet, thankful that Edith's knock gave her an excuse not to answer.

Aisley was not to be put off, however. "Please?" she asked, in a tone so sincere that Gillian felt herself wavering.

Then Gillian remembered that she would not be bidding this fine lady goodbye if it were not for Nicholas, and she found the strength to reply, "I do not think I can."

Gillian stared out the window, watching the ribbon of road long after Aisley and Piers had disappeared from view. She did not even stir when Edith came in quietly and set a cup of spiced wine down beside her.

"Come now, my lady. 'Tis not like you to mope," the old servant said, but Gillian did not respond to the gentle scolding.

"At least come down and have a look at the lord. He is a bit battered and bruised, and wants seeing after. His head took a knocking about on the tiles and no doubt pains him. He needs you, my lady. Perhaps you can make up something for him?"

Privately Gillian was surprised that her husband's head had not cracked the floor; it was certainly harder than stone. And even if she had not been forbidden to treat the sick, she knew, he would take nothing from her hand. She remained silent, gazing out over the rich demesne, which was like a shiny apple, bright and appealing, but home to the meanest of worms.

"As much as I hated to see my Aisley go, lady, it was not our lord who sent them away," Edith said, in a pleading tone. "That red devil she married is known for his frightful tempers, and he was the one who took her off, not our own lord." Gillian practically had to bite her tongue to keep from arguing over the blamelessness of Nicholas de Laci. No doubt Edith would excuse him anything short of murder.

The old servant sighed. "Well, you must at least come down to supper, or His Lordship will not be pleased." Gillian felt herself stir at that, but she kept her mouth shut. "Make no mistake, he is in a foul mood already, and if you do not do as he bids—"

Gillian whirled around, only to catch a gleam in the old servant's eye that startled her. "You are trying to goad me, Edith!" she cried. "Well, it will not work. I am not going down."

The servant put her hands upon her hips. "And just what shall I tell him? You know what a sour humor he has been in lately."

"Ha! You'd think he was a paragon, to hear you talk of him!" Gillian said, but she regretted the words instantly. Edith was grieving over Aisley's departure, too, and she was just trying to do her best. Gillian felt a flicker of anger in the breast that had known little besides heaviness today. Did her husband never think of anyone but himself? He made everyone around him unhappy, from his sister to the lowliest peasant. And might he be damned for it!

"I want no supper. Tell him that I am unwell. I will attend to myself and retire to my pallet," Gillian said. And tonight sleep might come to her early, she realized, for she knew no fear.

After last night, Gillian was assured that her husband would never come to her bed.

Chapter Eleven

Too bad he was not a drinking man, Nicholas thought, gazing speculatively at the wine. Although he knew it would wreak havoc on his stomach, he motioned for the servant to pour. Just a little, he thought, enough to ease the raw feeling that had come over him since his unwelcome guests had fled.

It was not guilt that gnawed at him, for Piers had started the fight, only to take off in a huff, with no more than a bloody lip and a few bruises. So much for the Red Knight! Nicholas would, at least, be spared any more of that one's preaching. And what need had he of his sister, or her mewling babe? He was well rid of them all!

Gingerly Nicholas touched his nose, glad to find that it was not swollen, then rubbed his sore knuckles. Although he had thought to feel better after besting his brother-in-law, the victory, like most of late, had left a bitter taste in his mouth.

Or maybe it was just a trace of blood.

Taking a swallow of wine, Nicholas hoped its fine flavor would remove the sour tang that lingered, yet he felt no ease. Angrily he tried to summon up the hatred that had driven him for so long, but it had deserted him, pushed aside by too many new sensations struggling for supremacy. Even the old emptiness that he had once despised seemed preferable to the tumult that assailed him now. He felt as if he had swallowed a swarm of bees, and since the wine dulled their sting, he drank more.

He was halfway through the meal when he realized she was not coming down. Distracted by the fine drink, he had not noticed the furtive glances of his household toward his lady's empty place. Damn the wench! He had made her duties clear, and she was to attend him! Did she believe that Aisley's comings and goings changed anything, or did she think to defy him?

Nicholas felt his temper roar to life, along with a shadow of disappointment at her absence. Why could she not give him ease from his troubles, instead of adding to them? Would she ever greet him as Aisley did Piers, with warmth and pleasure in her eyes? For a moment, he wanted everything his sister possessed, but then he cursed himself silently. His wits must be addled! Too much wine, he decided, and put the cup aside. The trencher soon joined it, for his taste for food had vanished.

He had been too lenient with his wife, but he was done with his coddling. If he had to take the lash to her, by the faith, he would! Surging to his feet, Nicholas ignored the wary looks that followed him and strode to the stairs, determined to bring Gillian to her knees at last.

The passageway was empty and his chamber silent when he threw open the door. If Gillian was gone . . . A vile oath sprang to his lips, but died unuttered when he saw her. She was standing by the fire, combing out her hair, in nothing except her shift, and the play of the light behind her revealed each curve of her woman's form.

Her hair was down at last, and the fiery waves cascaded over one breast, to the curve of her waist, bright and thick and beckoning. Nicholas's breath caught, and he stared like a man dazed—or drunk. Cursing his weakness, he sought the temper that had fled, and held on to it as if it were a shield protecting him against the temptation that was his wife. He groped for words, his mouth suddenly dry, while she tossed those beautiful locks behind her and regarded him with eyes that flashed defiance.

"How could you?"

Her heated question threw him off balance, as did the sway of her body beneath the shift when she moved. Nicholas swallowed hard and remembered his rage. "Where have you been? You were to attend me at supper!"

"I was grieving the loss of your family, tossed out onto the road like the meanest of vagabonds! How could you, Nicholas?" The accusation struck too close to the truth for consideration, so he lashed out at her instead, angry that she would dare question him. Perhaps he no longer could control his life as he once had, but he could control her, and by his faith, he would!

"'Tis not your business, wife. You need concern yourself with nothing but your own obedience, which has been sorely lacking. You were to attend me, and you did not!"

As he stood there, all of Nicholas's frustration focused on this one woman, who was so different from what he had expected...and so much more than he had ever wanted. His eyes narrowed, and he strode forward menacingly, stopping bare inches from her before whispering his threat. "I ought to thrash you within an inch of your life."

As usual, Gillian did not cower or flee, but met him face-to-face. Although her cheeks were flushed, she raised her chin. "Go ahead! I am tired of living under your constant threats. Do your worst, Nicholas de Laci, but heed this—I will never give way. You can take away my freedom, my friends, my privileges, and you can bully and beat me, but I will not surrender to you!"

Nicholas felt as if something inside him had exploded, and it must have shown on his face, for despite her brave words, Gillian took a step back. He reached for her, but instead of running away, she swung at him, and, caught off guard by the attack, Nicholas felt the blow hit its mark.

Although her spirit no longer surprised him, her abilities did. Somewhere along the line, she had learned to fight, because her fist slammed into his jaw with surprising force. Blinking in astonishment, he paused to move it experimentally. When he realized that she had done no real damage, he pinned her with a glare that promised retribution tenfold and lunged for her, but she was too quick, faster even than Piers had been, though she had none of the knight's discipline.

And the fight was not the same, for this was no petty feud, but a struggle for supremacy that he would ultimately win. He was not seeking an outlet for his frustrations; *she* was his frustrations, and his blood roared her name. He caught hold of her arms, pinning her against the bed until her knee slammed upward, nearly catching him in the groin. It was an act of violence, meant to do him injury, and Nicholas realized that.

His body did not.

When her leg brushed his thigh, Nicholas felt himself spring to life, heedless of Gillian's intentions. And the swiftness of his own response made him drop her on the bed as if she had burned him.

Stunned, Nicholas looked down at her. Although they were both panting, Gillian was not gasping in fear, and her eyes no longer flashed with defiance. Indeed, she made no move to escape him, but lay on his covers as if meant to be there, staring up at him. She was sprawled out in a pose he had seen before, but this time her shift rode up around her thighs, exposing incredibly long, creamy limbs. Her hair was spread wildly about her, and her breasts were rising and falling rapidly, as if straining to be free of the linen that covered them.

Desire surged through him, and Nicholas felt as though he had wanted her forever.... Without stopping to think, he reacted instinctively, as he so often did in her presence. Pressing one knee down on the mattress, he rose up over her, took the front of her shift in his hands and ripped it asunder. Then he pulled the edges aside, baring her body to his gaze, and drew in a ragged breath.

Heat washed over him, making him shudder as if fever raged through his body. By all the saints, she was beautiful, especially her creamy breasts, ripe and luscious, the nipples like berries, small and . . . hard.

"I thought you did not want me." The sound of her voice, a rough whisper, only inflamed him further, and Nicholas heard a noise rise up out of his chest in reply.

"I lied," he admitted, and, putting his hands on her outstretched wrists to hold her in place, he leaned forward and took one bright berry into his mouth. She moaned, and the low, husky sound urged him on. He suckled, and it was more intoxicating than anything he had ever done.

Nicholas had never been one to waste time pleasuring women, and to suck at their breasts like a babe had not been his sport, but now it became his life's blood. He licked and nibbled at the firm mounds, burying his face between them and groaning in ecstasy as his tarse hardened painfully.

He raised his other knee to the bed, so that he knelt between Gillian's spread legs, and released her wrists, running his hands down the length of her smooth arms and side to the curve of her waist. She arched toward his seeking mouth, gasping in pleasure, but then she erupted beneath him, rolling over so that he was thrown onto his back and she sat atop him.

Dazed, Nicholas watched as Gillian's hands came down upon his wrists in perfect mimicry of his own actions. He would have laughed at her puny attempts to hold him down, had he not been so aroused. This was no ordinary maid, but his spirited wife, and her antics made his heart pound and his member reach for her stiffly. He lifted his gaze to hers, where it was caught and held in silent challenge, and her words came back to him: *I will never surrender to you.*

Was she toying with him? Although she no longer feared his touch, Gillian's eyes clearly proclaimed that she would not yield her body to him. Nicholas's blood roared a protest, but before he could act, she released his wrists and pushed up his tunic. Her hands, soft yet strong, glided over his skin, and Nicholas swallowed hard. As he stared in astonishment, she lowered her head, sending ripples of bright locks over him, and put her mouth to his nipple.

Pleasure, piercing and fantastic, shot through him, and Nicholas realized that she was not refusing him. She might deny him conquest, but she would meet him as his equal, and Nicholas felt dizzy at the discovery. Another sound erupted from deep in his chest, and Gillian lifted her head. Green eyes fastened on his again, glimmering with shared desire, and he nodded his agreement.

As if his assent fueled her passion, Gillian tugged at his tunic, and Nicholas sat up, yanking it off with swift impatience. Although he usually folded his clothes neatly, this night they dropped, forgotten, from his fingers when Gillian shrugged out of her torn shift. Tossing it aside, she sat perched over his thighs, completely naked, her breasts swaying gently over her slender waist, and a bright thatch of red hair shining like a beacon at the juncture of her thighs.

She was not close enough. With a shout that conveyed his desperation, Nicholas pulled her down on top of him, reveling in the press of her firm mounds into his chest and the bright locks that flowed about them. Their passion exploded in a flurry of heat and wonder. He kissed her like one gone mad, knowing that he was mad, but uncaring. His tongue thrust frantically into her mouth, while his hands roamed over her shoulders, her back, the soft curve of her buttocks.

It was not enough. Muttering his need, he rolled her beneath him and pushed his swollen member against her, damning the braies that lay between them. He slid a hand down along the curve of her waist to her hip and along one slender thigh, then upward to where her legs joined. Anticipation seized him, and his fingers trembled as they trailed through the curls that covered her. He breathed deeper and delved lower, cupping her in his hand, and when she surged up against him, he shuddered.

The next thing he knew, he was on his back again, and Gillian was lying atop him, tugging at his hose. He let her remove them, along with his boots and braies, because he had long waited for her to attend him. And she suffered not under the task, but fumbled in her eagerness, sending a rush of blood to his groin. Her lovely face was flushed, and her lips parted to take in low, shallow breaths as her palms slid up his legs, reaching for him.

Nicholas thought he would explode in her hand when it closed around him. He clenched his teeth while her fingers explored his nether reaches until he bucked, unable to stand any more. Sweating and panting, he rolled again, but this time only onto his side. Then he and his bride faced one another, neither one beneath the other, neither one surrendering.

With swift impatience, he drew one of her knees high up over his thigh, glorying in its texture as it slid against his skin. Then he guided his tarse to her ready opening. Smooth, hot and wet, she closed around the tip, and he trembled at the ecstasy that flooded through him. He wanted . . . he needed to be deep inside her. Grasping her buttocks in one hand, he pulled her to him, even as he thrust past her barrier to bury himself to the root.

Gillian screamed and tried to pull away, but he held her fast, struggling to remain still as she pummeled his chest with her fists. "Would you rend me asunder?" she cried. Seeing the tears that pooled in her shining eyes, he drew her head down against his chest, whispering into the thick mass of fiery hair that flowed over his knuckles.

"Hush, we are not done yet."

"Damn you, I am done! You h-hurt me!" The broken admission smote Nicholas to the core. How often had he planned to give her pain? Yet now that he had accomplished that goal, Nicholas felt no triumph, only shared agony, as if he took her suffering into himself.

"Shh . . ." he whispered, before capturing her mouth to rekindle the passion that had raged so wildly and well between them. Wary at first, she remained stiff and unyielding, but then her tongue met his and her arms wrapped around him in a fierce grip that tested his patience.

His hand roved down her back and over her smooth thigh, then moved between them. She liked that, for he felt the gentle sway of her hips, reaching for him. He made a low sound of delight, and she echoed it, twining her fingers into his hair. Slowly Nicholas eased himself out and in fully again, and when she did not balk, he doubled the pace. But still he stroked her, for suddenly it was imperative that her pleasure equal his own.

She deserved no less.

The heat between them grew, driving Nicholas like a demon to thrust deeper, and he cursed the awkward position. His body screamed to move atop her, but he denied himself. And, as if to keep him there, she wound her leg around him, her calf tight against his buttocks.

He kissed her all the more fiercely, and the mouth that had so often spoken to him in anger whispered his name against his lips. It would never sound the same again to his ears. "What do you to me?" she asked, but he could not answer. He was beyond words, beyond thought, beyond anything but the rhythm of their mating.

Then, suddenly, she stiffened, clutching his hair in a fist. "Nick!" she cried, in a husky voice that inflamed his senses. Gasping, she tightened around him, milking his seed with her pleasure. And as he poured himself into her, Nicholas felt as if she, in turn, were filling up all the empty places in his soul. Or had she done that already?

Trembling in the aftermath of something that made a mockery of all his trysts with lemans and slave girls and noblewomen, Nicholas pressed his face against his wife's hair and, exhausted, slept.

Nicholas awoke in a tangle of arms and legs and luxurious red locks. For a long moment, he drifted, caught up in dreams of a passion beyond imagining, and he rubbed a long silken strand between his fingers. Was he enjoying the hospitality of some emir's harem? He sniffed the air, but detected no incense, only a fresh, alluring fragrance that was oddly familiar. Gillian's—along with the lingering scent of their mating!

The memory made him sit up abruptly, and he surged from the bed angrily. His wife lay sprawled upon his sheets, her virgin's blood staining them red, her mouth curved into a soft smile of contentment. Like some mythical goddess of old, she had enslaved him with his own greedy lusts, and Nicholas hated himself for it.

Without bothering to don his clothes, he flung open the door and called loudly for a bath. He wanted her scent and her blood off him. After using the chamber pot, he moved to the window and stared out, brooding over the night's misdeed.

Had he really taken her on his side, so that she would feel his equal? Faith, the wine had dulled his wits! Only a fool catered to a woman's whims, and this one was his enemy! Her voice, low and seductive, broke into his thoughts, as if his agitation had awakened her.

"You are beautiful, Nicholas de Laci, and yet you seem not to know it," she whispered. He stiffened, having expected anything but that husky compliment. He did not turn, not wanting her to see the swift response of his body. Her power over him.

"I give it no thought," he replied testily. "My mind is occupied with vengeance. That is what concerns me!" Gaining some measure of control over himself once more, he stalked to the bed and stood over her.

She was lying completely naked, the most shameless of nuns, the most tempting of wives. He forced his gaze away from the body that called to him, only to have it caught in her flaming hair, tousled from sleep, and her creamy shoulders, flawless but for a scattering of freckles. Suddenly those small flecks seemed incredibly erotic, and as he stared at them, Nicholas felt himself surge to life once more.

Damn her! She had no hold over him. He shuddered with the force of his need, and the denial that raged against it. Abruptly it all melded together. By his faith, he would show her his mastery! Without a word, Nicholas gripped her ankles and pulled her to him. Ignoring her gasp of surprise, he spread her thighs and thrust himself deep within her.

It was like entering heaven. Leaning back his head, he closed his eyes as he let white-hot pleasure wash over him.

Never before had he known such bliss. His fingers dug into her hips as he withdrew, only to sheathe himself fully once more.

"Nicholas." Her breathy whisper drew his attention, and he looked down at her. Her wary gaze brought him triumph, and he drew back and drove deeper, harder, as if he could hammer away whatever bound him to her. She flinched once, but then lifted up to greet him with a soft moan. An answering sound rose from somewhere deep inside him, and he was undone yet again.

"Nick." Her throaty, urgent call, reserved only for him, made him frantic, and he moved faster, reaching for what he experienced only with her. "Touch me...like you did last night."

Why should he? He cared only for his own pleasure, and yet, as if of their own accord, his hands slid around her thighs, his thumbs meeting and pressing there, where he knew she wanted them most. She cried out, arching off the bed in sudden climax, and he bucked against her frantically.

Through the heat of passion, Nicholas heard the opening of the door behind him, followed by a loud gasp, but he neither stopped nor slowed his pace. He pumped into her, and as soon as the door closed again, he threw his head back, a primal noise leaving his throat as his seed planted itself in her body. She was his. Now and always.

His long, pulsing climax was followed by small tremors that continued for so long that Nicholas fought the urge to collapse upon her. Although he could barely stand, he lingered at the edge of the bed, her legs still wrapped around him. When he finally withdrew from her body, he was trembling, his knees weak, and he turned away abruptly, unwilling to let her see how shaken he was by what they had done.

This was not mere sex. He had been to the East, and had tasted exotic arts never to be had in Britain, but this… This was beyond his experience.

Gillian watched him bathe, and the tingling returned to her body, heating her skin and driving her heartbeat until she wanted to go to him and slide her hands along his gleaming muscles. But that would not be enough. Not now that she knew what could follow. In truth, Gillian did not think she could touch her husband without feeding her growing appetite for him.

Never in all her life, especially her cloistered years at the nunnery, had she imagined such desire. What had happened between them was nothing at all like Master Freemantle's crude groping, but then, the burgher was not young and strong and beautiful….

He was not Nicholas.

Gillian was not so foolish as to believe that anyone but her husband could transform her into such a wanton creature. Although she craved him more fiercely than any whore, their union was perfectly legal, approved by the Church itself.

She nearly laughed aloud at the irony. Of all the odd turns her life had taken, this was truly the strangest. To be married, against her will, to a man who despised the very blood that flowed through her veins, only to find pleasures beyond imagining in his bed.

And that was not all. The heaviness in her chest was gone, lifted by the naked desire she had seen burning in his eyes. When Nicholas could no longer deny it, the ache that had plagued her had fled. Now her heart was filled with something else entirely.

But that was not necessarily an improvement. Although she knew nothing of such things, Gillian sensed that more than simple lust had fueled her passion. Along with the pleasure to be had in their merging bodies, Gillian had experienced a deeper, even more powerful bonding.

She had the sinking feeling that she had fallen in love with her beautiful, terrible husband.

Gillian let out a heavy breath that was more than a sigh. What a fool she had been to think she could live with such a man without being affected by him, to believe that his fiendish behavior would act as a barrier to her emotions. Her feelings had lain dormant for so long that she had thought them dead, believed herself safe from Cupid's arrows, when in truth she had been starved for human contact, a target of the simplest sort.

Oh, she had lived with others before, most recently a house full of nuns, but none of them had touched her heart. Only *he* could have managed such a feat, with his ravings and his demands and his boorish behavior... and sudden gentleness so unexpected that it transfixed her, a brief glimpse into the pain he endured daily and the ecstatic expression on his face when he entered her body.

All these things, the good and the ill, had woven themselves around her senses until she was lost. Her mind called it folly, but her body and her soul were enraptured.

Unfortunately, her husband obviously was not similarly affected, she thought as he shot her a look from his water that bespoke his contempt. Gillian forced herself to meet his glare evenly, but when he glanced away, she shivered. Hatred still burned in him, along with passion, and Gillian knew it would never die. To expect anything else from him was hopeless.

Damn, but she had wanted no part of this! She had only wanted to endure him, not to embrace him. *Too late,* her inner voice screamed. *You cannot go back.* Slowly Gillian lifted her chin. Well, maybe not. Perhaps she was already immersed too deeply to ever extricate herself, but she could still save herself from drowning.

She did not have to let him know.

If Nicholas de Laci ever divined her true feelings, Gillian knew, she would be lost, a puppet to his whims, and he would, at last, possess the means to defeat her.

Chapter Twelve

Gillian watched as her husband dressed swiftly and silently and stalked to the door. He halted there for a moment, turning to fix her with eyes no longer smoky with desire, but harsh and sharp. "Get yourself up and washed, wife, for you have duties to perform. I have not forgotten them, nor have I been sufficiently *distracted* to forgo them!"

Then he thrust wide the portal, only to stumble on the threshold. Pulling the blanket over her head, Gillian heard her husband's black oath, followed by his shout. "Edith! Why do you waylay me? Get yourself gone!"

"I beg your pardon, my lord!" the servant replied, without a trace of real contrition. "My, but you do look well this morning. Very well indeed." Gillian smiled in spite of herself, for she could imagine Nicholas's reaction to Edith's comment.

"What the devil do you want?"

"I would assist your lady with her bath," Edith answered mildly. Nicholas snorted, as if the thoughtfulness pained him.

"Very well, but heed me well, wife," he called toward the bed. "Once properly dressed, I will expect you to attend me!" The fierceness of his words was lost, upended by the bustling sounds of Edith as she rushed in, cackling like a happy hen.

"Well, my lady. 'Twas not so bad now, was it?" she asked.

Although she blushed scarlet, Gillian peeked out from the covers and laughed, the memory of the soul-stirring pleasure her husband had given her still clinging to her body.

Edith laughed, too, and clapped her hands with delight. "Now, then, you must get yourself into the tub before the water turns cold, and I shall put fresh linens on your bed. If I did not think Lord Nicholas might object, I would hang the sheets out for all to see."

As Gillian rose and crossed to the tub, she shook her head at the folly of such a notion. Nicholas had been reluctant to admit his desire even to her; she knew he would not approve of announcing it publicly. With a sigh at her husband's perversity, she slipped into the water he had only recently vacated. The knowledge of that tenancy made her draw in a quick breath, for the memory of him lingered, warm and compelling. Sinking down into the remnants of his heat, Gillian leaned back, content to listen to Edith babble.

"I knew you would have a fine time of it, my lady, for you are a beautiful young woman with strong passions. Now you must bind him to you every night—or day," Edith added with a chuckle. "And more than just his body will come round to you. You shall see!"

Smiling at the idea of Nicholas "coming round" to anything, Gillian leisurely washed herself with the scented soap Edith provided. As her hands moved over her skin, she dreamily wished that he was bathing her, and the image of her hard husband leaning over her captured her imagination. Surely his feelings for her did not matter, as long as they could reach such heights together....

"It does my heart good to see the two of you reconciled at last. And it will not be long now before we see a new de Laci at Belvry!" It took a moment for Edith's words to sink into Gillian's thoughts, but when they did, she nearly dropped the soap. A baby! Gillian placed a palm against her stomach and realized that the prediction might well be true.

Joy swept through her, even more potent than the emotions that her husband induced. A child. A family of her own, finally, just as she had dreamed! It seemed too good to be true, and Gillian glanced over at Edith's back, wondering about her chances. "How many...times do you think would...assure a baby?"

"Sometimes it takes only once, my lady, but to be sure, you must bed often and well!" Edith replied.

Blushing brightly, Gillian smiled. She had no difficulty with that plan, for she was eager once more for Nicholas's touch, for the openmouthed kisses that seared her soul, and for his body, hard and strong and beautiful.

Now, if only she could get her recalcitrant husband to agree...

Gillian sat in the great hall kicking her heels all morning, her duties coming to naught because the man she was to wait upon was not there. Bored and angry, she tried not to fume, even though, as the morning wore on, she began to feel as if she were some prize brood mare on display.

The tale of exactly what Osborn had interrupted this morning in the great chamber had spread, as news will, and Gillian received more than her share of happy smiles, sly winks and speculations upon a future heir. She told herself that the people of Belvry meant well, but she would rather be working in the garden, away from prying eyes, than waiting on a bench like some young page.

It was maddening, but every time she felt her temper stretch to the breaking point, Gillian recalled the look in her husband's eyes as he had taken her maidenhead. Then, when the fiend could have reveled in his triumph, she had seen no gloating. Instead, Nicholas had bared his tortured and needy soul in that moment, and let her see the bliss that he knew in their joining.

Gillian held the image close until at last he arrived, just in time for the midday meal. She rose when she saw him, though she wondered whether a proper slave ought not to prostrate herself. Gillian's lips quirked at the thought, for she had no intention of doing that. Let Nicholas content himself with her presence!

In truth, he did seem satisfied, turning toward her immediately and striding across the hall on long, strong legs that made Gillian's heart beat apace. She remembered the way those thick thighs had felt beneath her fingertips, and the curly, dark hair that covered so much of his body. She remembered him naked and aroused, and she sucked in a deep breath.

Nicholas seemed to be no less affected than she. He kept his head bent, his eyes hooded, but she could see his hands clenching at his sides when he stopped before her. Silence reigned for a moment before he spoke. "I would wash my hands, *wife!*" he snapped.

Gillian's chin came up. It was the duty of the servants to present bowls of water to the diners, but, gritting her teeth, she fetched one for her husband and stood while he took his time with the ritual cleansing. Her anger returned, only to fade away again, slowly but surely, as she watched those long, capable fingers, recalling how they had felt against her skin and just where they had touched her. She choked back a strangled sigh, and he lifted his head. Their gazes met, held and ignited, until Gillian felt as if she were engulfed in flames.

"My lord?" The sound of Osborn's voice made Gillian realize she was standing there, transfixed. Yet she could no more break away than she could stop the fire that raged through her.

It was Nicholas who finally wrenched his attention from her to the servant. "Yes?"

"A messenger, my lord, to see Lady Gillian," Osborn said, startling Gillian from her daze. Who would seek her out? She knew no one here, and even if she did, who would dare? Glancing behind the waiting servant, she was surprised and pleased to see young Will Bennett, who helped his father with the cows and sheep belonging to the abbey.

"Will!" she cried, stepping forward eagerly, only to be stopped in her tracks by her husband's shout.

"Hold!" he boomed, and the hall became silent. The people who had been busily laying out food backed toward the archways, and those already seated at the trestle tables froze in their places, fearful of Belvry's lord. Nicholas was oblivious of the reactions around him, however, his piercing gaze fixing upon poor Will.

"Who are you to beg audience with my wife?"

"I beg your pardon, my lord," the youth answered, his face gone white. "I would not offend you. 'Tis the abbess who sent me."

Gillian watched her husband's taut body lose some of its stiffness, and she relaxed slightly, too. Apparently he was not going to cut down the poor boy for running an errand, but neither did he looked pleased.

"State your message, then, and begone!" Nicholas snapped, and Gillian gasped at his discourtesy. Will had traveled a good distance in her service. He should be properly fed and rested before he was sent on his way. And besides, the message was for her, not her husband!

"Nonsense," she protested, stepping forward. "You do not want the abbess to think us inhospitable, husband. Come," she said, gesturing to Will, "and you may give me your tidings while we eat."

Nicholas erupted. "Nay!" Leaning toward her, he gripped her arm and yanked her back to his side.

Whirling on him, Gillian threw off his hold. "The message is for *me,* and I shall hear it! Give me my due!"

"You are due nothing!" he shouted.

Angered beyond caution, Gillian met his glittering gaze with her own, and this time, the only fire she felt was the flames of hell that rightly should be licking at his heels.

"Get to your chamber, wife!"

"I am not leaving!" Out of the corner of her eye, Gillian could see poor Will glancing from one to the other of them helplessly. The servants gaped from the archways while the food cooled and the diners left their seats. She knew her husband intimidated them all, but she did not move, facing him down as she glared up at him.

"'Tis only that a man has been to the abbey, asking questions about Gillian!" The words burst out of Will, suspending the battle that raged between the lord and lady, and they both turned to stare at him.

"Who?" Gillian asked in puzzlement.

Will shook his head. "He did not say, Gillian—I mean, my lady." He shot a fearful look at Nicholas. "My lord. The fellow came after word spread of her marriage, but he was not known in the town. None of us had seen him before. He was most insistent in his questioning. Very peculiar, the abbess said, and she thought you should know of his visit."

Nicholas's eyes glinted with accusation as he swiveled toward Gillian, and she knew his thoughts ere he spoke them aloud. "I know no such man!" she protested.

Scowling as if he thought the fellow some dalliance of hers, Nicholas said nothing, but fixed Will with a glare that made him quiver anew. Then, finally, he swung toward one of his men, who had brought the messenger into the hall and now stood at the doors.

"Have Darius take this fellow back to the abbey. Let us see if the Syrian can find out more about our mysterious questioner!" Nicholas shot her a swift, triumphant glance that told her he was glad to rid himself of both the boy and the handsome foreigner who had been kind to her. The bastard! Gillian glared at him while Will hurried to make his exit, the guard following closely behind, as if both were eager to leave the lord's presence.

Gillian could not blame them. She turned on her husband then, anger churning in her so forcefully that she wanted to knock him silly. Balling her fist, she raised it, but he was too quick this time. He snared her wrist in a fierce hold and glared at her.

"Remember where you are and who you are," he warned.

Gillian looked up at him, stunned by the reminder of her place in his life. Was this the same man who had entered her body with such desperation? "Oh, I am aware of myself well enough," she replied, pulling her hand from his. "But I know not what you are."

Nicholas's gaze swept over the faces in the hall, taking pleased note of his missing companion. Although he hardly thought it necessary to send someone to the abbey, Nicholas had learned to be wary. And if Darius was willing to go, so much the better. He would not have to worry about finding the Syrian holding his wife's hands in a darkened passage.

The memory made Nicholas tighten his hold on the cup in his hand, and he forced himself to loosen his grip on the empty vessel. His people seemed to think there was something to celebrate, for they lingered after supper, dancing and making merry, but Nicholas refused the wine that Osborn offered him.

He did not want a repetition of last night.

It was ironic that he, who feared nothing, worried over bedding his wife! But Nicholas knew that what had taken place between them was no simple union. He and his vixen bride had merged more than their bodies, and the experience had shaken him. It had no place in his disciplined, ordered world, just as Gillian played no part but that of a tool for his vengeance.

Yet already she had become more.

Nicholas slammed the cup down in angry denial. Although a servant stepped forward to fill it with ale, he shook his head, turning instead toward his wife, who, after a moment's hesitation, rose and filled it for him. She set the vessel before him neatly enough, but her eyes flashed fury.

Good! Nicholas had spent the better part of his day forcing her to wait upon him, if only to prove that he still had the upper hand and that she had not enslaved him with her body. Gillian had gritted her teeth and glared, but she had done his bidding, fetched his accounts and fed him morsels from their trencher... until he called a halt to that.

The intimacy of her fingers brushing against his lips had quickly become too much to bear, for Nicholas had wanted to take each digit into his mouth, instead of the food. Lustful fool! Surely he had lost his wits! Even when he looked at her, his palms grew damp, his tarse grew stiff and his reason fled.

So he refused to notice the way her new gown fell over curves he had molded with his hands. He denied his desire to tear the caul off her hair and let down each fiery strand, preferably over his naked body, and find his lost soul inside her.

For the first time in his life, Nicholas could not trust himself, and so he glared and made demands and argued with her, in the hope that her rage would protect him. And the hour grew later. If not for the knowing looks of his people, he would have gone to sleep with his horse. Or, mayhap, another trip. Coward, that he would flee her, yet again!

He could not, and so, when she stood up, Nicholas felt some measure of relief. He would let her go, and wait until she was asleep on her pallet before seeking his own bed. Perhaps, with temptation out of reach, he could regain control....

"Husband, I would retire for the night. Will you join me?" Nicholas felt his jaw drop open at the words, and he glanced up at his wife in startlement. She was standing beside his seat, completely composed, her eyes gleaming with bright challenge.

His body's response was swift and irrevocable. He hardened painfully, and rose to his feet so quickly that he nearly knocked over his chair. "Aye. I will escort you," he muttered and, taking her arm, he led her up the stairs to their chamber.

With each step, anticipation roared through his blood so forcefully that he had to clench his fists to stop himself from throwing her over his shoulder like some primitive warrior with his prize. The short journey seemed to take forever, strangling his patience as he went up behind her, his eyes locked upon the curves of her bottom.

When they finally reached the room, Nicholas's breath was coming fast and shallow. He shut the door behind him and leaned against it, trying to regain mastery over himself, but Gillian was there before him, so close he could feel her heightened breath against his face. And before he could react, she pulled his head down for a passionate kiss, thrusting her tongue inside his mouth and pressing against him.

Groaning, Nicholas cupped her buttocks, bringing her up against his erection. He ground his hips against hers, wanting and needing her so violently that he could not think. When she wound her arms around his neck and wrapped her legs around his waist, pushing the heated core of her against his desire, Nicholas realized that she was as eager as he.

The revelation stunned him and set his roaring blood ablaze. Something rose in his chest, breaking free into a triumphant shout, and he carried her, stumbling, to the bed, falling upon it with her, tearing at her clothes, even as she pulled at his.

Revenge, arguments and all else that passed between them were forgotten in his desperate urge to claim her as his own. Finally, they were both naked, and the silken heat of her skin, the feel and the taste of it, was making him mad for her. He moved over her, but she pushed at him as if she would deny him. For a moment, Nicholas was livid, until he found himself on his back and his wife straddling his hips.

"'Tis my turn to ride you, husband."

"What?" The word was a croak, his mouth useless but to stroke her. His mind felt fogged, apart from the rest of him, which was driven only to possess her.

"You had your way this morning," she whispered. Her voice was husky and exciting, making it hard for him to concentrate, but through the haze of desire it came back to him. Equal. Partners. By nature, Nicholas resisted, but then she lifted herself up and touched him, guiding him into her, and he knew no regrets. Hot. Tight. Ecstasy. The sight of her astride him, her long hair wild about her, made him buck against her, and she closed her eyes, leaned her head back and made a soft sound of delight.

God have mercy on him, for he would surely die from pleasure! The ends of her silky red mane stirred his thighs, and the creamy, milky globes of her breasts beckoned him. Groaning, Nicholas took them in his hands, and soon she was writhing over him, quickening her pace.

"Touch me, Nick," she begged, and he did not consider refusal. Grasping her thighs, he stroked her with his thumbs until she convulsed around him, calling out his name in a throaty shout that made him surge upward to join her in oblivion.

Nicholas looked up as a cup was set in front of him, surprised to see it placed there by his wife's hand. In the past few weeks, he had grown less demanding of her during the day. And why should he not? She more than made up for the slackening of her duties at night. In his bed. His groin tightened, and Nicholas forced his attention back to the vessel before him.

"What is it?"

"Something for your stomach," she whispered, and before he could react, she put her hand on his shoulder, squeezing it gently as she passed. His brief surge of anger faded as she took her seat beside him; he no longer felt threatened by her knowledge of his ailment.

Odd, how subtly things had changed. Nicholas no longer worried about her enslaving him with her body, either. Rather, he thought they had enslaved each other, for she was just as needy and eager as he, and the partnership thrived. If there was more to contemplate in that success, he did not want to pursue it.

"Are you sure it is not a spring tonic?" he asked teasingly.

She lifted her head, and her mouth curved into a wicked grin as she leaned close, her reply intended for his ears only. "I hardly think you are in need of such a drink. If your sap rises any higher, I will be unable to walk."

Her husky answer roared through his blood. Snaring her green gaze with his own, Nicholas lifted the cup and downed the mixture in one long swallow. Deliberately, he licked his lips, and watched her shiver. 'Twas a game they played between them, and oh, it was so enjoyable. "I would retire early tonight, wife," he said, rising to his feet, and she followed, nodding in mute agreement.

When they reached the great chamber, however, Nicholas was dismayed to see the tub filled with hot water, as if awaiting him. "A bath, at this hour? What are you about?" He had washed earlier and now wanted nothing more than to bury himself in her as quickly as possible. Perhaps he would not even undress her, but lift her in his arms and take her up against the wall. . . .

"I am bleeding," she said softly. She lifted her head to meet his gaze fearlessly, and it took Nicholas a moment to understand what she was talking about. "If you would have your way, 'tis best to do it there, unless you want to stain the bed linens."

Nicholas stared at her, stunned, as ever, by her behavior. Of course, he was familiar with a woman's monthly flow, but this was the first time one had offered herself to him in spite of it. "Well, what is it to be?" she asked, her green eyes gleaming in challenge. "Are you afraid of a little blood? It is not overmuch, warrior."

Nicholas laughed aloud at her taunting. "Me? I have seen more blood than you ever will, vixen, and it bothers me not." Indeed, he realized now that he was hard as a rock, and more eager for her than ever. Reaching down, he took his tunic by the hem and yanked it over his head, suddenly impatient, as she, too, removed her covering. Then they were both sinking down in the tub together, and Nicholas groaned at the sensation.

His bath had always been personal, private, but now he discovered it was an exotic, erotic place. He pulled her onto his lap, enjoying the slick wetness of her skin and the slide of her limbs. They joined, both seated, face-to-face, and the slightest rocking sent exquisite pleasure jolting through him. It built slowly, in a heated rhythm quite different from their usual frenzied mating, and for a moment, the change panicked him.

But she was bleeding, and he must be careful of her, Nicholas thought in some dim recess of his brain. How strange, for he, who had little use for women, had never thought to go to such lengths to have one. Yet he could not deny her, or go without the salvation of her body.

And as he watched her thick lashes drift down over dreamy eyes, Nicholas felt something heave in his chest, as if the heart he had thought long absent had begun to beat.

Chapter Thirteen

Lying in the huge bed, encased in soft blankets and cushioned on thick pillows, Gillian was miserable, even in the midst of luxury. And she felt guilty for it. There had been a time, after her mother died and before Master Abel took her on, when she was flung out onto the streets, and she remembered all too well the cold, the fear and the hunger. Back then, she would have given anything to be ensconced in such surroundings—even her heart.

She sighed, and that ragged release made her husband turn in the act of dressing to fix her with his gray gaze. Gillian met it, marveling absently at just how handsome he was, but taking no joy in the knowledge, for he was still ... Nicholas.

Oh, he no longer deliberately tormented her or made her act his slave, but his feelings for her had not changed. He remained rigid and unyielding and closed off from her, except when their bodies joined together. Gillian took what she could from him in the night, but during the day she had only the memory to sustain her, for the Nicholas she knew in the darkness was gone. Or mayhap she imagined that he was anything else.

Turning onto her back, she stared sightlessly up at the bed hangings and told herself she was a fool to expect anything from him. He was what he was, a hard creature, so obsessed with vengeance there was little room for anything else. At least he gave her pleasure. Gillian knew she should be content with that, and yet she wished he would give her a child, too.

And therein lay the source of her discontent. Even though Edith had told her that sometimes a woman did not conceive right away, Gillian had hoped that after so many passionate couplings she would be blessed with a baby. Her woman's flow had always been a nuisance, but now it took on another, depressing aspect, as if her body were grieving for the child that was not there.

A knock came at the door, and at Nicholas's shout, Edith entered, bustling in and clucking like a mother hen. "And how is it you are not yet up this morning, my lady?" she asked, giving Gillian a broad wink.

The sly insinuation brought down Nicholas's wrath, and he turned to glare at the old servant. "She is having her courses. Let her lie abed all day, if she will."

"Oh." Edith's disappointment echoed her own so vividly that Gillian did not properly appreciate her husband's indulgence. "Oh, well... Do not fret, my lady," the servant said, reaching out to pat Gillian's hand. "Sooner or later, we will see you round with child!"

Nicholas was poised at the entrance to the great chamber, but the servant's words made him turn, and Gillian went rigid with wariness. Even now, she would not willingly divulge any of her weaknesses, for he still might use them against her. Love him though she did, she trusted him not.

Gillian's fears were realized when she met his eyes. They glittered, painfully sharp, in a face set as cold and hard as stone. "If you think breeding will make me forget your tainted blood, think again, Hexham's heir!'' he warned. "You do yourself and the brat a disservice by such folly.''

He turned and slammed the door, and Gillian felt as if a part of her had been closed off, as well, never to open again. The hope she had nurtured died, slain by her husband's hand, for how could she bring a baby into the world, knowing that he would hate it? How could she let an innocent child suffer his revenge?

"Come, lady,'' Edith said finally. The old servant's perpetually cheery voice sounded shaky, but she flashed Gillian an encouraging smile. "He will come around, lady, you shall see. Meanwhile, I will not have you lie abed. There is sickness in the village, and even though he has forbidden you to aid his people, I thought perhaps you could give me instructions, that I might make up something for them.''

So Gillian roused herself, refusing to dwell on her own devastation when others, less fortunate, were suffering. She let Edith help her dress, and then she listened as the old servant recounted the illness that had struck several of the poorer families.

Gillian had Edith make up some barley water for the fever and black currant to relieve the sore throats several of the victims were suffering, but soon diarrhea appeared, too, and rashes. Although Gillian wracked her brain for anything that might help, this sickness had never been visited upon the nunnery or its local people. And despite her best efforts, the news of deaths soon reached her.

Within weeks, it had moved into the castle itself, striking one of the cooks, who had relatives in the village, and Gillian searched the abandoned garden for some new remedy—to no avail.

When Edith herself fell ill, Gillian had no choice but to take on the duties of healer, dispensing treatment to those who had once gone to Edith for her mixtures. And whenever she was able, she slipped away to join Edith's husband at the woman's bedside. The sight of the old soldier so tenderly holding his wife's hand made Gillian blink back tears, and she vowed that, no matter what, Edith was going to survive.

At first the fever and chills that wracked the old woman's body were so alarming that Gillian feared the worst, but after a week, it eased. Then the spots appeared, and Gillian was frightened anew, for she knew the cook had died not long after breaking out with the rash. Each day Gillian hoped and prayed to find the old servant clinging to life, and each day she had been rewarded.

This afternoon, Gillian studied Edith closely, while Willie brushed out his wife's graying locks. Were the marks fading? They seemed to come in waves, but today they appeared fainter to her hopeful eyes.

"Willie! Would you yank the very hair from my scalp?" Edith's rasping voice, sharp with irritation, brought them both up short, and their eyes met over her head in surprised delight, for she had not been awake and alert for days. Blinking, the servant focused on Gillian and frowned. "My lady! What are you doing here?"

Gillian smiled down at the older woman, her throat tight with emotion. "I am tending to you, of course."

"But you should not be here. If the lord finds out, he will be sorely aggrieved." Gillian bit back a laugh at the woman's understatement. In the face of life and death, Nicholas's temper had lost its importance.

"Go on, now. I will not be the cause of more fighting between you," Edith said, tilting her head.

"Very well," Gillian answered, squeezing the older woman's hand. "I will let Willie listen to your scolding."

"As well he should," Edith murmured, before closing her eyes again. With a last tender look at her friend, Gillian turned to leave, but before she lifted the heavy drape that curtained off the tiny room, Willie joined her.

"She is better, eh?" he whispered.

Although Gillian's first inclination was to agree, she knew that those near death sometimes rallied before making their final exit. As desperately as she wanted Edith's recovery, she was unsure, so she said nothing.

The lack of her reply made Willie turn his grizzled head away, and, unable to bear his grief along with her own, Gillian slipped into the passageway and leaned against the wall, fighting back her tears. She had no time for them, for she had other patients to tend. The people of Belvry had begun asking for her, and she complied, knowing all the while that it would not be long before word of her healing reached her husband.

And he would not be pleased.

Nicholas returned to find the hall empty, and it did not ease his mood. He had taken some of his men into the fields to help with the harvest, because several of the peasants had fallen ill. Tired and sweaty and unused to such labor, he wanted a bath and his wife's attention, not necessarily in that order. Her absence provoked him all the more.

She had been moody of late, listless and lacking her usual liveliness, and he had been lenient with her, but his temper was wearing thin. If she thought to abandon her duties simply because she continued to please him in bed, he would have none of it. By God, he would remind her of her place!

"Osborn!" he roared, but his bellow echoed off the walls, summoning not his most favored servant, but only a young boy.

"Osborn is ill, my lord," the youth reported.

Damn. The knowledge that whatever was killing the villeins had entered the castle frustrated him. It was his duty to protect his people, but what could he do against an unseen invader?

"But do not worry, my lord, your lady is with him."

Nicholas whirled on the youth. *"What?"*

"Your lady. She is well versed in healing," the boy said, backing away.

Nicholas's rage was such that he could hardly find his voice. "Fetch her. Fetch my wife to me in our chamber. At once." As the boy ran off to do his bidding, Nicholas strode up the stairs to await her. By his faith, he would teach the vixen to obey him, if he had to lock her away and bind her to his bed!

Charging into the room, Nicholas clenched his fists to keep from slamming them into the wall. He had thought her complacent at last, when she had really been sneaking about behind his back! The knowledge infuriated him. And the more he contemplated the blatant betrayal, the angrier he grew. The saints be thanked, Darius was still away, or he would wonder about her fidelity, too. The very idea made the stomach that had eased its torment in the past weeks churn painfully.

When the door opened, Nicholas tried to master himself, for she looked perfectly serene and composed, damn her! He would have her as distressed as himself, at least! As usual, she approached without a flicker of trepidation and stood before him fearlessly.

"You summoned me," she stated, with just enough sarcasm in her voice to send him over the edge.

"Aye, I summoned you, vixen, from your patient's sickbed! How dare you defy me?" he snarled, circling her slowly. "I forbid you to treat my people, and yet I hear that you are tending to Osborn, against my orders!"

She showed no regret or remorse, but faced him calmly. "Your people are falling ill, and they come to me for help. How can I deny them?"

"Would you have me lock you up, away from everything and everyone? Is that the only way I can assure your obedience?" Nicholas shouted.

She stiffened at his words, but held both her ground and her bland expression. "These are your own people, Nicholas. Have you no care for them?"

"Aye, perhaps they are better off without your interference!" he snapped. She flinched at that, and Nicholas felt a bizarre moment of regret before she recovered. Her eyes, cool and intelligent, met his, and he knew an urge to shake her, to force a reaction from her inanimate body.

"Has your stomach pain not eased?" she asked, her tone soft and reasonable.

"Yes," he muttered absently. What had happened to the woman he had married? Where was the fire that he had come to expect from her? It had faded since her courses, and although Nicholas suspected the reason behind the change in her, he did not care to acknowledge it.

His hands clenching into fists, Nicholas whirled away from her. By God, what did she want from him? He had already granted her the status of his wife. Surely she could not expect him to welcome a child of Hexham's blood into his life? It was too much!

From behind him, he heard her voice, low and sensible. "I cannot totally ignore the teachings of the convent, Nicholas. I cannot stand by and let these people die without trying to help them."

Resisting her explanation, he turned on her, frustration whipping him to a new fury. "Who appointed you to sainthood? You are my wife, and you are to attend solely to me! I will not have you—"

"Selfish bastard!"

Nicholas stopped and gaped at her, for although she was reacting at last, there was no heat in her curse. "That is not the issue," he answered harshly. "You defied me, and you shall suffer for it, heir of Hexham."

Even the reminder of her place did not set her after him, and Nicholas could not believe she had once thrown drinking vessels at his head. Now she seemed but a lifeless shell. The thought made him pause, and his anger faded, to be replaced by sudden anxiety.

"How long have you been tending the sick?" he asked, his voice rising on a wave of emotion.

"I have personally tended none but Osborn and Edith," she answered stiffly.

"But there have been others here in the castle?"

"One of the cooks is dead. Several of the servants are now ill."

Stepping forward, Nicholas reached out and grasped her chin to eye her closely. She tried to jerk away—a small show of strength that eased his mounting tension—but there were dark smudges of weariness under her eyes. He dropped his hand.

"You are confined to this chamber, and if I find that you have defied me once more, I will tie you to my bed."

He expected her to fly at him, nails sharp, but she only stood staring at him, as if dumbfounded.

"No wonder your people prefer Piers," she whispered. "You do not deserve to be lord of Belvry."

Selfish she had called him, and it was true, Nicholas admitted as he walked along the walls of his castle. He had never developed a connection to anyone or anything. His mother was a memory, his father a legacy of lessons, and the land they had left him nothing more than a place to rest his head.

Aisley, as his only living relative, was little more than a blood tie, and even the Syrian woman who nursed him back to health had earned but grudging gratitude. Although he knew she longed for more, Nicholas had distanced himself from her as quickly as possible. She had seen him at his most vulnerable, and he wanted no reminder of those helpless days.

As for Darius... Nicholas recognized that the Syrian was as close to a friend as he had ever known, despite the jealousy that had come between them. And yet Nicholas felt no ties binding him to his companion, nothing even remotely resembling the selfish need that his wife aroused in him.

Lifting his face into the breeze, Nicholas felt his possession of her like a thrumming in his blood. Gillian was his, and he did not wish to share her with anyone, not with Darius or Edith or her attendants or his people, ill or no. He wanted her—*needed her*—all to himself, so desperately that it was unnerving. She was the first thing in his life to hold meaning, and he would covet her, whether she liked it or not.

If locking her away was his only course, then he would make no apologies for it. His eyes narrowing with determination, Nicholas strode back along the walls and down into the bailey. He had made sure that her supper was sent up to the great chamber, for she would not be leaving it, even for meals. Then he had met with his steward concerning the sickness that was plaguing the demesne. They had agreed to send to the city for a physician, since Nicholas had made it clear that his wife was no longer to administer treatment.

It was growing late when he mounted the stairs, and Nicholas felt his anticipation grow as well. No matter what arguments raged between them during the daylight hours, at night he and Gillian came together in his great bed, spending themselves in each other. Only then did her passionate nature still assert itself. And only then was Nicholas able to take all she gave him, feel everything she meant to him. . . .

Yanking open the door impatiently, he shut it behind him quickly, eagerness roaring in his blood. Selfish, aye, he would possess her as he never had before and as no one else ever would.

When at first he did not see her, Nicholas knew a trickle of panic, but the candlelight showed her slender form already in his bed. He smiled in satisfaction. Her pallet was long gone, for he liked to hold her close in the darkness, her breath gentle against him, her body stirring beside him.

Walking to the edge of the mattress, Nicholas stood over her, but his excitement turned to dismay when he realized she was asleep. Already? She always waited up for him, as frantic as he for their coupling, and night had not yet settled upon the castle.

Tempted to wake her, Nicholas leaned over her and noticed again the dark circles beneath her eyes. Her skin was pale, too, and he felt a jolt in his gut. She was tired and, selfish bastard that he was, he had thought only of himself. Reaching out a hand, he smoothed a few errant strands of hair from her forehead, only to halt in the act, his entire body stiffening. She was warm, her flesh heated to the touch, as if feverish . . . *like someone who was ill*. . . .

Nicholas swayed on his feet as he felt his very heart being torn from his chest. Death reached up to strike him more savagely than any infidel blade. He opened his mouth to scream for Osborn or Edith, but nothing came out. They could not answer him.

He, who had been alone all his life, had never felt so bereft. He, who had never needed anyone, suddenly knew his lack. Aisley was gone, driven away by his foul temper, and even Darius, banished by his jealousy, could offer him nothing. No one remained but an assortment of servants and castle tenants who meant far too little to him to be entrusted with his wife.

A noise startled him, and Nicholas wakened, blinking blearily into the dimness of the great chamber. *Gillian.* He leaned toward her, holding his breath until he saw her chest rise and fall fitfully. She lived, and he let out a long, ragged sigh of relief. Was the rash worse or better? he wondered, studying the marks that marred her. Would they ever fade? Nicholas realized that he did not care whether she was spotted or pink or blue, if only she would recover. A low, harsh sound of pain erupted from his chest into the stillness.

"Hush now, my lord. I will sit with her for a spell. You must go get something to eat." Dazedly Nicholas turned to face the speaker. Edith, looking worn and weary, was standing by the window, opening the shutters enough to let some light into the room. When had she arrived?

And what time was it? Nicholas rubbed his eyes with his palms. He could not remember where night began or ended, for he had rarely left this room, the hours running into days—mayhap even weeks—as his wife grew worse. He must have dozed off, for threads of brightness were streaming into the room. How could the sun shine? It seemed a blasphemy, and he cursed a world that went on about him when his own was crumbling.

The sound of shuffling footsteps made him turn, and he found Edith standing before the chair where he was slumped. "You must eat, my lord. Go on down, and I shall get someone to air out the room and clean it. I will stay with her," she said, laying a hand on his shoulder.

No one ever touched him. No one but his wife. He knew that, and not too long ago he would have shrugged off the old woman's attempt at comfort, leaping to his feet in a fury, but now he only stared at her as he struggled to digest her words. Food. He stood, though he wanted nothing in his burning gut.

"Go on now," she said, and he went. But in the great hall, the soulful gazes of Belvry's residents were too much for Nicholas to bear, and he strode to the doors, stepping out into the autumn sunshine. Still, he imagined their reproachful eyes following him, looking to their lord for protection against this scourge.

Damn! Frustration coiled in him, strangling his insides. He had been a warrior all his life, a knight, a holy crusader and an instrument of revenge. Fighting was all that he knew, and he wanted to kill something and hack it to pieces, but this time his foe was unseen. All he could do was take his sword and bury it in the ground, bellowing his rage to the skies.

"My lord?" The anxious looks of his men made Nicholas seek to master himself, though discipline seemed a part of his past. Dismissing their queries with a glance, he pulled his weapon from the soil and sheathed it again. With a sigh, he ran a hand through his hair and down over the stubble on his face. More than food, he needed a bath, but not the usual hot tub in his chamber. Barking an order to a lad to fetch him some fresh clothes, Nicholas headed toward the stream that flowed behind the castle walls.

It was ice-cold, but it revived him from his lethargy and sent his blood pumping again. Although the air chilled him further, it was a welcome contrast from the heat that raged in his stomach and farther up, in the depths of his chest.

When he returned to the hall, he felt better able to greet his people, and he saw not reproach in their faces, but concern. It was almost worse, yet Nicholas steeled himself to accept their wishes for his wife's recovery, and when one old woman pressed a bunch of flowers upon him for Gillian, he managed to thank her instead of sending her flying across the room.

He had not realized how much they cared for her, and the discovery made him swallow hard. In the brief time Gillian had been at Belvry, she had touched them all with the vibrant life that was waning even now.... Turning on his heel, Nicholas strode toward the stairs, and the great chamber where his wife lay abed. Suddenly he needed to know that she still breathed, to see for himself that she had not left him.

The door to their room was open, and he stopped at the threshold, his belly burning and his lungs heaving with more than the slight exertion of his climb. Edith sat beside the bed, bathing Gillian's face with cool water, as he had done so often during the past few days. A male servant, a gangly youth with lanky blond hair, stopped laying fresh rushes and leaned against the wall. His negligent attitude was enough to make Nicholas stiffen, but then he glanced dismissively toward Gillian, firing Nicholas's blood.

"You are wasting your time, Edith," the youth said with a shrug. "That one will not be with us long, no matter what you do, and the lord will get himself a new bride soon enough to breed the babies you want. Too bad this one could not give him an heir. Better that she die in childbirth than—"

Nicholas was not even aware of his own movement, but suddenly he was standing in the room, dragging the miscreant off his feet by the neck of his tunic. With a vicious oath, he slammed the bastard's head against the wall.

"You...will...not...speak...of...her!" The walls closed around him, crimson with his own rage, until he felt Edith's hand, surprisingly strong, upon his arm, restraining him. His eyesight cleared then, and he blew out a breath, realizing that if not for her, he would have killed the man who quailed before him. He did not care. "Your name?" he snarled.

"'Tis Eudo, my lord, a freeman's son from the village, called in to help us," Edith answered.

"We need not his kind of help," Nicholas spat. He turned back to the youth he still held against the wall. "Get you gone! You are banished from Belvry, from the castle, from my land, from any grain of soil that belongs to me. Do you understand?"

Nicholas gripped the fellow so tightly by the neck that he could barely speak, but Eudo finally nodded and squeaked his assent. With a growl, Nicholas tossed him toward the door, and the youth went sprawling among the rushes before struggling to his feet. Shooting Nicholas a last sullen look, he ran from the room.

Silence hung in the air, and Nicholas turned his head toward the bed, uneasy until he heard her ragged breathing. He should not have created a disturbance, when she was so ill. She needed peace and quiet, and when had he ever given her those? Something hurt inside his chest again, and Nicholas looked away. Dear God, would he lose his composure in front of that old harridan Edith?

"Leave us," he muttered.

"But, my lord, you must rest yourself, else you, too, will grow ill," she protested.

Nicholas gave her a warning glare that told her what he thought of her words. If he sickened and died, what did it matter? He had nothing, really, for which to live.

For a moment, she hesitated, as if she would say something, but then she released a heavy sigh and was gone, shutting the door quietly behind her.

Nicholas was alone with his wife. He gazed down at her, but the niece of his old enemy did not even notice his presence. She had rarely been lucid over the past couple of days, either slipping into a deep sleep that frightened him or mumbling in delirium. How far she had come from the brave woman he had married—yet Nicholas took no joy in her fall.

Indeed, despite all his plans to torment her, he had never taken pleasure in her travails. His revenge had come to mean less to him as the woman herself came to mean more. His delight was culled from other things: from her unpredictable behavior, from the way her eyes flashed when she faced him, from the look in them, all dreamy and erotic, when he sank into her body, her strength, her beauty, her passion....

At last, Nicholas admitted that he no longer wanted vengeance, only a resurgence of *her*. He had heard her laugh, although she had never done so with him, and he wanted to make her laugh, to see her smile again, to argue with her, to lose himself inside her.... A harsh sound Nicholas did not recognize erupted from his chest as he stood over his wife's prone body. And silently he vowed to forget his vengeance, if only she would recover.

Nicholas took no oath lightly, and especially not this one, for revenge had driven him for years. Yet he did not fear the emptiness that had once plagued him in its absence, because Gillian had given him things to take its place.

Aye, his wife had filled him with feelings that he had never known before, and the strongest of them right now was pain.

Chapter Fourteen

Nicholas did not know what he expected, certainly not for the heavens to open, but something, anything... And yet his vow changed nothing. His wife still lay there, feverish and restless, as sick as before, totally oblivious of his momentous decision. He laughed—it was a harsh, bitter sound—at the enormity of his arrogance, and Gillian turned her head toward the noise. Taking her hand, Nicholas murmured an apology that at first was for disturbing her rest and continued on through every black deed he had ever done her, until finally he rested his forehead against the pillow, silent once more.

Weary as he was, he nearly drifted off, but when Gillian moved, he was alert again. Hope burgeoned and died as he looked up to find her thrashing and babbling in delirium. She had called out names before, presumably those of her companions at the convent, and once she had even mentioned Edith, but she had never spoken to him...until now.

"Nicholas." He stiffened at her side, wondering if he had dreamed the word, and rubbed a palm roughly against his eyes. His other hand still clutched Gillian's, and he squeezed it lightly.

"I am here, Gillian," he answered.

She mumbled something unintelligible, and Nicholas leaned close to catch her whisper. "Must not tell..."

"Tell who? What?" Nicholas asked, even though he knew she was likely out of her head. To see his wife, who had been so bright and clever, reduced to this raving made his throat tighten.

"Must not tell Nicholas," she muttered, growing agitated.

Nicholas froze where he was, leaning half over her, his face only inches from hers, uncertain what to think. Would he now discover some perfidy that he had not expected? Or would his worst suspicions about his wife and the Syrian be confirmed? His stomach clenched and burned. God, but the emptiness would be welcome now, for he liked not being so full of feelings!

Gillian tossed her head back and forth against the pillow, and Nicholas put a hand to her damp curls to gentle her. Despite his sudden misgivings, her discomfort upset him. Would that she were well, and all could be as it was between them!

"He despises me," she whispered.

"Who?"

"Nicholas," she said, breaking into a sob, and Nicholas's fingers curled into her locks.

"Nay. Nay, Gillian. He does not hate you."

"You always say that, Edith, but you have not seen the way he looks at me." She shuddered. "His eyes glitter with his hatred!"

"Nay," Nicholas said, his own voice wavering. "'Tis not Edith, but I, Nicholas, and I swear to you, Gillian, I do not hate you."

Although she did not seem to understand, she turned her unseeing eyes toward his. So green they were, and yet they had so lost their brightness that it hurt him to look at them.

"You must promise not to tell him, Edith!" she whispered fiercely, grabbing at his arm.

"'Tis your husband, Gillian. 'Tis I, Nicholas!"

"Promise me!"

Her ravaged face took on an expression of such urgency that Nicholas pressed her hand to his chest. "I promise," he whispered.

She relaxed at the words and turned her head away, her thick lashes drifting shut in such an imitation of death that Nicholas's blood roared a protest. Desperate to keep her talking, even if she spoke nothing but ravings, he gripped her hand tightly. "What is the secret that we guard so closely?"

For a long moment, she did not respond. Then he heard her voice, in the barest of soft replies. "You must not tell Nicholas."

"Tell him what?"

"Do not tell him—" she moved again, her lashes fluttering to reveal tears pooling in the corners of her once vivid eyes " I love him."

Nicholas was stunned to silence by her admission, and when she slipped back into dreams, he did not rouse her again. He stayed where he was, bent over her, holding a hand that was suddenly wet with tears. And the tears were not his wife's.

Nicholas lost all track of time. Once, he heard Edith at the door, but he would not open it. He felt delirious himself, as if his insides were burning up, and ready to explode whenever he looked at his wife's still form.

She was dying. It was time he faced the fact. Nicholas thought of the moment when he had first learned of her, how her very name had dragged him out of his empty hell and how, over the weeks that followed, she had filled him with her vitality, her boundless passion. He pictured life without her, and he wanted to tear down the castle walls around him with his bare hands.

The irony of it all did not escape him, and a wild, strangled laugh erupted from his throat. He had set out to defeat her, and instead she was destroying him. And not with superior strength or cunning or even with the considerable wiles of her body that she wielded so unknowingly. Nay, his wife laid waste to her husband by wasting away.

Nicholas could not bear it. With an angry bellow, he turned on her, and he saw not the frail creature in the bed, but the untamed spirit that resided within. "Do not think you can free yourself of me, wife!" he shouted. "You will not die! I told you so before, and I meant it well! Do you hear me?"

He raised his fist into the air. "You are mine, vixen. You belong to me, and I will not let you leave me! By God and all the saints, you will do as I say for once, Gillian Hexham de Laci! You will not die!"

Nicholas raged, no longer worried about disturbing her rest, but determined to rouse her. He paced the room, ranting like a madman, ignoring the sound of knocking at the chamber door. He was determined, by the very force of his will, to make her do his bidding at last.

And he bade her to live.

Was he dreaming? Nicholas blinked, but the vision persisted. Emerald eyes, weary yet clear, studied him, and the soft sound of his name fluttered along the edges of his awareness. Rolling onto his back, he rubbed his eyes. He was lying on the bed beside his wife, yet he was fully clothed, while she was beneath the covers. He was puzzled until he glanced at her and saw her as if for the first time, weary and wan and covered with spots. *Gillian!*

He sat up abruptly. "Gillian!"

"Hmm?" She looked at him, and he felt as though he might burst from the force of his emotions. Her expression was wary but alert, and he wanted to shout in triumph. She was awake! She knew him!

"Gillian! Gillian!" he said, even as his throat tightened, threatening to halt his speech. Leaning over her, he took her hand and brought her fingers to his cheek. They were cool and smooth and more precious to him than life. "Gillian. Gillian..." he murmured as he pressed his lips into her palm.

"Nicholas? What is it?" she whispered, her eyes growing big in her pale face. "Do you... weep?"

"Nay." He choked out the word and gently replaced her hand on the cover before swiping at his eyes with the back of his own. "Nay. 'Tis the smoke from the hearth. They must be burning green wood again," he muttered. "How do you feel?"

"Terrible. Could you... Water..." Before she had even finished speaking, Nicholas was out of the bed, pouring her a cup and lifting her head so that she could drink. Her feeble efforts were more exquisite than the most elegant of gestures. She was alive! And she was his, never to leave him.

A sense of peace such as Nicholas had never known settled over him, as if all were right with the world for the first time since his arrival in it. Nothing drove him anymore, nor was he hollow and aching inside. He was whole, for she was well.

After her brief burst of energy, Gillian leaned back and closed her eyes once more, but Nicholas was too excited to be discouraged. "You will need food—some broth, mayhap. I will summon Edith."

In just a few strides, he was at the door, calling the old servant, and when she did not appear soon enough to suit him, he went searching for her, yelling her name. He took the stairs two at a time down to the great hall. After his long absence, shut away in his chamber, everything seemed changed. His father's hall appeared bigger, better, more familiar and welcoming, than ever before. And the faces that eyed him from the edges of the room no longer looked wary, but seemed relieved to see him.

"Edith! Attend your lady!" he ordered when he spied the servant. Even her plain countenance had taken on a pleasing aspect, and Nicholas nearly smiled at the old witch before he caught himself. He sent her on her way with a gruff nod, and ran a hand over his face. He needed a shave and a bath, or perhaps another swim in the river, to revive himself.

Nicholas was halfway across the tiles when he saw Darius moving toward him, and he hurried to greet his companion. Stifling an urge to embrace the man who was his friend, Nicholas reached up and grasped the Syrian's arm instead. If Darius was surprised at the abrupt contact from someone who had never touched him before, he did not show it.

"You are back," Nicholas said.

"Yes," Darius replied, his lips curving into a smile. "Walk with me, and I will tell you of my journey."

Outside, the sky was overcast and threatening rain, but the world had never looked so fresh to Nicholas. The autumn air felt brisk and clean, and he sucked great drafts into lungs that seemed starved for it. He was aware of the presence of the Syrian beside him, and although they had walked together countless times in foreign lands and finally here in Britain, Nicholas knew a heightened appreciation of the ease with which they fell into step.

"'Tis a strange tale," Darius said seriously. "I did as you bade and went to the abbey, and by all accounts, a young man had been there before me, seeking information about your wife."

Nicholas tensed, alert to the nuances no one else would have detected in the Syrian's manner. Although others might not have seen it, he could tell Darius was puzzled, and he liked it not. "Go on," he urged.

"The man was of medium build, lean and black-haired, and all at the convent claim never to have seen him before."

"What kind of questions did he ask?"

"How many years Gillian spent at the nunnery, where she lived before, her background, her family. He sought details, and he was persistent enough to worry the abbess."

"What did she think?" Nicholas asked, for the holy woman had seemed wiser than most.

"She did not hazard a guess. Indeed, no one could suggest why he would be asking after Gillian, unless he was a former acquaintance."

Nicholas caught Darius's assessing glance and saw the dark eyes waiting to judge his reaction to such news. He remained composed, however, the fires of his violent jealousy banked for now, and his restraint earned a nearly imperceptible nod of respect from his companion.

"Working under the assumption that he was someone your wife knew, I looked farther into her past for traces of this fellow," the Syrian said. "I spoke with the abbess about where she lived before the convent."

Nicholas jerked his head around to look at Darius, but the foreigner's features revealed nothing. "I learned that she served in the household of a burgher named Abel Freemantle. And after some coaxing, I was able to get the man to speak to me."

Nicholas's mouth curved upward as he pictured the type of persuasion involved.

"According to the burgher, a man with black hair also came to his home and asked about his former servant.

Again, the fellow was very interested in your wife's family."

Nicholas's eyes narrowed. More than common curiosity was involved, when a man went to so much trouble to ask questions. He felt the unease of a threat, yet unseen, at his back.

"Although hesitant, the burgher related to me another strange incident involving Gillian Hexham. It seems that a knight of obvious wealth and power barged into his home not long ago and berated him for his treatment of her. Although he claimed not to know the identity of this fierce warrior, he is terrified of the knight's return and would not speak willingly of the matter."

Nicholas's lips curved as he remembered the burgher's fright. Apparently the filthy creature was keeping his word, as well he should, if he cared to continue his existence. "And?" Nicholas prodded, refusing to rise to Darius's bait.

The dark man appeared bemused, but continued. "I followed the trail back to your wife's birthplace, where I spoke to neighbors. Again, the black-haired one had been there before me, though none knew him. And there the track ended."

Nicholas stopped and stared out over his lands, the fertile ground that provided a good harvest for his people, and beyond, past the boundaries of his demesne and toward a foe he could not name. "What do you make of it?" he asked softly.

Darius was silent for a long time. "I do not know, lord of Belvry, but I would advise you to watch your back."

Nicholas nodded grimly. "As I have well learned."

"And what of you?" Darius asked. "I returned two days ago, but have seen you not. The castle has been rife with all manner of rumors that you had fallen ill. Or that you had locked yourself in your chamber with your wife's dead body.''

Nicholas flinched at that. "She still lives, and I did not lock myself in with her. I merely oversaw her treatment. She is, after all, my wife."

"Aye," Darius said, and a slow grin broke over his normally expressionless face. "She is that."

Nicholas took one glance at his wife's stubborn expression and nearly turned on his heel and left the great chamber. She was becoming more difficult daily, and he was weary of arguing with her. And if he was weary, he could not imagine the toll these outbursts were taking on her. His eyes narrowed.

"You wished to speak with me," he snapped.

"I *wish* to get up!" she said, managing to appear both exasperated and extremely beautiful. She was sitting up in bed, her hair tumbling about her shoulders in lovely disarray, and her color had returned at last, cream and rose...and freckles. He hardened himself against her appeal, but before he could answer, she was at him again.

"Nicholas, I am well! Look," she said, stretching out an arm toward him, "even the spots are gone!" He looked, and he saw that she was wearing only her shift. He looked away. "You cannot mean to confine me here forever," she protested. Her voice lowered ominously. "Unless this is some new course of your revenge."

Nicholas whirled toward her, outraged at the train of her thoughts. His plans for vengeance were over. Could she not see that? He was concerned for her, and he did not trust her to mend herself!

Convinced that the force of his own will had saved her from death, Nicholas was determined that only he could keep her alive. He eyed her warily at every turn, and if she coughed, he glared. If she closed her eyes, he panicked. When she wanted to get out of bed, he forbade it. He gritted his teeth. "You must take this slowly, so as not to task yourself," he explained.

"Nicholas, it has been weeks!" she said, throwing up her hands in disgust. "If I do not get up soon, I shall grow sores and become crippled!"

His lips twitched at that, but he kept control of himself. "I am willing to . . . compromise," he said slowly.

Immediately her chin lifted. "What do you want?" she demanded.

Your health. "Nothing," Nicholas answered innocently. "I will allow you to rise, if you remain in this chamber." He held up a hand to forestall her argument. "If your condition continues to improve, then we shall see."

"So you *do* mean to imprison me!" she cried accusingly.

"Nay. I will not hold you here when you are well." He did not mention that for her freedom, she must promise him never to treat the sick again. That discussion could wait for another day. The illness that had struck the castle had finally ended, but there would be other diseases, and Nicholas vowed that she would not suffer them.

She gave him a sulky look that told him she was mollified for now, and he relaxed his stance. She lived, and he would make sure that she continued to do so. Unfortunately, he suspected that he was going to have his hands full with the task.

Gillian lay awake, silently counting the golden stitches that edged the elaborate bed hangings. Fully recovered from her illness, she had been up and around for weeks and had resumed all her previous activities, with the notable exception of one.

She had not made love to her husband.

Nicholas had not sent her back to her pallet. He slept with her, as before, but he did not touch her. They neither coupled passionately nor curled up together in the aftermath, for he stayed firmly entrenched on one side of the huge bed.

At first, Gillian had been too tired to care, but when she grew better, she had reached out to him, only to be rebuffed. Her husband had insisted she rest, and then he had started coming to bed later and later, until she could not stay awake for him. In the morning he was gone, and the sheets were cold and empty.

Gillian sighed. She would have thought him weary of her charms, but during the day he did not avoid her. In fact, he spent more time with her than ever. Just yesterday, he had taken her hawking, patiently explaining the finer points of the sport to her, for no reason other than her expressed interest. She had been so stunned that she could barely listen.

And the outings were not all of it. No matter where she was, he would appear throughout the hours, popping his head into the room as if to check up on her. Often Gillian caught his eyes upon her, so intense that she felt seared through to the heart.

It was not hate, or the desire she had glimpsed many times, but something else entirely, that burned in those gray depths. Yet, just when she felt as if a momentous discovery were imminent, it would be gone, his gaze shuttered again and whatever feelings he might harbor locked away from her.

Gillian was not sure how to deal with this new Nicholas. Oh, they argued still, and especially long and hard over her treatment of the sick, but there was some underlying change in him that she could not quite understand. If he was a little less fierce, he was moodier, more prone to sudden sullen spells and to silence rather than shouting...to sleeping rather than loving.

The absence of his rather demanding passion had left Gillian floundering. She was not quite sure how to initiate either a discussion of the problem or a resolution of it. She had sent Nicholas plenty of hot looks, and brushed against him countless times, all to no avail. She had even considered giving him the tonic that she had once concocted at Edith's insistence, but she was getting too desperate to waste time with subtlety.

Alive and healthy, Gillian missed what they had made between them. During the day Nicholas had held himself apart from her, but at night he had always shared himself with her. Gillian drew in a sharp breath at the memories. She wanted him. She wanted that peek into his soul that she took when they came together. She wanted the pure physical pleasure that he gave her with his hands, his mouth and his beautiful body.

And she refused to wait any longer. Just this afternoon, she had snuck a nap while he was out riding, so that she would be wide awake when he finally came to bed. Tonight was the night, and she was determined.

The slow creak of the door was her reward, and Gillian smiled in the darkness before closing her eyes. Nicholas undressed in silence, as if he did not want to disturb her, and Gillian felt a precarious twisting of her heart that had become all too familiar. Nicholas, thoughtful? She must be dreaming!

But the gentle dip of the bed told her she was not, and the rustling of covers signaled his presence. Gillian was sprawled in the middle of the mattress, and he hugged the edge of it, as if he dared not come closer. Perhaps he did not want to wake her, she thought, with no little wonder. When at last he had settled down and his breathing had became slow and easy, Gillian made her move.

Still feigning sleep, she turned onto her side and snuggled against him. She was not wearing her shift, and the slow glide of her naked skin against his sent heat shooting through her. Ah, how she had missed this! Running her fingers lightly across the thick mat of hair on his chest, she sighed softly, only to feel him stiffen beside her. To her astonishment, he jerked away as if she had burned him, and rolled onto the floor.

Gillian sat up and stared at him, crouched by the bed, his face hidden from her in the darkness. "Nicholas?"

"Gillian! I thought you were asleep," he muttered. But still he made no move to join her.

"Come back to bed," she whispered, her voice husky with need. The night made her bold, and she stretched out her arms, wrapped them around his neck and tugged him down on top of her.

The kiss was just as she remembered, hot and fierce and soul-searing. Without preamble, his tongue thrust into her mouth, claiming her fiercely. Their naked bodies fit together, hers soft, his hard. It had been so long.... "Nick," she said with a sigh.

He broke the kiss to rest his forehead against hers. Gillian could hear his swift breathing, could feel his arousal pressing against her. He stayed still for a moment, and she ran her hands along the smooth sides of his muscled body, urging it against hers.

"Gillian!" His voice was sharp, and he eased away from her, disengaging her arms from around him.

"What is it?" she asked, bereft, as he sat up, swinging his legs over the side of the bed.

"You have been ill."

"I am well now, Nicholas, as I would show you."

"Nay!" His denial sounded harsh and final.

Gillian fell back against the pillows, stunned. Whatever else was between them, they had always had the passion. Or had he just played with her, making her want something only to take it from her? Was this all part of his revenge?

She was glad he could not see her face well in the firelight and revel in his triumph. Damn him for a fiend! Gathering all her resources, she turned on him, taunting him as he would her. "Why not? Are you afraid you might act human for a change?"

"Gillian!" He shouted her name in outrage, and she thought he might lunge for her. She hoped he would, for if they grappled together naked, she might get what she wanted, if only for this night. But he suddenly halted, regaining control of himself once more, and, muttering foul oaths, he surged from the bed. She could hear him dressing, and she rolled onto her side, pulling the covers over her head.

This time, he did not slam the door, but Gillian still heard it shut behind him. Only then did she bury her face in the pillows and weep.

Chapter Fifteen

Nicholas strode through the bailey, ignoring the low, surprised greetings of the sentinels. He did not stop walking until he was far from any activity, alone in the darkness. Then he bent over, blew out a ragged breath and willed his painfully hard body to dormancy.

Damn! When forced to marry Hexham's heir, he had abstained from any physical relationship, and he had thought to do so again. Unfortunately, it was not so easy the second time around, for now he was familiar with each creamy inch of Gillian's skin, each tantalizing freckle, each gentle sigh and pulse of her body. He knew just what awaited him, if he would only relax his guard. Even so, he had been doing well enough avoiding temptation until tonight, when he realized that there was something else he had not taken into consideration.

Gillian. Nicholas had never thought that she would try to seduce him, but he should have guessed. His wife was no shy little nun. She was bold and brave and accustomed to fighting for what she wanted. And, apparently, she wanted him. He should not have been so surprised. After all, she loved him, and to her their lovemaking would mean only pleasure.

To him it was a frightful proposition.

Aye, he admitted for the first time in his life, he was afraid. Oh, he had suffered aplenty in those long days and nights after Hexham abandoned him, but revenge had consumed him, fueled him, and in truth he had not feared his own death.

He feared Gillian's. Those helpless, hopeless hours at her bedside had proved one thing to him. He did not want to face a life without her. He was determined to keep her well and with him forever, unharmed, unhurt, and content in her devotion to him.

To that end, Nicholas had already increased the number of guards and outriders who protected his demesne, just in case the stranger who had asked after her turned out to be a threat. And he had secured her promise that she would not tend the sick. Indeed, he had ordered the stiffest penalties for anyone who came near her with the slightest cold or the simplest wart.

The Syrian had eyed him askance and told him he could not control the Fates, but Nicholas would not listen. He had yanked his wife back from the arms of death, and he would see that no harm or disease came to her ever again. But there were other killers that stole the lives of women in their beds, and Nicholas was well aware of them. Had not his own mother died giving birth? The risk was too great for him to ignore, and so he would not allow it.

Gillian would never carry his child.

The decision, made when she lay pale and prone, had seemed reasonable at the time. Then his need had not been for her body, but for her soul. Now, however, she was up and about, her lovely form weaving in and out of his vision, her scent, fresh and beguiling, wafting through the air, and her voice, low and sultry, working upon his humors more strongly than any tonic.

He thought he would burst.

Leaning his head against the wall in frustration, Nicholas envisioned a lifetime of this torment and did not think he could endure it. What if she tested him again? He knew very well that his wife was more stubborn than an ox. If she was determined to bed him, she would, and only the strength of his own will could save her.

That will was already stretched to the breaking point.

There had to be another way, Nicholas thought, banging the stone angrily. He had heard of men who withdrew at the last moment to spill their seed outside the woman's body, but he did not know how well it might work. Nor did he trust himself, lost in the throes of passion, to act at the appropriate time. In the East, there had been whispers of certain herbs that could prevent conception, but he knew not the truth of the tales. If such a potion existed, women kept the knowledge to themselves, and rightly so, for most men wanted heirs.

Nicholas snorted. Not he! Here was one man who would pay dearly for such a recipe, if only he could find it. He thought of the women he might turn to for the information. Edith, for all her flighty ways, was wise in some things. She would certainly not approve of his request, however, and so would deny him the knowledge, if she possessed it. And the old healer in the village was long dead.

Indeed, the only woman at Belvry who was steeped in herb lore was Gillian, and he could hardly ask her for it. She wanted a child. Had she not told him so? Nicholas flinched at the thought of denying her, but she was not the best judge of her own well-being. She had proved that already. He was her husband, and it was his job to keep her safe.

Setting his jaw tightly, Nicholas pushed aside any doubt, and resolved to find a way to both have his wife and keep her. If no one here possessed the proper knowledge, he would venture forth for it, or send Darius looking, by God.

Maybe even to Dunmurrow. Although he had heard no word from Aisley since her abrupt departure, he knew that his sister had a canny way with plants.

Nicholas straightened abruptly. He would write to Aisley first, for she would surely know what he needed. He did not like asking her for anything, especially in light of their quarrel, but they were tied by blood. And, once upon a time, he had saved the life of the pompous husband she so doted upon. She owed him.

Smiling grimly, Nicholas began the long walk back to his hall. Aye, Aisley would do her duty by him, and when he discovered the secret, he would slip it into his wife's wine. And she would never be the wiser.

It seemed to Gillian that she had just drifted off to sleep at last when Edith was at the door, waking her again. She jerked upright, opened bleary eyes, looked around the empty room and wondered where her husband had spent the night. It had better not have been in the arms of some other willing wench, or she would kill them both!

"My lady?"

Gillian snapped at Edith to enter as she dragged herself from the bed. Anger and humiliation heightened the effects of her lack of sleep so that she could not even summon up a smile for the hapless Edith as she reached for a shift.

"What is it, my lady?"

"What is it always?" Gillian retorted, yanking the garment over her head so that she nearly rent the fabric. She poked her head out. "Nothing but him!" She thrust one arm through, and then the other. "I thought he had changed, just a little bit, but he is up to his old tricks, tormenting me for his amusement, the fiend!"

Edith's mouth gaped open for a moment before she shut it firmly and frowned at her charge. "My lady, how can you say that, after what he did for you?"

"And what exactly did he do?" Gillian asked impatiently as she chose a gown for the day. "He snatched me from my home, vilified and frightened me, and ordered me about as his slave!" *And, worst of all, he made me fall in love with him....*

"Surely you remember, my lady!" Edith chided, pushing away Gillian's clumsy hands to take the dress herself. "Why, everyone knows that he was at your side all through your illness, day and night, from the very first. I was still abed myself, so he took care of your needs, washed you down when you were feverish and changed the linens. When I finally saw him, the poor man looked as if he had not slept for weeks. He sat right there and held your hand," she noted, pointing to a chair that stood near the massive bed.

Gillian grew pensive as she let the servant help her into her clothes. Her illness was little more than a blur, with snatches of visions that she had thought brought on by fever. Now she studied them more closely. She recalled her husband shouting at her so loudly that he made her head hurt, but she also remembered him pressing a cool cloth to her face and murmuring softly to her. In fact, when she looked back at her care, she saw only Nicholas at her side, tender and gentle and wholly unlike himself. Once, she would have sworn he was crying. She truly must have been dreaming!

But she could not put down all of it to her fancy. Nicholas must have tended her, at least part of the time. But why? Why go to such lengths for someone he claimed to despise? With a chill, Gillian remembered other times when he had comforted her for base reasons of his own. "He just wanted to keep his vengeance alive," she said bitterly.

"Oh, no, my lady," Edith said, looking so disappointed in her that Gillian actually felt guilty. For what? For assuming the worst about her husband? Just when had he proved her wrong? Even his attention of late, the hawking, the riding, the looking in on her, seemed part of some insidious plan now. Whatever he gave her, he meant to take away sooner or later.

Edith gently urged Gillian onto the settle and faced her, hands on ample hips. "My lady, 'tis time you heard the truth about your lord. I have never seen a man suffering so in my life, and I hope never to again. When you were ill, no one could get him to eat or sleep or even to leave your bedside. When a servant dared speak of your death, he banished the man from Belvry. And I was not the only one to hear him howling like a beast who has lost his mate."

Gillian dropped her eyes, uncomfortable with the stark truth to be found in Edith's. It was too much for her to grasp. "But why?" she whispered.

"Why?" Edith laughed gently. "For such a clever woman, you seem to be fair dense where His Lordship is concerned. My lady, Nicholas has changed, make no mistake about it, and it is you who has changed him. Our lord is in love."

It was Gillian's turn to gape, for the servant's words made her mouth fall open in stunned surprise. "Do not look so shocked, my lady. Surely you have seen the difference in him!" Edith insisted. Gillian closed her lips, but she was still too stunned to answer.

"Why, everyone at Belvry knows it. In fact," Edith said, leaning closer, "I have collected quite a nice little bag of coins from our more skeptical residents."

"Coins . . ." Gillian echoed dully.

"Yes, my lady. I knew from the very beginning that you would turn our Nicholas around, and I was not afraid to put my money on it. At first, I wagered only with Willie, but as word got around, well . . . And after your illness, everyone was forced to pay up, of course, for even a blind man could see that our lord is in love with his wife.''

Gillian sat slumped on the settle, staring at the far wall, while she tried to make sense of Edith's rambling. Nicholas in *love?* With *her?* Even though her heart desperately wanted to believe it, her mind warned her to beware. He had toyed with her before, deliberately, and with evil intent. Perhaps this was all an elaborate ruse to gain her trust. But why? To destroy her, Gillian answered, shaking herself dazedly.

Just as he had last night. The memory made Gillian stiffen and straighten, for there was proof enough of her husband's perfidy. A man in love did not reject his wife's . . . advances. Gillian lifted her chin. "Nonsense, Edith," she said, rising from her seat.

"But, my lady—"

"I wish to hear no more of this!" Righteous anger made her answer more sharply than perhaps was warranted.

"But, my lady—"

She rounded on Edith. "And this man you say is swooning with love for me, just where did he spend the night, and with whom? He was not here. He will not . . . stay with me. He refuses me!" Gillian turned away, unwilling to let the servant see her distress.

She soon felt the comforting pat of Edith's hand, however. "My lady, he has been concerned about you. You know how he has striven to see you well. Give him time. He wants to be certain that you are fully recovered before having his way with you."

Gillian was torn. Although she did not want to listen, her heart bade her heed the servant's words. And as much as she wanted to reject Edith's explanation outright, something in it rang true. Oh, she did not for a moment believe that Nicholas had fallen in love with her, but he might have changed just a little. Her perpetual optimism reared its head, only to be warned away by her good sense. Perhaps all the attention he had paid her did spring from concern, although it would take her a while to adjust to that kind of thinking.

"Give him time," Edith repeated, as if reading her thoughts. "And if you are not willing, then there are ways to hurry him along," she added with a chuckle. Then she leaned close to whisper in Gillian's ear.

Gillian drew in a sharp breath as she listened to some of the servant's suggestions. They whirled in her head, conjuring up visions of herself and Nicholas together, making her heart beat apace, making her *want.* If only she could believe the old woman. If only she could believe in Nicholas! But what if she did try to... seduce her husband, only to be rejected again?

Gillian did not think she could bear it.

Nicholas waited until Gillian was busy sewing with the other women before he called for his bath. Although he felt like the basest coward, hiding away from his wife, he wanted no interruptions, and the river outside was turning too cold even for him. His steward had elevated another servant to take Osborn's place, but the man was slow, and Nicholas snapped for him to hurry.

Before the fellow finished filling the tub, Nicholas had doffed his clothes and was ready to step in. He sank into the relaxing heat even as the door closed behind the new man, Rowland by name.

Nicholas had just leaned back his head and closed his eyes, reveling in the nearly forgotten pleasure of his bath, when the door creaked open. "You may go. I will attend myself," he muttered, realizing that he had taken Osborn for granted. And now that good servant was dead. . . .

"Will you?" That husky purr belonged to no man, and Nicholas shot straight up, sloshing water over the sides, to find his wife standing before him. He had avoided her since the previous night's debacle, for he well remembered her ire. Had she come to drown him? Although Nicholas would not have put it past her, he knew better than to reveal his suspicions to his wife.

"Aye, I need no assistance, as well you know, vixen. Now begone!"

"Why?" she asked, stepping closer. "I have sworn to attend you, and I would but do my duty."

"Nay," Nicholas said. He watched her warily as she knelt by the tub and rubbed the soap between her hands. Beneath those thick lashes, her green eyes sparked dangerously. "What ails you, Gillian? I warn you, if you are up to some mischief, you will know my wrath."

"Will I?" she asked, but her smile belied her seemingly meek answer. She rose to her feet, moving behind him, and Nicholas thought himself rid of her, but then her hands settled upon his shoulders, kneading and spreading the soap along them with her bare hands. Her touch held him paralyzed, unable to move or protest, as she washed his neck and then the length of one arm.

Something tickled his skin, and he turned to see that her hair was down. Damn! Had she dropped it apurpose, to torment him? The wild red locks fell over her shoulders like fire, and he longed to reached out and grab them, to pull her down atop him, fully clothed. His tarse hardened painfully, and he shifted, remembering all too well the times they had spent together in this very tub.

Temptation. It stood beside him in the form of his wife, slender and firm and close. It wove into his senses, stealing

away his will, but he held firm. Although they had made no
child before, he could not take the chance again. He would
not lose her because of his own lack of discipline, he resolved, his eyes narrowing. Gillian still had hold of his wrist
and now was massaging each finger in a way that made him
reconsider the merit of stimulating such extremities.

He pulled his hand away. "I need no help," he croaked.
"Go fetch me some ale."

Although Nicholas was certain that she would not defy
the order, she did, without blinking an eye. "In a moment," she replied softly. Then she soaped her hands again
and laid them on his chest. Her palms caressed him, her
thumb flicking his nipples into stiffness, and that was not all
that was stiff. His groin was aching. "Gillian!" he growled.

"Hmm?" Nicholas recognized the low hum of her desire, and the sound was enough to set him teetering on the
brink, caught between need and duty. Without volition,
his hips rose in the water, just as her hand drifted down his
stomach.

Nicholas snatched her wrist in a fierce grip as he drew in
ragged breaths. "I know not what game you play, but
cease!" The words came out harsh and rasping, as he
struggled to maintain the last vestiges of his control.

She stepped back from him, her eyes flashing too brightly.
"How could you not know this game, for 'tis one that you
taught me?" she taunted. Flinging her wild mane over her
shoulder, she lifted her chin. Angry. Defiant. His tarse grew
until it pained him, for he wanted her just like this.... "But
if you no longer wish to play, then perhaps I shall have to
find another partner."

"Gillian!" Nicholas surged upward, sending water flying in all directions as he stood upright in the tub, his hands
fisted at his side, his wrath enough to frighten an army of
men.

Gillian did not blink. She lifted her delicately arched brows in challenge. "If you no longer want me—"

"Want you?" The wave of powerful anger ebbed as he stepped from the water, his erection fully visible. "I want you well enough, as you can see, and if I could, in all good conscience, I would have you now. Right here. Right now."

She blinked then, her breath coming faster, and Nicholas struggled against the fire that would rage between them. Her emerald eyes grew dreamy with desire, and Nicholas had to stop himself from reaching for her. Gritting his teeth, he grabbed up a length of linen instead, wrapping it around the evidence of his lust.

Gillian stiffened immediately, the longing gone from her gaze. "You have no conscience."

Nicholas could find nothing else to say. All his strength was required simply to stand there, frustrated and hard, staring at the woman he wanted but could not have. His wife.

"Damn you for a coward!" She threw the curse at him, her voice breaking.

For a long moment, they faced off, wills clashing as they so often did. Then Nicholas laughed harshly. "You are right. I am a coward. And damn you for making me one."

And this time it was not he, but Gillian, who fled, slamming the door behind her, leaving him alone in the vast chamber to ponder his loss.

Gillian tossed and turned upon her pallet. She had dragged it out and placed it at the foot of the massive bed once more, determined never to sleep with Nicholas again. Perhaps she could not help loving him, but she need not torture herself by lying with him any longer. The more distance she put between herself and her husband, the better for her wounded pride—and her aching heart.

Unfortunately, the nest that had once been so cozy now seemed cold and hard and...empty. After having shared Nicholas's bed, Gillian suspected that all others would fall short. It was not only the passion she missed, but also the feel of his strong arms around her, safe and secure, and the heat of him beside her in the night.

Gillian blinked back the tears that had threatened all day, unwilling to give in to them. Tears and torment were what Nicholas craved. They fed his revenge, and she would not let him have them. He might have triumphed, but she did not intend to let him see it.

As if he somehow knew of her defiance and had come to harry her for it, the chamber door opened to admit the fiend himself. Her husband. Gillian lay still, feigning sleep, while he stalked across the room. Soon the sound of him undressing made her breathe easier.

His quiet actions surprised her. Considering his body's response to hers, she knew Nicholas would be well rid of her presence in his bed. Yet Gillian had expected him to be annoyed by her return to the pallet, simply because it was her own idea and not one of his almighty orders. Although she told herself that she was glad he let her be, she could not help feeling a prick of pique at being so ignored.

She was pondering his lack of reaction when he let out a string of low oaths that told her he had just noticed her absence. Although her nest was visible by the light of the nearby hearth, Nicholas had gone by without seeing her. Now his footsteps moved closer, stopping just short of where she lay.

"Gillian!" He roared loud enough to wake her—or deafen her.

Biting back a smile at his response, Gillian rolled over to eye him coolly. Unfortunately, the sight of his naked body, tinged golden by the glow of the fire, made her swallow hard. "What?"

"Get back in my bed!"

"Why?"

"Because I said so, that is why!"

"No."

"What?"

"I have no wish to sleep with you. Go away and leave me in peace." Gillian started to turn away from him, but found herself being lifted off the floor instead. As if she weighed no more than a feather, her husband hefted her into his arms and tossed onto the bed. Shouting in fury, she scrambled to leave it.

"Nay!" Nicholas commanded, and before Gillian realized what he was about, he had launched himself at her. He landed beside her, sparing her the weight of his fall, but one of his arms was snaked around her and one of his legs entangled with her own.

Gillian was trapped. She drew in a sharp breath as he moved over her, pinning her inexorably upon the mattress. Although she was wearing her shift, it was a thin covering at best, and she was acutely aware of his nudity as the length of his body pressed against her.

All else fled under the force of her desire, and Gillian was too dazed to do anything but stare as her husband raised his head over her own to look down at her. As she took in the harshness of his features and the angry glint in his eyes, his expression changed. He opened his mouth as if to speak, but then it came down upon her own, hot, rough and frantic.

Holding her wrists hostage, Nicholas thrust his tongue deep, and her senses soared. Under his fierce assault, Gillian felt alive for the first time since her illness. She wanted to wrap her arms and legs around him, but he kept her still beneath him while his kisses grew more wild and erotic.

Frustrated, Gillian lifted her hips, and he groaned, pushing his hard member against her stomach. Gasping in heated anticipation, she shifted, trying to position herself to receive him, but in the next moment he was gone, releasing her hands and rolling away from her to spring from the bed.

A low sigh of protest escaped her before Gillian could stop it. Damn him! Her body still burned, aching for him. Swallowing hard, she struggled to shake off the bonds of passion and think clearly. With some effort, she managed to push down the hem of her shift and turn toward him. Although his back was to her, Gillian suspected he was still ready for her. At least she had the satisfaction of knowing that he wanted her, too, small comfort that it was.

"Mayhap your revenge is not so sweet," she whispered bitterly.

"What?" He turned toward her then, his body a study in masculine strength and grace, with its sleek muscles and dark hair—and full erection.

"You punish yourself, as well as me, with your schemes of vengeance," Gillian said, sitting up and sliding to the edge of the mattress. She had no intention of sleeping with him ever again, no matter how loud he bellowed.

"Is that what you think I am doing? Punishing you?" he asked her, with a fine show of indignation.

"Are you not?"

"Nay! I am done with revenge." He blew out a seemingly frustrated breath. "'Tis the child I might give you that holds me back, as it should you, as well."

Although she was seated on the side of the bed and he was a few feet away, Gillian felt as if he had struck her. She knew the color drained from her face, even as all the hope drained from her heart. He had told her before that he wanted no heir of hers, and yet she had allowed herself to cling to a dream. Oh, what a fool she had been!

Gillian rose slowly, as if her whole body were empty and lifeless. The rushes were cold against her bare feet, chilling her to the bone as she had not been since her homeless days, when she had been so very alone and frightened.

Somehow, she managed to walk to the hearth and stretch out her hands. They felt numb, as did the rest of her. "So that is it. You have decided that you want no heir with my tainted blood." When the heat did nothing for her, Gillian straightened her shoulders and turned to face him. "It is best, of course. I would have no innocent baby be tormented because you think your precious Hexham lives on in him."

"You believe I would torment an infant?" he asked, with an incredulous expression that soon hardened at the sight of her even stare. "You are wrong, Gillian. I would harm no baby. And I am done with my revenge. 'Tis over." He uttered the words with a conviction that gave Gillian pause. But she knew well his clever schemes. She could not trust him.

"Why?"

Nicholas stared at her a long moment, his gray eyes clouded, his jaw working as if *he* were the one who was distressed. "Because!" he snapped. "I am weary of it."

Then, to her astonishment, he sank down onto the edge of the bed and put his head in his hands, stifling a strange sound that rumbled from his chest. Gillian stared, stunned, at this pose she had never thought to see her warrior husband take.

Nicholas, weak and vulnerable.

Perhaps he was human, after all. Gillian closed her eyes against the sight that threatened to wrench her heart in two. *She* was the one who had been wronged time and time again. Why should she care if the man she thought incapable of feeling anything looked to be in pain? Why should she go to him with comfort?

Because she loved him, despite all. And because she loved him, Gillian moved toward him, stopping only when she stood in front of his silent figure. "Nicholas..."

At the sound of his name, he lifted his head, his eyes blazing with the fierceness of his conviction once more. "You are mine, Gillian, and I will not let you leave me, even in death!" he whispered fiercely.

"I stood here and watched you try to get away, but I pulled you back," he said, making a fist, as if to clutch her life in his hand. "And I will not let it happen again. I will protect you from all that may do you harm, and I will not get you with child."

Gillian reeled from the force of the revelation. He feared for her life? She released a long, low, shuddering breath of relief. Dared she believe him? She dropped to her knees before him and looked up into his face. "Is that what this all is about? You are anxious for my health?"

"You belong to me, and I will not have you endangered."

"But, Nicholas, I do not understand." Gillian's mind was spinning in confusion. She reached out to touch him. "You say you are done with your revenge, yet you are determined to keep me alive and well."

Gillian sought his eyes, and the gray depths she had once thought as cold and sharp as blades seemed now more like smoke, warm and encompassing. "You are my wife. That is reason enough," he said before looking away.

It was not exactly a confirmation of Edith's suspicions, but neither was it a vow of hatred. And Gillian knew she could not allow herself to hope for his affection; that would surely lead her to madness. She rested her hands upon his knees, her heart twisting within her breast at the ingenuous declaration. She was his wife; it was better than being his enemy. Taking a deep breath, she raised her face to him once more.

"I am very grateful for your concern, but, oh, Nicholas, only God has the power of life and death, and as much as you would like to believe otherwise, you are only a man. Perhaps the force of your will did give me the strength to get well again, but you cannot take God's matters into your own hands and decide that we are to have no children."

"Perhaps there is a way, Gillian," he said with sudden urgency. "Know you of herbs that can prevent a man's seed from growing inside you?"

Gillian dropped her head, shaking it sadly at his fierce stubbornness. She could argue until she was blue in the face and still not sway him. In truth, she could think of nothing to say but what was foremost in her heart. "Oh, Nicholas, I would so like to have a baby of my own, with beautiful dark hair and silver eyes like his father. Like you."

The admission, wrung from her very soul, made him groan, and suddenly Gillian was aware of her position, kneeling on the floor before him, her hands upon his knees. He was still naked, his legs parted before her, and straight ahead was the instrument of her desire that could so readily give her what she wanted. While she watched, it grew and rose before her, as if in agreement.

Nicholas mumbled a protest, but Gillian ignored it, sliding her palms along his inner thighs as she leaned forward, pressing kisses along his hair-roughened skin. When she put her mouth on him, his denial dissolved into a growl of hunger that sounded as if it were torn from his chest. He fell back upon the bed, pulling her with him, but Gillian kept to her task, fascinated by it. And then his hands tangled in her hair, holding her head in place as he groaned and thrust himself into her mouth.

"Gillian...Gillian..." She heard Nicholas mutter her name, softly at first, and then more urgently. "If you want a baby, this is not the way to get one."

Chapter Sixteen

Gillian was a woman with a mission. Although she had had her way with her husband, she could see he still had doubts about making a family. And she was determined to remove them. Simple capitulation to her wishes would not be enough, Gillian had decided. Although she knew Nicholas would never want a baby as much as she did, nonetheless, she planned to convince him that a child was just what he needed in his life.

Her task was not as difficult as it sounded, for her stubborn husband was, for once, indecisive. Although his commands had always been swift and sure, now she noticed the glimmer of uncertainty in his eyes when he looked at her. And Gillian seized upon it, harrying him relentlessly.

At night, Nicholas pressed her again for some recipe that might prevent conception, until Gillian took matters in her own hands. She knew that once his passions were stirred, he forgot all else, and afterward, she robbed him of his regrets by snuggling close and murmuring of her desire for the child he could give her.

Nicholas was not unaware of her stratagems. And although at one time her constant harping would have driven him to violence, now he could only admire her relentless drive, equal to his own. And her aggressive behavior in bed

fueled his passions. Coupled with his knowledge of her love
for him, her actions made their unions even more pleasur-
able.

There was something infinitely exciting in the knowledge
that his brave and beautiful wife did not merely tolerate his
attentions because of her precarious position in his household. She wanted him. And not for his wealth or his name
or his title, but for who he was, God help her.

Unfortunately, his trebled passions carried with them a
risk that Nicholas was still loath to take. Even though he had
succumbed to his lust for two nights, he could not blithely
ignore the fear for her safety that lived within him now. She
was his, and he was responsible for her.

"My own mother died in childbed," he whispered, pulling Gillian to him, in the bittersweet aftermath of their wild
mating. Nicholas watched the firelight dance through her
hair, as bright and shiny as it had once been. She was alive
and well now, but what of tomorrow? What of nine months
from now? His hold upon her tightened.

"But my mother survived it," she argued. "Women give
birth every day, Nicholas, more often than not without incident. And there are other ills in the world. Why, I might
be struck by lightning, too, or did you plan to cage me in my
room?"

"'Tis not a bad notion," he muttered, his mouth moving
against her red mane. His palm slid possessively down her
back, as though to protect her for all that might threaten
her, now and forever.

"And then how would I get my exercise?" she purred.
Her fingers tangled through the hair that marked his torso,
leaving him in no doubt as to just how she intended to exercise herself, if kept to the chamber with him. When she
lifted her head to gaze down at him, however, the teasing
light was gone from her eyes. What he saw was so open and

honest that he wanted to turn away, rather than face it. "I want a baby, like Aisley's."

Nicholas snorted, grateful for a distraction from the need he saw so clearly in her green depths. "That brat is a noisy nuisance," he said, but he remembered all too well the poignant picture of his wife holding Sybil. It had stayed with him, and now it taunted him to give her what she wanted, to want what she did.

Refusing to rise to his bait, Gillian laughed. "Our child might be noisy, but it would not be a nuisance. Would you not like a lad to trail after you, to follow in your footsteps, to hug you and—?"

"My father never hugged me."

"More's the pity," Gillian said. As if to make up for his supposed loss, she wound her arms around him and squeezed him tightly. It felt much better than he would ever admit. "But you do not have to be like him. Look at Aisley and Piers!"

The mention of his sister and her pompous husband offended him. "Faith, vixen, I pray that I would never become like those sentimental fools!"

"Then be yourself," Gillian whispered. She lifted a hand to his cheek, her fingers just barely brushing his skin. Her lips followed, in the lightest of touches along his chin, against his mouth, and he felt himself weakening. *She loved him,* and she had never asked for anything but this. Nicholas wanted to give it to her, and his blood roared agreement, but even as he rolled her beneath him, spreading her legs wide, he knew the bitter taste of doubt.

If only he could be sure that his seed would not take her from him.

The night had not convinced Nicholas of anything except his own lack of discipline. He had let lust rule his head more than once, and he was loath to face the consequences. Yet, even as he berated himself, Gillian laughed at his grim expression and teased away his foul mood. In the bright light of day, she was so vivid, so full of life, it was difficult to imagine anything threatening her health, especially such a commonplace act as childbirth.

He needed time to think. With an impatient sound, Nicholas strode from the chamber, but his wife followed him, her fragrance teasing at his nostrils. "What of a girl? A daughter to look up to you, to bounce upon your knee?" she asked from behind him.

Without even deigning to answer, Nicholas walked through the great hall and out the huge doors to his men and his lands, where he was the master of his world and his destiny and his flame-haired wife did not rule.

Once outside, he felt better, although the sky was overcast, presaging rain or even snow. It had taken Nicholas a while to grow accustomed to Britain's weather upon his return from the East, but now he wore no cloak against the chill autumn air, thick with the smoke of many fires.

He had gone no more than a few paces when he was heralded by an old man leaning against one of the outbuildings in the bailey. Nicholas's eyes narrowed as he recognized the wiry figure. Willie, was it not? The fellow was Edith's husband and, as such, aroused his suspicions. Although Nicholas had come to an uneasy truce with the servant, he would have no more of her meddling.

"Psst! My lord!" Willie said, jerking his grizzled head in invitation.

"What is it?" Nicholas snapped.

"Well, now, I've been hearing some things," the older man whispered, glancing about as if he wished to keep their conversation private. "They might not be true, but if they are, I've a mind to help you."

"You are Edith's husband, Willie, are you not?" Nicholas demanded. When the old man nodded, he asked, "Why would you assist me?"

Willie chuckled. "Aye, I can understand your wariness, my lord. Indeed, you're a sharp one, as I've always thought. Never would have got back from the East, if you were not." He paused, his gaze assessing Nicholas in a shrewd manner that both judged and accepted. "Let us just say that we men must stick together sometimes."

His frank speech won Nicholas's attention. "Go on. What is this knowledge you share with me?"

Willie ducked his head, as if he were now reluctant to continue. "Well, you see, there's the rub, my lord," he muttered, his brown, wrinkled face flushing a deeper color. "'Tis not a subject that I normally would be discussing with you."

Impatience made Nicholas's temper rise. "Speak up, man!"

"Well, now . . . you see . . ." Willie stammered until Nicholas was certain he was dealing with a doddering old fool, rather than a sharp-eyed, intelligent fellow. He had turned on his heel, ready to walk away in exasperation, when Willie's voice halted him in his steps.

"Ah, hell," he muttered. "My lord, you must wash it in vinegar."

Slowly Nicholas turned to stare at the old man. "What?"

"If you wish to kill the seed," Willie explained, apparently warming to his topic. "Either that or put a cap on it. Now, a little cap will cool the blood, you see, and reduce the strength of the semen."

"*What?*"

"Or you could pull out, of course." Willie scratched his salt-and-pepper hair in a gesture of puzzlement at his own suggestion. "That is the most common way, and I've got great admiration for them that can do it, but for myself..." He shook his head in resignation.

As Nicholas stared, stunned, the old man continued. "Then, there's the act itself," he said, stroking his beard-bristled face as if in thought. "Now there's two schools of thought on that, you know. The one claims that you can prevent conception by doing it without the passion, which is rather a contradiction in terms, don't you think? If you have no lust for the gal, why do it in the first place?"

Nicholas was so outraged at the man's speech, he could not even sputter an answer. Although he wanted this sort of information, and badly, he had never thought to stand here listening to it being spouted by Edith's husband.

"And then there's them that lean toward the other direction, that the more violent the mating, the less chance you have of making a child. That may be true, but—" Willie smiled, shrugging helplessly "—at my age, it's too late to find out."

Nicholas opened his mouth to put an end to the old man's words, but this last bit of news drew him up short. With few exceptions, he and Gillian were lusty in their zeal for each other, and because of that, perhaps, there would be no child between them.

Nicholas knew just how often he had taken her before her illness, and no baby had been made then, or as yet. Hope burgeoned into near certainty. Mayhap, if they kept to their vigorous lovemaking, she would be safe! Despite his excitement, Nicholas schooled his features into a cool, impassive expressions. "I will think upon what you have said," he told Willie in curt dismissal.

"Very good, my lord," the older man answered. And because Nicholas turned away quickly, he did not see the grin that split the wrinkled face from ear to ear or suspect Edith's fine hand in the advice he had just received.

* * *

"I put it to you, Darius, does not Nicholas need some children to give him comfort in his old age?"

Nicholas choked upon his ale, nearly spewing it out upon his dinner, and turned to glare at his wife. She was wearing what he had come to think of as her perpetually innocent expression, though her bright eyes betrayed her guilt. She was as innocent as a fox among the hens.

"I am not in my dotage yet, vixen," he muttered, irritated that she had drawn the Syrian into such a personal discussion, and at table, too.

"But would not a family be wonderful?"

"And what could you possibly know of a family, living in a convent as you did?" he asked, surveying her coolly. She was going too far with this business. Perhaps it was time to put a stop to it, here and now.

She refused to rise to the bait, but smiled gently. "When I was small, there was love and warmth between us, before Father drank so much and we had so little money...and death took them all."

She looked so wistful that it pained him. He thought of that bastard Hexham living in his luxurious manor, spending money on trinkets and soldiers and his quest for more and more land, but not on his own brother.

Nicholas tightened the grip upon his cup. Yet had he shown any more familial loyalty? Of his mother, he remembered little but cool beauty and a light, pleasing fragrance. His father had been strict and distant, his brothers good companions...until they left. His own fostering had taken place under the aegis of a cruel man, who had been best avoided, and Nicholas had always been in competition with the other boys there. No love had been lost between any of them.

Nicholas frowned. Perhaps there was something to Aisley's idea of keeping children at home. The thought of his sister brought him mixed emotions. For the first time in his life, he wondered how she had felt, all alone after his father's death, keeping Belvry together by herself, facing marriage to a stranger... He could have returned sooner. Instead of nursing his grievances in the East, he should have come back and taken his rightful place with his sire. The knowledge had been long in coming, and it was bitter in taste.

"You are not ancient yet," Gillian said teasingly. "But someday you will need a younger sword at your side."

He lifted his head and fixed her with a serious gaze. "And who is to say that any son of mine will do his duty?"

Gillian looked taken aback by his sharp question, but Darius, whom Nicholas had almost forgotten, filled the silence. "I cannot believe that a child of Lady de Laci would do anything less."

Nicholas switched his gaze to the Syrian's dark one. Although the man showed no expression, his eyebrows lifted slightly, as if he dared Nicholas to dispute his words. Perhaps Darius was right. He could certainly not imagine anyone Gillian loved embracing vengeance or violence, as he once had.

"Blood is thicker than water," Gillian said softly. "No matter what is between you and Piers, if you needed him, he would come. I know it. That is family."

Nicholas's pensive mood fled at the mention of the Red Knight. "I will never need that pompous ass!"

"He would come! I know it!" Gillian repeated, more vehemently.

"Enough!" Nicholas snapped. "If I hear another word about family or children, I shall lock you up in the dungeon, where you shall find no one to impregnate you!"

Gillian's lips parted on a gasp, and her eyes flashed fury. For a moment, Nicholas thought she might toss her food at him. Her fingers twitched, as if reaching for her half of the trencher, but, obviously thinking better of it, she stood and straightened, her chin lifting.

"And you, Nicholas de Laci, may sleep with the other beasts tonight, where no one will press you for services rendered!" She stalked away just as Darius burst out laughing, and, for once, Nicholas joined in. Then he pushed aside his meal and strode after her, intent upon finishing this battle in bed.

Despite her twitching lips, Gillian tried to take a stern tone with the laughing Edith. "Really, that was too bad of Willie," she scolded.

"'Tis nothing more than the truth, my lady," Edith said. "Why, my Willie did not make up a word of it. Everything that he told Lord Nicholas is accepted practice."

Gillian shook her head as she fought back a chuckle. "Well, some men might take the trouble to wash their wicks in vinegar, but I cannot imagine Nicholas doing it!"

"Just so, my lady. Just so," Edith said, wiping her streaming eyes. "I'll wager that my Willie has put him off that nonsense for good."

Gillian smiled. Although she appreciated Edith's efforts, she did not think the meddling was wise. If truth be told, her campaign was coming along nicely, and she did not want any interference, no matter how well-intentioned. Unfortunately, Edith seemed to excel at making things worse.

The servant collapsed into a chair, overtaken by her own amusement, and Gillian said nothing to dampen her spirits. When silence descended, however, Gillian looked up, surprised to see that Edith had moved to the window.

"Visitors!" she said, turning an excited grin toward Gillian.

"Really?" Gillian hurried to join the older woman. Because of the upheaval a few years ago, and Nicholas's resulting reign as baron, visitors to Belvry were unusual, especially this late in the season. From her vantage point, Gillian could see that the approaching group did not bear the colors of the king's messengers; nor, unfortunately, was it large enough to signal the return of Aisley and Piers, for which Gillian still hoped.

"Pilgrims, perhaps," Edith said.

"Still, it will be nice to hear some news!" Gillian answered. The two women quickly put away their sewing and headed down to the great hall to await the coming of the troop. Below, they met several residents and servants as anxious as they for a look at the new arrivals, and Gillian suppressed a smile as the once deserted room filled.

Stepping into the kitchens to call for bread and ale, Gillian nearly bumped into her husband, newly come from outside. Handsome as ever, with his cheeks bright with cold, Nicholas stomped his feet and threw his cloak to a young boy.

"Who comes?" Gillian asked.

"I know not," Nicholas answered. "'Tis a raw day to be on the roads." He rubbed his hands together, then pressed them to her cheeks.

"Ah!" Gillian sucked in a breath, startled by the chill feel of his fingers against her skin. She was even more stunned to see the slow curving of his lips at her discomfort. He had changed, and truly for the better, thought Gillian, as was evidenced by this bit of play. Grinning happily, she followed him into the great hall.

They did not have long to wait before a single man, obviously the head of the procession, was ushered before them. Smiling in a friendly fashion, he doffed his cloak as Nicholas urged him forward. He was of average height, rather slender, with black hair and dark eyes that Gillian could not quite discern.

"Greetings to you, my lord," he said, bowing slightly in deference. "And to you, lady," he said to Gillian. He flashed a white grin at her, singling her out in a way that she knew would make Nicholas jealous, and her own smile faltered.

"Who are you, and what is your business here?" Nicholas asked. Instead of answering, the man turned toward her. "Gillian, do not you know me?"

Startled, Gillian sent Nicholas a wary look. "Nay. I know you not," she said.

"I am hurt," he said, clutching his chest dramatically. "I know that it has been many years, but I was hoping..."

"Who are you?" Nicholas's angry tone rang out over the hall, making his own people shudder, but the visitor showed no fear. In fact, he seemed to taunt Nicholas by turning, yet again, toward his wife.

"Gillian, surely you recognize me," he said, spreading out his arms in exaggerated supplication. "'Tis Hawis, your brother."

Stunned silence met the man's words, following by a buzzing of soft voices that swiftly rose to a cacophony within the hall. With growing alarm, Gillian listened to the speculation that a brother of hers was heir to the neighboring lands that had once belonged to Hexham, and, worse yet, heir to Hexham!

Stifling a gasp, Gillian sent a fearful glance toward her husband. Although outwardly Nicholas looked impassive, she could see the sharp glitter of his eyes that told her of his rage. She knew, just as surely as if he had spoken it, that he wanted to kill the man who stood before them.

Gillian watched him bring himself under control with massive effort, only to turn on her. Before he could even speak, she shook her head. "Nay, 'tis not true. I have no brother!"

"Gillian," the black-haired man said softly, "surely you have not forgotten me."

Normally she would never have attacked a stranger, but the precarious peace of her marriage teetered in the balance. Rising to her feet, Gillian pointed a shaking finger at the man. "How dare you disturb my household?"

Instead of shouting back at her, the fellow looked oddly forlorn. "Aw, Gilly," he said, and suddenly, Gillian felt as if the earth beneath her feet had shifted. She was seized by a memory of dark curls pressed close, smelling of grass and horse. *Aw Gilly,* a high voice whispered. *Quit chasing after me. Stay with Mum, now.*

Gillian swayed upon her feet, then fell back into her chair, collapsing under the weight of her discovery. "Hawis," she mumbled.

The silence that followed was deafening, as was the bellow that soon rent the air. "Do you know this man?" Nicholas demanded. "Is he your brother?"

Gillian's head felt thick as she struggled to think. She pressed fingers to her temple, searching for images that were so deeply buried in the past that they seemed just out of reach.

"My lord, I have—" The man tried to speak, but Nicholas cut him off.

"Silence!" he shouted. "I would hear from my wife."

Gillian lifted her pounding head to meet the gentle, beseeching gaze of the stranger. Then she turned to her husband, whose thunderous expression stood in stark contrast to that of the man who claimed to be her brother.

"Well?" Nicholas said, goading her.

Gillian swallowed hard. "I had a brother, but he died long ago." She turned an apologetic glance toward the man who stood before them.

"Nay, sister. I died not, but was sent away by our father," he protested. Gillian tried to warn the fellow with her eyes. Whoever he was, could he not see he was playing with fire? Kin or no, he would be wise to leave before Nicholas struck him down.

As if reading her thoughts, her husband pinned her with a cold gray gaze that twisted her heart. "When did he die?"

"I do not remember," Gillian answered, helplessly. "I was very young!"

"Gilly—"

"What killed him? Did you see the body?"

Gillian put her hands over her ears. "Stop it! I cannot remember. I know only that he died, as did my younger sister... and my father... and my mother." She was shaking now, with both grief and rage. How could the man she loved turn against her so easily?

"Gilly!" Ignoring Nicholas's black expression, the stranger knelt down before her chair and took her hands in his own. "Gilly. I never meant to cause any harm, I swear it. I was very young when I was fostered out, and when the man who held me fell to his enemies, I lost all touch with my true family. It has taken me years to remember, and now, finally, to find you."

This time the stillness that followed his words seemed unnatural, for even Nicholas held his tongue. Gillian felt as if everyone in the hall were holding their breath, awaiting her response. She knew she ought to say nothing, to show nothing, to feel nothing, but despite her best intention, a tear trickled down her face.

Silently she looked upon the sibling she had thought long dead, the last member of the family she had thought lost to her many years past, and she reached out to embrace him.

Chapter Seventeen

Nicholas paced. Back and forth, forward and again, seeking order amid his turbulent thoughts. For once in his life, he was in a quandary. The discipline and swift decisions that had marked his life before Gillian seemed a thing of the past, but never had he been so confused! And all because of one man's arrival.

Gillian's brother. Nicholas's eyes narrowed, and he clenched his fists in frustration. His first inclination had been to kill the bastard, and he had nearly leapt from his chair to do it. Only iron will had prevented the spilling of Hawis Hexham's blood then and there.

Such an end would be too swift and clean for Hexham's treacherous line, Nicholas had decided. He had leaned, instead, toward tossing the fellow into the dungeon to torture and torment him, to see Hexham's heir suffer as he had, at last. Revenge, his old companion, called to him in a tempting refrain, rife with possibilities. Nicholas could strike Hawis down or string him up, and no one would say him nay.

No one except his wife.

Cursing softly, Nicholas turned to stalk the length of the room again, stopping only when a voice broke into his reverie. He looked up in surprise, for he had been so absorbed in his thoughts that he had forgotten Darius's presence.

"'Tis a puzzle, is it not?" the Syrian said. "If you had discovered the brother first, you could have killed him and still taken the sister as spoils, but now…" Darius shrugged, as if distressed, yet he sounded more amused than dismayed.

Nicholas scowled. "If you have no counsel to offer, then begone with you."

The Syrian ignored the harsh words, just as though Nicholas had not spoken. "Will you slay him?"

"Nay!" Nicholas answered abruptly. He remembered Gillian's face, her tears at the reunion, and knew he could not destroy her brother. He wanted to do it. Indeed, every fiber of his being cried out for vengeance that could finally be his. But something else was stronger, a nameless something that had planted itself inside him when he first looked upon his red-haired bride. It had sprouted in the days and nights after his wedding until it had grown greater than his need for reprisals, greater than himself. And now it demanded that he protect Gillian at all costs, even at the price of his once treasured goal.

"You mean to let him go?" Darius asked, as if reading his thoughts. "What if he runs to Edward, demanding his inheritance?"

"The claim has been settled already," Nicholas snapped.

"True," Darius answered. "But, if I recall, you, too, rose from the dead to succeed your father."

"That was different!"

"Was it?" Darius mused. "Still, even if he eventually gains those lands, 'tis not as if they would be any great loss to you. Belvry is vast and prosperous without them. You have no need of them, do you?"

Yes! Nicholas wanted to answer. Belvry, his heritage, provided him with wealth and power, but even if he had no financial need for Hexham's demesne, he would not part with it. He had a personal interest in every acre that had belonged to the scheming bastard who had once been his neighbor, and they were his—by right of suffering, battle and vengeance. Nicholas's feelings were too strong to put into words, too gripping to shake off like a bad investment. Even as he tried to express them, Darius went on, seemingly oblivious of his struggle.

"It is not as though you would have to ally yourself with the nephew of your old nemesis. You could bar this Hawis from Belvry, keep him from his sister, make war upon him..."

Nicholas's head jerked toward the Syrian. Although his stomach had healed, he felt his gut churn at the thought of depriving Gillian of her brother, through death or any other means. Did not the vixen rant daily about her need for a family? If he kept this newly discovered sibling from her, he would know her displeasure soon enough. Aye, would he not lose her love? Nicholas swore and whirled on his heel. Although it was not something he had ever sought, now that he possessed it, he found himself loath to destroy this affection she felt for him.

His mouth tightened, for he was unwilling to share such sentiments with the Syrian, who would, no doubt, laugh in delight at the prospect of Nicholas bowing to his wife's wishes. Nicholas ground his teeth, unable to believe it himself, yet he could not bring himself to do anything else. Gillian came first.

As the realization sank in, a new thought struck him. "Where did Hawis say he served?"

"The marches, under a man named Mollison."

"Where there has been so much upheaval?"

"Britain and Wales are at peace now, as I understand it," Darius said, giving Nicholas a puzzled look.

"Still, they were at war but a few years ago, resulting in much destruction of those lands."

"What? Do you suspect this Hawis of some nefarious deed, besides being born a Hexham?"

Nicholas scowled at the ill-advised jest. "Let us say that I would like to know a little about Hawis's past. Yet it will be hard to trace a man along the marches." He whirled toward his companion. "Why do you suppose it took so long for him to find his sister?"

Darius shrugged. "Perhaps he waited to see if you would kill her before daring to claim his own." Nicholas stiffened, disliking the reminder of what he found so easy to forget. Yes, Gillian was of Hexham's blood, but she was different—better and finer than anything that bastard could have produced. And Hawis? Nicholas did not like to think that perhaps he misjudged her brother, too, so he turned on the Syrian angrily.

"Just because he is Gillian's brother, that does not mean he is a good man," Nicholas argued. "Indeed, the opposite is more likely! You may scoff at his bad blood, but it is there, and it may run true. I would know what kind of man he is, lest he do my wife ill! Where was he when she was thrown into the streets, or when she was forced to be a servant, tormented by her master?"

Darius did not blink, his dark eyes fathomless. "He claims to have been bound to his lord on the marches, which made it impossible for him to come back earlier, but if you would know more of him, I shall seek it."

Nicholas was surprised at the wave of feeling that swept over him at his companion's offer. Although they had sworn no oaths between them, Darius gave him full measure, and more. "I would go myself, but I must protect my wife and my home," Nicholas said gruffly.

"Your place is here," Darius replied. "I will go, not only for you, but for your lady."

Nicholas nodded his thanks before his thoughts returned, inexorably, to Hawis Hexham, and the problems his arrival had engendered. "I would know, too, how he found her after all these years," Nicholas muttered.

"I suspect that he is the dark-haired man who asked after her so often and led me such a merry chase in search of him."

"Aye," Nicholas agreed. "But why so many questions? And why did he cover his trail so well that you could not find him? There are too many unusual circumstances that trouble me about our Hawis."

Darius shrugged. "I will find out what I can, but you must realize that it may all be as he says. And then what? What if he is not the villain you would paint him?"

Nicholas paused, annoyed, as usual, by the Syrian's insight, but he refused to be drawn into such speculation until he knew the facts. That much, at least, of his training remained with him, despite the effects of flashing emerald eyes and fiery hair.

"We shall see," he said. "Until I hear from you or decide otherwise, I will let this Hawis stay here, where I can keep an eye on him."

Darius lifted his dark brows slightly. "Do you think it wise to give him your hospitality? What if your lady wife grows more attached to him? It will make it harder for her to accept what may come."

Attached. Nicholas's eyes narrowed. He did not like the word, or the idea, as Darius well knew. The jealousy that had been gnawing at him ever since he saw his wife put her arms around another man, albeit her brother, burst full-blown into his chest. He whirled and paced again, going over the same limited choices.

If he sent Hawis Hexham away, he might lose Gillian's love, and if he let the bastard stay, he might lose that love as it was divided, shared . . . She would have her precious family, and he would have what? Suddenly, Nicholas's lips curled wickedly. He knew of a way to keep his wife's attention focused solely on him and his, and give her what she most desired in the process.

He would get her with child.

It was what she wanted, after all, and she would be more concerned over the seed growing in her belly than about her adult sibling. Nicholas's smile grew. It would not be such a bad thing to have an heir of his own, and Gillian was strong. She had told him often enough that his doubts about her safety were foolish. The threat from Hawis was real and here and now, while the problems of birthing were vague and in the future.

Grinning, Nicholas made his decision.

"And what has made you suddenly so cheerful?" the Syrian asked.

"Congratulate me, Darius, for I am going to sire an heir on my wife."

Nicholas felt an unfamiliar twinge of anxiety as he entered the great chamber. He told himself that this night was no different from any other, and yet the knowledge of the resolution he had made weighed upon him. Tonight, he would not just let Gillian have her way, he was determined to give her what she wanted. His lips curled in anticipation of the task.

But he remembered Willie's advice, and knew that if he was to be successful, he must be sure that events progressed at a quiet pace. Tender, gentle, slow. Those were words that did not describe his usual behavior. His smile turned into a frown as he realized that what he planned might not be that easy.

"Nicholas?" Gillian's voice from the bed made him start. "Yes?"

"Thank you for not killing him."

So concerned was he with what lay ahead that it took Nicholas a moment to remember what she was talking about. "Your brother."

"Yes," she replied, as he began to remove his clothing. "'Tis so strange to see him after all these years. I wonder how Aisley felt when you rose from the dead." Nicholas halted, his tunic dangling from one hand. He had never stopped to consider his sister's feelings when he stormed back into her life. Frowning, he dropped the garment and bent to remove his braies.

"I can barely remember him. A face, snatches of impressions. It is frustrating, but I am glad he is alive, and I... thank you for letting him stay."

Grunting in acknowledgment, Nicholas slipped into bed beside his wife. Her brother was not what he wanted to discuss. Indeed, he did not wish to talk at all. He would rather spread her thighs and... Slowly, Nicholas told himself, swallowing an oath of frustration.

His hand snaked out to find her slender curves and glide over them in the darkness. Her skin was smooth and supple, and he threw off the covers to see it touched by the firelight. But the sight of her body fueled his passion, and Nicholas struggled to hold himself in check. Closing his eyes was little relief, for her scent wafted through his nostrils and into his blood, making it soar and thunder in his ears. Burying his face in her hair, he sought to slow the lust that threatened to run rampant. Easy, he told himself, but Gillian made it difficult.

"Nick," she whispered, inflaming him with the sound of his name, eager and joyous, on her lips. Her fingers trailed down his torso, settling over his hard nipples, and he lifted his head to kiss her. She met him greedily, her tongue mating with his own, and soon his breath came quickly, and he wanted only to roll atop her, to feel her under him as he pounded into her.

Tearing his lips away, Nicholas gasped for breath. He needed a moment to gather his resources, but Gillian knew no such hesitation. She pressed her mobile mouth against his chin, his throat, his chest, and her hands moved down his back, clutching his buttocks.

Damn. Blowing out a harsh sigh, Nicholas decided that Gillian would soon have him mindless and frantic. Better to get on with it, before he became too feverish. Pulling her to him as gently as he could, Nicholas threw her leg over his thigh and entered her warmth.

It was ecstasy. Nicholas bit his lip in an effort to be still. He might have succeeded, but for his wife, who was moving her hips and grabbing at him like the lusty wench that she was, and for once he did not welcome her wildness.

"Gillian," he croaked.

"Hmm?"

"Gillian!"

"What?"

"Calm down."

"What? Why? Are you hurt?" She drew back to study him, and Nicholas gritted his teeth at the exquisite sensation of her body sliding away from him.

"Nay," he answered, and she took him back into her warmth, stealing his wits. "I would give you what you want, vixen, but I... Ah!" He had not realized that this would be torment akin to roasting. In about one more minute, he was going to abandon his scheme and sate himself.

"Nicholas." Apparently he had got her attention, for she took his face in her hands, forcing him to look at her. Green eyes, dark with passion, met his own. "What is it?"

He could speak, if she just would not clench him so tightly. And she was not even moving. "Gillian!"

"What?"

Nicholas released a ragged sigh. "To make a child, we must go slowly."

Of course, he should have known better than to expect his wife to acquiesce to anything. Instead of nodding in agreement, she burst out laughing, so forcefully that he nearly slipped from inside her. Nicholas might have taken offense, had the sound not been so welcome, the look on her face so lovely. His chest swelled with affection for her, his wife.

"Oh, Nicholas," she said between gasps for breath. "You cannot believe those old wives' tales."

"'Twas no old wife, but Willie, who told—"

His words were interrupted by Gillian's fresh gale of laughter. Then she buried her face against his shoulder, giggling uncontrollably. Nicholas had never seen her this way. Perhaps the strain of her brother's arrival had unnerved her.

"Gillian?"

"Oh, Nicholas, you cannot mean to believe Willie?"

Nicholas frowned. Now that he thought about it, he supposed there was no reason the old soldier should have any expertise upon the subject. Still, the man sounded knowledgeable. "'Tis not true, then?" he asked gruffly.

To her credit, Gillian tried to compose herself. "No," she said gently. Nicholas thought of eastern women who had been raped and yet produced children from those most violent of unions, and he knew she was right. To his own surprise, he felt disappointed. "How then do we assure you a child?"

Gillian gave him a slow, seductive smile that reminded him forcibly that they were still joined. "I suppose we must double our efforts," she whispered.

Nicholas's blood surged and heated in response, and he slid his hands over the curves of her buttocks, pulling her tight against him so that he was buried deep. "And we do not have to go slowly?"

"No." Her answer was breathy with pleasure.

"Good!" Nicholas replied, as he rolled her beneath him and thrust hard. She lifted her hips and put her legs around him until he was wrapped in her warmth. He wished he could stay there forever.

"I love you," she whispered.

Nicholas stilled, once more, at the sound of the soft admission he had never thought to hear again. He looked down at her face, flushed and bright-eyed, and he longed to tell her what the words meant to him. He wanted her to know that he, too, felt affection for her, but he was no clever-tongued bard.

"Yes," he said, staring down at her helplessly until the heat between them grew so sharp that it could not be denied. And then he filled her body, even as she filled his soul.

Long after she could hear the even breathing that told her Nicholas was asleep, Gillian lay awake, wondering what had possessed her. She had sworn herself never to tell her husband of her love, and yet tonight she had done so, willingly, and without regret.

Common sense told her she had just handed him the weapon that could bring about her destruction. Yet her heart, the part of her that knew no sense where Nicholas was concerned, beat merrily with the rightness of it.

Nicholas had not thrown her words back in her face or mocked her. He had looked down on her so intently that he had stolen her breath away. Gillian, in turn, had felt her heart swell at his quiet answer. "Yes," he had said.

Was that reason enough to trust him?

No... The usual denial rose in her mind, but not with as much certainty as before. Nicholas had come a long way from the cold man who had threatened his new bride mercilessly. He had taken care of her when she was ill and had developed a misguided protectiveness that nearly denied her children. Yet he had even given way on that issue, too, and Gillian smiled at the memory of him actually trying one of Willie's ridiculous stratagems in order to give her what she wanted.

Gillian sighed. There was no doubt that she was truly, hopelessly, in love with him, a condition that could easily affect her judgement. She wanted to believe in him, but now she had not just herself to consider, but perhaps also an infant, and certainly her brother.

The thought of Hawis made Gillian frown thoughtfully in the darkness. Nicholas had invited her brother into his home, when she knew he wanted nothing better than to strike down any man of Hexham's blood. He had spared her brother's life for her; was that not a sign of his devotion? Gillian wanted to think so, and yet she knew not what Nicholas might have planned. His complex motivations were often a mystery to her.

Gillian eased away from her husband's heat and tried to sort out her tangled emotions. The face of her brother, long forgotten, danced in front of her eyes, as did the features of the man who lay beside her, and a sense of foreboding filled her. Nicholas's hatred of Hexham's heirs was bone-deep, while the bond that had grown between them was new and tenuous. Would it be strong enough to prevent the bloodshed he craved? Gillian shivered. Not too long ago, she had been surrounded by women, but now two men claimed her loyalty.

She hoped that she would never be forced to choose between them.

Aisley was drifting dreamily near sleep when the knock came upon the great chamber door, rousing her. Beside her, Piers stirred, shouting for Cecil to enter as she hurriedly covered herself. Her husband had no sense of propriety, whereas she still blushed to be caught abed at midday by the servants.

"A message from Belvry, my lord," Cecil said, with his usual aplomb. Aisley lifted her head, startled. She had received no word from her old home since Nicholas had assumed the barony. Her brother was not one for words, and after the way they had parted, she had never expected to hear from him again. Panic rushed through her at the thought that only dire need would compel him to write.

"Piers," she murmured, automatically seeking her husband's strength to bolster her own. When she looked up, they were alone once more, and he was handing the missive to her. Tearing open the seal, Aisley scanned the sheet, and her fears were confirmed.

"There has been sickness at Belvry!" she said, glancing up at Piers in dismay. He sat down on the bed beside her, silently giving her his support, and she steeled herself to read on.

"Osborn has been taken! Oh, Piers, he was a good man.... And several of the villagers, too, are dead. And Nicholas says Edith and Willie, and even Gillian were ill, but are recovered."

Aisley began to breathe easier, as the worst of the news appeared to be past, but Nicholas's next words distressed her further. "Oh, Piers, he does not think Gillian strong enough to carry a child! He wants a recipe to prevent conception!'' She looked up at her husband in dismay.

''The sickness must have been bad indeed, to affect her so, for she looked strong and healthy.''

''Oh, Piers, we must go to her. What if she is still abed? Maybe I can help.''

Piers's blue eyes darkened. ''Tis not the season for travel, Aisley. I would not take Sybil out in such changeable weather.''

Aisley bit her lip, uncertain. Piers was right, of course. She did not want to expose the baby to the sudden snows that could blow out of the east. Nor could she leave her behind. She lifted her head again. ''Would you go?''

Piers swore softly. ''I have no love for your brother.''

''I know.''

He stood up, and the dogs, Castor and Pollux, immediately gathered around his feet. ''Somehow I cannot imagine Nicholas's wife reduced to an invalid! Methinks that you de Lacis are too often searching for potions better left alone.''

Aisley held his stare, even though she knew he was referring to her own experience with the local healer. She had gone to the woman to break the love spell she thought Piers had put upon her. Though she had not intended to take the remedy, she had become very ill from it.

''Piers, the situation must be drastic if Nicholas is writing to me for help.''

Piers frowned, as if considering her words. ''Yet when last I spoke with him, your brother swore he never would get an heir of Hexham's blood,'' Piers said, ignoring the dogs, who clamored for his attention. He looked grim. ''Perhaps he still feels the same, but would enjoy his wife's bed nonetheless.''

Aisley worried her lip. Piers had never detailed the fight between him and her brother, but she suspected that this was the cause. Her gallant husband would naturally defend Gillian's honor, while Nicholas would resent any interference, especially in his plans for revenge.

"He wrote to me, Piers," she said softly. "Surely that means something." Whatever the reason, Nicholas must have felt deeply to put aside the quarrel and ask for her help.

Piers scowled. "It means that he wants something from you, something that goes against all the laws of God and man. Do you know of such a recipe?"

Aisley did not flinch from his accusing look. Piers could never imagine anyone not wanting a child, but she knew that some women risked their lives in childbed. "There are old stories, herbs that are said to render a man sterile. I will not tender advice until I see Gillian."

Piers scowled ferociously. "You mean until I see Gillian."

"Yes," Aisley said, smiling. He was weakening. "For her sake, you should go. She is part of the family now, as is my brother. And as cold and cruel as Nicholas can be, he did save your life."

Piers slanted a dark glance at her that told her he did not appreciate the reminder. "I will consider the journey," he said. "And now, the day grows late, and I have tarried overlong at my midday meal."

"Especially since you never touched your food," Aisley said with a smile. She knew her husband, and she knew that eventually, he would be persuaded to go to Belvry.

And then it would be up to Nicholas to set things right.

Chapter Eighteen

After Hawis settled in to stay, an uneasy truce was declared, but Gillian could not relax. As much as she had longed for a family, sometimes she just wanted her brother to leave, so that the relative peace she had known before his arrival might return to Belvry. And when she felt selfish for having such thoughts, she had only to consider Hawis's welfare, as well as her own. More than once, she had been tempted to beg him to flee before her husband's wrath.

For Nicholas was not pleased with his guest. Outwardly, he was curt, but civil. Inwardly, he was seething, as Gillian could tell. She could see his eyes burning with a cold fire whenever they turned upon her brother, and she could feel the heightened emotions that emanated from his taut body. Hawis had revived Nicholas's hatred for his enemy's line, and though she felt none of his enmity herself, still the knowledge hurt her. As yet, her husband had done nothing to harm her brother, but Gillian remained edgy and fearful.

Unwillingly, she had been thrust in the middle. Although Nicholas had not expressly forbidden her to meet alone with her brother, he was a dark presence whenever they were together. She told herself that the cooler weather had forced him inside, because it was easier to believe than the alternative: that he did not trust her. Yet why should he? Gillian was not so sure of him, either, especially when it came to Hawis's fate.

Gillian swallowed a sigh. Although their union had been fraught with suspicion and strife more often than not, they had come so far that this new setback was doubly frustrating. At night they made love with unrestrained emotion, but during the day the tension was palpable, especially when the three of them were cooped up in the solar because of the foul weather, as they were today.

The strained silence that reigned was beginning to tell upon Gillian. Hawis was kind but reserved. While he spoke haltingly of his knighthood under Baron Mollison, he said little about his life before, and he looked so bleak and grim when she brought up her parents that she decided the subject was too painful for him.

Since Nicholas could rarely be coaxed into conversation, that left Gillian to fill in the quiet. Despite her husband's fierce glares, she had talked endlessly about Belvry, and touched upon her past at the convent. After a week, however, even she had run out of things to say.

And so the crackling of the fire and the sound of the rain falling outside were all that was heard until Hawis spoke at last, startling Gillian into poking her sewing needle into a finger. Biting back one of Nicholas's oaths, she sucked the blood from the sore digit while trying to pay attention to her brother's words.

"The rain has stopped," he said, lighting upon one of the few neutral topics that comprised their discussions.

"Has it?" Gillian asked, trying to sound interested, yet again, in the weather.

Hawis turned suddenly from his position by the window. "Do you feel like a ride, sister? The ground should not be too soft."

Gillian's heart leapt at the chance to escape the stifling atmosphere of the castle, but before she could open her mouth, Nicholas spoke for her.

"'Tis too cold and wet for Gillian to be out," he snapped. Although seated on a settle by the fire, he looked as restless as she felt, and infinitely more threatening. He fixed Hawis with a fierce gaze that practically accused the younger man of trying to kill his wife.

Hawis ignored both the fearsome stare and the sharp retort, just as he usually did, and Gillian wondered how he was able. She could only imagine that since his hair was as dark of their father's, he had inherited none of the fiery temper that came with their mother's red coloring. He met all Nicholas's barbs with equanimity, refusing to be drawn into an argument with his host. And Gillian admired him for it, even as she struggled against her own, far from serene reactions.

"What about you, Nicholas? Will you go with me?" Hawis asked, ever polite.

"You have seen enough of my demesne," Nicholas grumbled.

"Then let us venture farther afield," Hawis suggested. He turned again toward the open shutters, his hands clasped behind his back as he looked out. "I have a mind to see my uncle's manor."

At the mention of Nicholas's enemy, Gillian dropped her needlework into her lap. She shot a troubled glance at her husband, who surged to life. "Why?" he demanded.

"Why not?" Hawis countered easily. "By rights, the property should fall to me, should it not?"

"No," Nicholas said in a low snarl. "'Tis mine."

Hawis appeared to be oblivious of the heated possessiveness that sounded in his host's voice. "I understand why it would have passed to Gillian, and hence to you, by her marriage, when no male heir was found, but now that I have returned . . ." He let the words trail off, and Gillian's heart pounded in frantic dismay.

"Those lands are mine," Nicholas said. What little softness had graced his features fell away, and Gillian recognized, all too well, the cold, hard man who had come to claim her at the convent. She tried to catch her brother's eye in warning, but he continued to gaze out the window with apparent calm.

"I do not see why you would stand in the way of my ownership, when you acquired Belvry in the same way," he reasoned.

"That was different," Gillian said hastily, before her husband could erupt in fury. "Piers never made a claim on Belvry, but ceded it back to the de Lacis when Nicholas returned. Our uncle's manor was in dispute before his death, because he made war upon Belvry and was defeated."

Although she tried to convey both the foolishness and the danger of his persistence with her words, Hawis seemed unperturbed. "Still, I hardly see how that affects me," he said.

Gillian wondered if her brother was feeble-witted, or if he thought to play upon Nicholas's sympathies. She had only to glance at her husband to see the folly of that course. Nicholas had no sympathies. In fact, her husband looked as if he would gladly strike down her brother where he stood. While Gillian watched in horror, he leapt to his feet.

"That is why you are here, is it not, nephew of Hexham? You did not come to see Gillian, but to sniff around your uncle's property, like one of his bastard hounds. All those years you stayed away, without a care to the welfare of your own sister, but as soon as you heard of an inheritance, you came running back."

"Nicholas—" Gillian began, but he cut her off, his eyes chilling with the force of his fury.

"Only a cold-blooded bastard would leave his sister to the likes of me!"

"Really?" Hawis said. He turned, his hands falling to his sides, but he did not flinch. "'Tis a strange accusation, coming from you, is it not? I had good reason to stay away. Can you say the same? What kept you from Belvry while your own sister was thrown to the Red Knight, a man whose reputation is blacker than any's?"

Gillian gasped in shock, rising from her seat as if she could somehow prevent her brother's words. But it was too late. Nicholas faltered, quivering like a solid oak that has been struck to the core, and the blood drained from his face. For a moment, he was the man she knew in her bed, vulnerable and human, but he collected himself quickly. The cool, harsh mask descended, and he stepped menacingly toward Hawis, his hand dropping to the dagger that rested at his waist.

"Enough! The only heritage that awaits you here is my vengeance. By rights, you should die for your uncle's sins, but I have spared you, for your sister's sake. Do not test my patience. Edward gave me those lands, and they will remain in my possession. If you make a claim upon them, then you pronounce yourself my enemy!" He stepped closer, as if stalking the silent Hawis with deadly intent. "How will it be?"

Before her brother could answer, Gillian moved forward in an attempt to come between him and her husband, but her breath caught, and she swayed, struggling to take in air. The sound of her labored breathing made Nicholas turn toward her, and she saw the fury on his hard features fade. He was beside her in an instant.

"Breathe, Gillian!" he shouted. His strong arms supported her as he pushed her down upon her seat. Her fierce husband looked so stricken with anxiety that Gillian's heart twisted in her breast, and she began to relax under the gentle touch of his callused hands. They stroked her face and slid down her arms to take her fingers in his. "Hush. It will be all right. Nothing is wrong." He was lying, of course, but his voice, gentle now, coaxed her breathing back to normal as only he could do.

Finally, when she no longer felt the terrible press of panic, Gillian leaned back. "There, that is better," Nicholas whispered. "All is well now, my—" At the abrupt halt in his speech, Gillian lifted her head. She stared into the smoky depths of his eyes and saw more than she had ever hoped to see.

"What happened? Has she fits?" Hawis asked. Gillian blinked, having forgotten his presence. She saw Nicholas's eyes narrow. Although he remained kneeling in front of her, his hands holding hers, he turned toward her brother.

"And how is it that you, her brother, have no knowledge of her malady?" he asked, his voice deceptively mild.

As usual, Hawis did not take offense. "Perhaps this came upon you later in life, Gillian?" he suggested.

Gillian could not remember. She had been but a child when Hawis left, and he little more than one. "Perhaps," she answered, aware of the fragile peace that had descended over the solar. For once, she was glad of the shortness of breath that plagued her, because it just might have saved Hawis's life.

He did not look the slightest bit grateful, however. Concerned, yes, but about her, not about his own threatened existence. How could he be so calm, so oblivious of the danger that was Nicholas? "Are you well now?" Hawis asked solicitously. "Let me call Edith for you. She will know what to do."

Although her husband was the only one who could help her, Gillian did not argue. She let him leave, eager to dissipate the tensions that still ran high in the room. When Edith came bustling in, Nicholas rose to his feet.

"Do you go after him?" she whispered, afraid again.

Nicholas sighed. "Nay, but he must decide, and I would have his answer . . . soon."

Gillian nodded. Surely, after what happened today, Hawis would see the folly of pursuing their uncle's lands. Perhaps, if she could talk to him alone, she could convince him, but when and how? Suddenly, she felt overwhelmed, and so very tired that when Nicholas left and Edith propped up her feet, she did not protest.

It seemed to Gillian that she closed her eyes for just a moment, yet she opened them to the sight of afternoon sun slanting through the windows, lighting an elegant thick tapestry that draped from a coffer onto the floor. Shaking her head groggily, she blinked at Edith, who was sitting on the settle, grinning from ear to ear.

"Congratulations, my lady," she said. Although Gillian had become accustomed to Edith's eccentricities, she could make no sense of the older woman's words.

"What?"

Edith threw up her hands in glee. "My lady, you were sleeping during the day!"

Gillian nodded slowly, bewildered. Although normally she did not nap, she failed to see the significance of this instance. Nor could she fathom the servant's odd behavior.

Edith continued grinning like the veriest fool and leaned forward expectantly. When Gillian did not speak, she chuckled giddily. "And you have not had your courses!"

Gillian blushed at the old woman's plain speaking. And just how did Edith know that her monthly flow was past due? "Are you keeping track?" she asked, suspiciously.

The servant did not even bother to deny it. "Yes! Are you not?"

"No, I—" Gillian paused. Of course, she should have been more aware of her personal habits, since she so desperately wanted a child, but she had never thought to count the days. And with the arrival of her brother, her attention had been diverted. She lifted her head, hardly daring to believe what Edith was telling her. "Do you really think 'tis possible?"

Edith nodded eagerly. "I do, my lady."

Gillian looked down at herself in wonder. Did she carry Nicholas's heir? Even as she smiled, her vision blurred with tears at the thought of all that this child might mean. Not only did this baby represent the future of Belvry and its people, but Gillian also had her own hopes for him, beyond those of any good mother.

Silently and fervently, she wished that this tiny life that flowed with the blood of the de Lacis and the Hexhams could bring an end to the feud between them.

Nicholas left the heaving horse with his groom and strode back toward the great hall. Keeping his distance, he had followed Gillian's brother as far as the old border marking Hexham's former demesne. Then he had turned away, riding hard and fast toward home, for he was afraid that if he got any closer, he would slit the bastard's throat, whether Gillian liked it or not.

Treachery. Deceit. It was ever a Hexham trait, and it ran true in this Hawis, who had taken advantage of Nicholas's hospitality while scheming to steal his lands. Damn the bastard's black soul! Nicholas stormed through the hall and up to the solar, determined to tell Gillian that he had come to a decision.

Her brother must go, for he would nurture no viper in his own home. As soon as Hawis returned from his uncle's former holdings, he could pack up his things and count himself lucky to leave with his life! And woe betide the man if Nicholas ever caught him on Belvry land again. Clenching his fists angrily, Nicholas stalked into the room, only to pause as his wife rose from her chair to greet him.

"Nicholas," she whispered. She looked different from when he had left her, softer and less strained, somehow. Her mouth was curved into a gentle smile, and her eyes shone with a new light, bright and yearning.

Closing the door behind him, Nicholas stepped forward, puzzled by the change that had occurred in his absence. She had been gasping for air before, but now she was a glowing vision that nearly stole away *his* breath. "What is it? What has happened?" he asked.

She moved toward him gracefully, her hand drifting over her stomach in a gesture he had never seen before. "Edith thinks that . . . I might be . . . I do not know for certain, but I hope that . . ."

Her stammered words caught him by surprise. Was she with child already? Nicholas felt rather numb at the knowledge that it was done at last and out of his hands.

"A family, Nicholas," Gillian said softly, drawing his attention back to her face. She watched him warily, as if uncertain of his reaction, and Nicholas put aside his doubts. Like so many of the gentler emotions, happiness was not something he had ever put much stock in, but now he could see it in his wife's eyes. It reached out to touch something deep inside him, as if she would infuse him with the feeling, too.

And why not? Gillian had filled his empty soul with life and warmth and all sorts of elusive sentiments that he had never thought possible. Perhaps her dreams of a family were not so foolish. He would willingly indulge her, as long as she took no harm. "Are you well?" he asked gruffly.

She laughed—it was a low husky sound that made him think of the noises she made in his bed—and he shifted his body uncomfortably. "I am fine. Put aside your fears for me. In fact, I would celebrate this good fortune!"

Before Nicholas knew what she was about, Gillian was whirling around the room, arms outstretched, as if to encompass the world. Frowning at her giddiness, he reached out to stop her, but she danced out of his way, knocking some thick pillows onto a carpet that was draped upon the floor.

"Be careful," he snapped, but as with all his orders, Gillian would have none of it. Instead, she dropped down onto the thick pelt, as if to inspect it.

"I have never seen something so beautiful tossed upon the tiles," she murmured, running her hand across the thick pile in a way that made his thoughts turn, again, toward the night.

"'Tis not uncommon in the East."

"Ah, the East," she whispered. Giving him a sultry look that quickened his blood, she leaned back against the fallen pillows. "Teach me some of the erotic arts that you learned there."

Erotic arts? Nicholas laughed. Indeed, he knew none, for sex had always been a straightforward act of lust for him, and he had not been one to dally at pleasuring a woman. Until Gillian. "I believe that what you are referring to is the same the world over."

His wife looked disappointed. "There must be something exotic and...wicked we can do," she breathed, and there was no mistaking the light in her eyes. She had never looked less like an inmate of a convent.

Nicholas's lips curved in amusement, but when Gillian did not return his smile, he realized that his fiery wife was serious. He had never dallied during the day! The afternoon's light was filtering through the half-open shutters, beckoning him to much unfinished business, including the onerous problem of Hawis Hexham, yet one glance at Gillian sprawled before him wantonly made all else seem unimportant.

He wanted her, here and now. He wanted to claim her, and the child, as his own, to lift her hips and bury himself inside her welcoming heat until nothing existed but Gillian. He had only to think about it, and he was ready—aye, more than ready—for her, and he took a step forward, only to halt himself.

She wanted something exotic.

Nicholas wracked his desire-fogged brain for memories of eastern practices. His lips quirked. "We could shave off all your body hair."

"Ugh!" She made a face, and he laughed, the once unusual reaction coming freely to him. How easy it was with her! Although he had rarely smiled before his marriage, Nicholas found himself often grinning at his wife's antics. She was alternately infuriating, amusing and exhilarating, he decided.

Right now, she was eying him expectantly, and he realized he was going to have to come up with something. Darius was a self-proclaimed great lover, so he tried to recollect some of the Syrian's lewd exploits.

"Honey," he said, abruptly. "I could dribble it all over your body and lick it off."

She frowned. "Too sticky."

"Crushed fruit?"

"What a mess!"

"Wine?"

Gillian shook her brilliant curls. "I would smell like a winery." Nicholas grinned, for they were much alike, he and his wife. None of those suggestions particularly appealed to him, either, for he was not one for exotic treats.

"'Tis just as well. Your skin tastes fine as it is, and needs no additional flavoring."

She blushed. "Do you think so?" she asked, rather breathlessly. "I like the feel of your tongue, without...all those extras." Although her pale coloring flamed even brighter at this admission, his little nun did not look away.

Of course! Did she even know what she asked for? Nicholas doubted it, but he remembered his own fevered pleasure when she had taken him in her mouth. And he knew, with certainty, that she would gain the same delight from him.

Nicholas's glance raked her slim form, coming to rest at the juncture of her thighs, and his breath came sharp and quick. He had never done it before, had never wanted to, but right now the prospect of kissing her heated center seemed infinitely appealing. He lifted his gaze to her face. Her green eyes were wide, and she shuddered. "What?" she whispered.

"This," Nicholas answered, and he sank down on his knees before her. Closing his hands around her slender ankles, he heard the low hiss of air leaving her lungs. Then he slid his palms along her stockings and higher, to the skin above them—bare and smooth. Impatiently his arms pushed her gown and shift out of the way, bunching it up around her waist until he could see the thatch of red curls that marked her woman's place.

Often had he played there, but never had he looked upon it in the light of day, and he found himself drawn there, fascinated. He parted her legs, dipping his head low to rub against the tender skin of her thighs, pale and soft.

"Nicholas . . ." She called to him, and he raised his head once more. Her breasts were rising and falling with the speed of her breath, her lips were parted, her eyes were luminous and wary. Although she looked unsure, Nicholas had never been more certain of anything. Suddenly, he had to do this, had to know the taste of her.

"Lie back," he ordered roughly. Although she rarely did as he told her, after a long moment, Gillian sank shakily onto the pillows behind her. Nicholas arranged her skirts out of his way and turned his attention back to her fiery core. He stroked her sleek thighs, then spread them wide and kissed the curls that crowned her.

She gasped, but he ignored it, too intent now upon his goal. Her scent wafted up to him, giving him greeting, and he nuzzled the spot where her legs joined her body. Having no experience to guide him, Nicholas moved on instinct, pressing his lips against the delicate folds of her body, his heart pounding in a furious rhythm as he acquainted himself with the source of her delight.

He opened his mouth, kissing her fully, and she cried out, lifting her hips in agitation, so he slid his hands beneath her to cup the curves of her buttocks and raise her to him. He snaked out his tongue tentatively, then more boldly. She tasted musky and sweet. Hot. And wet.

Nicholas's body tightened painfully, and soon he was licking her lustily and delving inside her, while Gillian writhed beneath the onslaught. Her hands twisted into his hair, holding his head to her, and she called his name, over and over, interspersed with pleas that made his blood roar its assent. When she cried out in fulfillment, it was all he could do not to spill his seed upon the carpet.

Her fingers pulled at his shoulders, dragging him up to her, but Nicholas required no urging. Still on his knees, he lowered her hips to his and, in a single thrust, buried himself deep. Gillian's ankles dangled over his shoulders, and in the seconds before his violent climax began, he recalled his wife's request.

This was, he decided, as exotic as he could take.

Chapter Nineteen

Nicholas strode into the great hall, calling impatiently for his wife. Why was she never here to greet him? His mood was poor, for he had been out scouting the damages from the late-autumn storm that had struck yesterday, toppling trees and destroying a villein's hut. Although the rain had stopped for now, the river behind the castle was still rising, and he had sent some men to ride along its banks to assess the danger.

Now he was cold and hungry and his wife was nowhere to be seen. He had just opened his mouth to shout again when he saw Rowland approaching him, looking glum. "Where is she?" Nicholas snarled.

"My lord, your lady has gone out riding with her brother, I believe," the servant replied.

"What? In this weather?" Nicholas clenched his fists in frustration. He did not like Gillian to ride in her condition, especially on a day like this. Damn that bastard brother of hers! He should have tossed Hawis Hexham out on his ear a week ago—after the villain asked after his uncle's property.

But Gillian had made soothing noises, Hawis had backed down, and, feeling magnanimous because of his wife's pregnancy, Nicholas had let her brother remain. He had regretted his decision ever since, but never more than at this moment. Not only was it too cold for Gillian to be outside, but the ground was still soft and treacherous in places, where the saturated grass had frosted over as temperatures dropped.

Nicholas whirled around, prepared to go after them, when Rowland cleared his throat. "There is something else, my lord."

"What?" Nicholas snapped.

The servant, apparently inured to his foul tempers, did not quail, but pointed to the hearth. "You have a visitor," he said. Then, without even waiting for a dismissal, he hurried away.

Nicholas's eyes narrowed as he looked toward the fire, where a large bulk of a man was warming his hands, unattended by any guards. Damn! His pregnant wife was galloping the frozen countryside, and strangers were wandering in the hall. What next? Nicholas thought, his temper fraying.

With a low oath, he stepped forward, only to halt in his tracks when the fellow turned slowly to face him. As he recognized the tall, broad figure, Nicholas stiffened in astonishment. What was Piers Montmorency doing here?

Nicholas's first thought was for Aisley and her child. Were they here? Or had his brother by marriage brought ill news? "My sister?" he asked harshly.

"She is well," Piers answered, looking faintly surprised at the question. "She sent me to you."

Silence descended at the Red Knight's quiet explanation, and Nicholas was aware of the tension that stretched between them. They had not parted on good terms after brawling on these very tiles. What brought the Red Knight back to Belvry?

As if reading his thoughts, Piers fixed him with those clear blue eyes that always seemed to see too much. "Aisley was concerned about you and your wife after receiving your letter."

Nicholas felt himself flush and glanced away, unable to hold Pier's gaze. He had forgotten that missive and its contents. "All is well. The sickness has passed."

"Good," Piers said. "And your wife?"

"Is fine," Nicholas muttered.

"I thought as much," Piers said, turning to rub his hands near the fire. Nicholas realized that the Red Knight must have been caught in the storm yesterday, and he felt vaguely guilty for having caused the man discomfort, albeit inadvertently. "I saw her riding from the bailey, but did not hail her. I wanted to see you first."

Nicholas nodded. Piers's caution was understandable considering the conditions under which he had left de Laci land. Yet Nicholas could hardly even remember the argument that had precipitated the violence between them. He suspected that he ought to apologize, but he was in no mood for it.

"She seemed happy and healthy," Piers said, prompting him. He eyed Nicholas closely, as though searching for deeper truths, and Nicholas volunteered one.

"She is with child," he said.

Piers's surprise was evident, but it was followed swiftly by a wide grin. "Congratulations, Nicholas."

Nicholas nodded, grudgingly. "'Tis good news, as long as she remains well. I...I would not wish for anything to go wrong."

Again Nicholas caught the flare of surprise in Piers's eyes before the man smiled. "All will be well. But, if you are concerned, mayhap we should bring her back to the hall.

The roads were foul and slippery as I journeyed here, and I saw some flooding.''

Nicholas released a sharp oath. "I would that she had not gone, but he would persuade her in my absence."

"He? The man who was with her?" Piers paused to rub his chin thoughtfully. "I have seen him before, but I cannot think where or when."

Nicholas turned, and was already heading for the doors when Piers's words penetrated his brain. He stopped short. "What do you mean?"

"I remember! 'Twas on the marches. He was squire to one of the knights, but was turned off in disgrace. What does he here?"

Nicholas felt his stomach seize up, and for a moment he thought he might vomit. He, who had not blinked an eye in the face of battle or its bloody aftermath, suddenly felt the kind of fear that made grown men sick. He forced his mouth to speech. "Are you certain? The man claims to be someone else."

The flash of confusion and alarm that crossed the Red Knight's face made bile rise in Nicholas's throat. He swallowed hard, gritting his teeth against the panic that threatened to engulf him.

"I saw his face only from a distance, but I could swear it was the same man," Piers said slowly. "Black of hair and eyes, he was, of medium height and build. Swithun was his name, I think. I remember well when he was turned off, because 'twas due to his own negligence. He sent his master off to battle with a loose cinch that cost the man's life, and he was lucky to escape with his own, for soldiers are not a forgiving lot."

Some of what Nicholas felt must have shown on his face, for Piers stepped forward to grasp his arm. "What? What is it?" he demanded.

For a long moment, Nicholas could not reply, as all his suspicions about Hawis Hexham had fallen into place. Why had the man waited so long without sending any word to his sister? Because he was not her brother. Undoubtedly he was the dark-haired man who had asked so diligently about Gillian, and the reason for his many questions was clear. He had needed every bit of information he could gather in order to act the part of her sibling. Still, there were things he had not discovered—her breathlessness, for instance.

But why would someone pose as Gillian's brother? The answer came, swift and painful: Hexham's former demesne was rich enough to satisfy any knight, let alone an errant squire. And the only people who stood between him and the lands he lusted for were Nicholas . . . and Gillian.

The wife he had sworn to protect was in more danger than Nicholas had ever imagined.

Gillian urged her mount after Hawis's, but the climb toward high ground was difficult. Nicholas would not approve, Gillian realized, and she felt a twinge of guilt. She had accepted Hawis's invitation to ride in the hope of speaking to him privately at last—and making it clear that he must forget about their uncle's property.

Although her intentions were noble, Gillian sensed that Nicholas would not appreciate her efforts, which, unfortunately, had come to naught so far. Not only had she failed to broach the painful subject of their heritage to her brother, she had barely conversed with him at all. Despite the cold weather and the muddy and slippery ground, Hawis seemed determined to ride, rather than talk.

"Hawis, slow down," she called to him, but the wind that was picking up again must have swallowed her words, for he did not turn. How typical of a man to forge ahead on a single course without stopping to consider his actions—or those of anyone around him!

Gillian glanced upward to get her bearings. Hawis was obviously making for the small gorge at the top of the hill. Apparently her brother wanted to get a good look at the rising river, but why he had dragged her along, she did not know.

Gillian frowned at the thought, which rang, sadly, with truth. Even after weeks in his company, there was still much she did not know about her brother. And, try as she might to feel the appropriate familial attachment to him, she could not. Guilt nagged at her for her failing.

She told herself that it was only natural that such sentiments be slow to develop, for she had only a vague memory of a curly-haired boy to put to the grown man who had returned to her a stranger. Still, Hawis deserved better. Kind and gentle and even-tempered, he seemed to possess all the fine traits that her husband lacked.

Yet she loved Nicholas more. So very much more. Of course, what Gillian felt for her husband was different from that she would feel for a sibling, but she could not rid herself of the impression that for all his foul-tempered blustering, Nicholas was far more *worth* loving than the warm, friendly Hawis.

Gillian shook her head at her own perversity. Perhaps her own character was flawed, but she preferred the company of her harsh husband. He might be moody and bullying and argumentative, but he would never bore her. Life flowed between them. Whether with anger or excitement or passion, they fired each other's spirits with a constant give-and-take.

Gillian was jarred from her thoughts by the struggle to reach the rise. Her saddle slipped, and she knew a moment's worry that she might lose her seat. Digging her heels in, she sent her palfrey the last few feet to high ground, and breathed a sigh of relief. A glance behind her, down the muddy incline, showed her just how dangerous a fall would have been.

She sucked in a strangled breath, regretting her unwise decision to come along. This was a hard ride, better suited to men and their destriers, and she had not only herself, but also the child, to think about.

"Hawis," she gasped.

"Over here!" he yelled. He was looking out over the gorge, as she had suspected, but she had no desire to go near the edge, where the earth fell away to the rushing river below.

She hesitated, then started in surprise as a horse and rider burst through the trees to the left and galloped up the hill at breakneck speed.

It had to be Nicholas, Gillian thought grimly. A very angry, very jealous Nicholas, who no doubt thought she was conspiring with her brother to take over the world—or at least this small part of it. When he reached the top, he was forced to slow down, and he reined in the massive destrier not far from her, his glance darting around the clearing suspiciously.

Gillian glanced at him dubiously, but he did not look particularly enraged. His face was bone white, and his eyes were dark against the colorless skin. Was he ill, or was this a new facet of his ever-changing temperament?

"Gillian, come to me," he said.

The vehemence in his tone surprised her. Was there more involved here than her simple ride with Hawis? Weary as she was of Nicholas's petty jealousies, her first inclination was to refuse, but the starkness of his features made her pause. If she had not known better, she would have thought fear drove him. Yet Nicholas was afraid of nothing.

"Gillian, over here!" Hawis called.

"Stay away from him, Gillian," Nicholas said. "Come to me. Now."

Bewildered, Gillian glanced back at Hawis. He was closer to her and, ignoring Nicholas's insult, as usual, he urged his mount forward. Gillian looked from one man to the other, from her brother's friendly countenance to her husband's forbidding one, and she realized that if she would trust one of them, it must be Nicholas.

The discovery made her blink, for though long had she loved him, never would she have thought to put her blind faith in her husband. Yet she knew that what flowed between them was stronger, more powerful, than anger and revenge, and she turned her palfrey toward him.

A noise made her start, and she looked up to see Hawis spurring his horse forward, frightening her little mount into sidestepping. Gillian tried to regain control, only to feel her saddle slip again. She gasped for breath, and might have fallen, but for Nicholas, who somehow reached her side in an instant and lifted her into his strong arms.

Cradled on his lap, Gillian watched as his great destrier swept from the fray, just as Hawis's big horse nearly ran down her poor little palfrey. It struggled valiantly for footing on the slippery ground, and Gillian released a long, ragged sigh, thankful that she had not been seated on the saddle that now hung crookedly from its back.

The incident had transpired so swiftly that Gillian was unsure what had precipitated it. Had Hawis's horse been spooked? The slippery ground was enough to make any beast skittish, but what would send it straight toward hers? She knew it was no unruly stallion, but an even-tempered gelding.

Slowly Gillian became aware of the tension emanating from her husband. He held her crushed against his chest, one arm wound around her so tightly that she could not move, and she could feel the thundering of his heart. He remained silent, however, his gaze firmly fixed upon Hawis as he maneuvered them a good distance away. When he did speak, his tone sent a chill down Gillian's back.

"Did you think to improve your chances for Hexham's lands by getting rid of Gillian and the child she carries?" he asked in a deceptively smooth voice.

Gillian gasped, stunned by his words, but Hawis only smiled.

"Obviously, your arrival scared my mount. You cannot charge that huge destrier into a clearing and expect the other horses not to react."

Gillian felt an icy cold descend upon her that was not due to the weather. Why did Hawis not ask her pardon or express his concern?

"That does not explain her saddle, does it?" Nicholas asked. He was as still as stone now, and just as unyielding. "Did you cut the cinch, or just loosen it? Was she to fall into the gorge, or were you going to push her?"

Gillian felt the air leave her lungs in a rush, but she refused to succumb to the horror that threatened to assail her. She breathed in and out, slowly, for her baby's sake, as well as her own. Only when she had regained control of herself could she look at her brother. He seemed as relaxed as ever. Did nothing affect him? Why was he not screaming his denial?

"I do not know what you mean," he said, a smile playing about his lips. Did he think this all a jest?

"Did you really believe I would let her death go unavenged?"

"You are imagining things," Hawis said.

"Nay. You are the one imagining things, if you thought to kill my wife and child and take my lands. The game is done, Swithun, for I know who you are."

For the first time, Gillian saw a brief flicker of reaction in Hawis's dark eyes, but he spoke evenly. "You can prove nothing."

"I have a man at Belvry who knows you, who can vouch that you are no brother to my wife, but a cowardly squire, turned off for poor service to his master. Or did you murder him, as you tried to Gillian?"

Hawis licked his lips, but held his ground. "He must be mistaken," he said, his mouth curving into a smirk. And, as Gillian watched in stunned silence, he stripped off his gauntlet and tossed it on the ground in front of Nicholas's great destrier.

"You insult me, Nicholas. I deny your words, and what's more, I challenge you to the Hexham lands, mine by right of inheritance."

Gillian gasped in horror, her eyes fixed upon the fallen glove, for even she, sheltered as she had been, knew the meaning of such a challenge. Trial by combat, it was called, and it was fought to the death.

Pulling her fur-lined cloak around her, Gillian turned toward the doors that led from the great hall outside, though Edith would have held her back.

"But, my lady, you cannot mean to go!" the servant protested, yet again.

Gillian silenced the older woman's protests with a single look, and Edith fell back, muttering something about the lady being as stubborn as the lord. It gave Gillian her first, and no doubt last, smile of this day, for before the morning was through, someone dear to her would be dead.

It was not what she would have, and the walls had rung with shouts as she and Nicholas had argued over the challenge. He had listed all the evidence against Hawis, and she had been forced to accept what her heart had suspected all along: The man who claimed to be her brother was not. It had hurt, and to hear of his crimes against her had been even more painful, but she would not have him cut down by her husband.

Nor would she have Nicholas hurt.

That admission had pulled her husband up short for a while, but he was still adamant. Honor demanded that he go forward with the duel, he insisted, although Gillian cared nothing for such knightly rituals. If truth be told, she could hardly believe that this barbaric contest was legal. If Hawis was an impostor, then trial by battle was an easy way for him to gain a vast estate by murdering the owner.

And that was what tormented Gillian. Although Nicholas scorned any suggestion that he would be defeated, she could not help but worry. What if he was not invincible? She knew him to be a skilled warrior, strong and clever and quick, but what if something went awry? The thought of anything happening to him made her gasp for breath, for she could not imagine a life without the harsh man she had grown to love. And what of the baby she carried? Would it ever know its father?

Only her own fierce pride had kept Gillian from begging him not to go through with it, and though she tried mightily, she could not sway him. Nicholas had stormed off, and she had succumbed to the drowsiness that plagued her. When she had awakened this morning, he was already gone, depriving her of any final protests. Or parting words.

Gillian let out a ragged sigh at the memory and forced herself to step outside. Despite Edith's dire warnings, she had no intention of cringing in her room while her husband

and the man purporting to be her brother fought to the death. Motioning for the old servant to attend her, she walked out into the bailey.

Although it had rained no more, the sky was dull and overcast and the wind cool, promising a cloudburst or perhaps snow later. The weather did not appear to be keeping anyone from the event, however, for the procession grew as they neared the field where the battle was to be held. Gillian might have accused them all of a ghoulish curiosity, but for the serious expressions worn by most. These were Nicholas's people, and though they had been slow to take him to their hearts, they were fiercely loyal.

From the whispered comments she overheard, Gillian could tell that few shared her concerns about the contest. Not only was Nicholas a skilled and seasoned warrior, but it was well-known that God aided the combatant with the just cause. That alone should have been enough to ease her fears, but Gillian knew that God did not always behave as man might expect or want, and none knew his ways clearly.

And so she doubted and was afraid. Still, she held her head up high as she made her way to her seat upon one of the benches that had been placed near the battle area. She knew that she must act the part of the lady of Belvry, even though she wanted to wail and sob and beat her breast in terror.

A hush fell over the crowd as Piers took his place as judge, though the position was strictly titular. The fight that ensued would be the real judge, and death the final decision. Gillian watched as Piers received the gloves of both men. Then Nicholas took a position to the north, Hawis to the south, and the two faced each other. Although both were large men, they looked small and vulnerable without their war-horses and armor. This was no joust, but a duel, and each held a single baton as his only weapon.

Piers signaled for the battle to begin, and Gillian felt her breath quicken. Despite her best intentions, her thoughts swiftly disintegrated into a jumble of prayers and pleas and her heart became an unruly thing that beat far too wildly within her chest. If Gillian had ever been uncertain, she knew the truth now full well. She loved the hard man who had come to the convent to claim her, and she would have him grow old with her, forever at her side, bullying and blustering and meeting her passion with his own.

It began. Nicholas thrust. Hawis parried. And Gillian felt the telltale hitching of her breath. She closed her eyes, trying to concentrate on taking in air, but her efforts were too fast, too shallow. Dear God, but she could not succumb to her fear! Not here. Not now. Not when Nicholas was in danger.

Gillian clung to her last thought, and with a strength she had not thought to possess, she blew out a ragged sigh and opened her eyes. She had to breathe, not just for herself, but for her baby. And for Nicholas.

He staggered under a heavy blow, and though Gillian flinched, she did not gasp. She felt someone's fingers close over her own, and looked down in surprise to see that Edith was holding her hand. Gillian squeezed the older woman's in reassurance, knowing that she, too, was anxious. And she breathed. Slowly. And, curiously, with each breath came new power, until she could face the grim battle without blinking.

Hawis, who had gained some ground with fancy maneuvering, was neither as big nor as strong as Nicholas. Nor did he have the endurance of such a seasoned knight. Gillian had seen her husband work with his men for hours, but she saw no such stamina in Hawis, who had spent his time at Belvry in idleness, for the most part.

It soon became apparent that Hawis was rapidly tiring, but, as usual, he showed no dismay. Although a solid blow from Nicholas cracked his own weapon in two, Hawis fought on, swinging one end wildly, for the rules of combat were clear. The fight would continue, if only with fists and feet and teeth.

Nicholas struck, but despite his weariness, Hawis moved quickly, avoiding the blow and dancing around his opponent. In the blink of an eye, he sent the cudgel crashing down on Nicholas's head. Nicholas swayed and fell to his knees as a murmur of protest rose from the crowd.

Gleefully circling for the kill, Hawis lifted his broken weapon high, the jagged end traveling downward in a deadly arc, straight for Nicholas's face. Gillian's fist tightened so tightly around Edith's hand that the old woman squeaked in protest, and it was as if time stopped, as everyone leaned forward to watch what might be the final feat of the battle.

Then, suddenly, Nicholas lifted his arms, his own baton receiving the blow and breaking before he was up and throwing himself against Hawis, who lost his weapon in the fall. The two rolled around on the ground, fists flying, and again Nicholas proved himself to be the better man, despite the blood that trickled from the wound on his head.

Still, Hawis did not seem frightened, not even when Nicholas knocked him to the ground, hands closed around his neck. For a moment, Gillian wondered if the man was mad, or uncommonly brave, but the reason for his confidence became obvious when his fingers inched toward the top of his boot. Abruptly, silver flashed, and, as if the forbidden weapon gave him renewed energy, Hawis struck, throwing Nicholas off and leaping on him with a vengeance. Nicholas fell onto his back, one arm up to catch the hand that gripped the knife poised at his throat.

The audience gasped, collectively, whether in horror at this breach of the rules or in fear for Nicholas, Gillian never knew. Another flash of silver caught her eye, and she watched it fly through the air from where Piers had risen to his feet to Hawis's back, embedding itself neatly between his shoulder blades. He fell, releasing his grip on Nicholas, and the crowd roared its approval.

Gillian remained where she was, unable to move, as Piers strode forward. He pronounced Hawis dead and Nicholas the victor, and Gillian felt the world swim before her eyes. She struggled to stand, with Edith's help, and then, as if the life that had been suspended rushed through her again, she found herself running across the chill grass toward her husband.

Chapter Twenty

Nicholas wiped the sweat from his eyes and stared at the large hand that was extended to him. He wanted to wave away Piers's misguided assistance, for he would rise by himself, with dignity. And yet he could not. He was shaken and unsure his legs could support him, even though he had walked away from worse skirmishes. Indeed, he had come closer to death many times.

But never before had he feared it.

It had almost done him in, this near-paralyzing fright that had begun even before the fight. Nicholas had heard of soldiers who froze in battle, unable to do their duty, but he had scoffed at the cowards, never thinking to join their ranks—until today.

It was not as if his own life meant so much, even though it was livable at last, fresh and full, as it had never been before his marriage. Nay, precious as it had become, Nicholas would give it up with honor, if not for Gillian and the child. His fear was for their future, for if he should lose, what would become of them?

Such thoughts had plagued him from the moment he accepted the challenge, and he had found himself wondering whether there might be something to this business of family that Gillian was always prattling about. Had he relatives to whom he could entrust his wife and unborn babe, perhaps he would not suffer under the suffocating dread that had nearly cost him the contest.

The hand reached for him still. Although Nicholas refused it, denying his need for assistance, it remained outstretched before him, steady, unwavering. Like Piers himself. With reluctant admiration, Nicholas lifted his head to look at the man who had saved his life. Reminded of his own timely appearance when Piers was under siege, he said, "We are even now."

The Red Knight shook his head in denial. "We are brothers."

The realization was long in coming, but perhaps all the sharper for it. Suddenly Nicholas knew that he had never really been alone, for here was the family he could turn to, if need be. All he had to do was grasp it. Eyeing the palm that was presented to him, Nicholas reached out to take it, letting Piers's massive strength drag him to his feet.

Their gazes met, and Nicholas saw a wealth of understanding in that of the other man, but for once he did not flinch from that knowledge, and Piers nodded, satisfied. Then Nicholas saw Gillian running toward him, her cloak billowing behind her, and he opened his arms. She came into them in a rush, and he gathered her to him, burying his face in her fiery hair.

Shakily, reverently, he breathed in the essence of her, and it was so heady that, if not for their audience, he might have wept into her precious locks and babbled all sorts of nonsense. Like how much she meant to him.

"Nicholas!" she whispered, her voice a gentle comfort. "Thank God!"

"My lord!" Edith's grating tone interrupted their tender reunion, and Nicholas groaned in annoyance. "The villain's servants are fled," she said, nodding toward the dead man. "And who did I see among them but Eudo, whom you banished from Belvry! He must have kept out of sight."

Nicholas's head jerked up, though he kept one arm around his wife. "That explains where he received some of his information, at least." All eyes turned to the body of his slain opponent, and Nicholas realized that he took no joy in the man's death, only in his own survival. So much for his long-awaited revenge.

"I suppose we will never know now if he was my lady's brother or not," Edith said, and Gillian leaned into him, pressing her face against his shoulder with a choking sound that made Nicholas curse the old servant's loose tongue.

"Hush," he said, stroking her back. "He will receive a proper burial." For her sake, Nicholas was willing to go through the motions, but he knew that the man was no kin to his wife. Although others might doubt Piers's memory, Nicholas did not. The great knight was too shrewd to be in error. If Gillian needed more proof, however, he would give it to her in good time. "We shall know," he said grimly, "when Darius returns."

Gillian released a sad sigh. "Now I have no family again," she murmured brokenly.

"Nay," Nicholas said. He slid a hand beneath her chin and lifted it, so that she was forced to look at him, her emerald eyes awash with tears. "Your family is here," he said, nodding toward the Red Knight. "Piers and Aisley and their child. Our baby." She blinked. "And we will make more between us. Gillian, I am your family," he whispered.

She stood there on the field of battle, with the wind tugging her cloak and sending long tendrils of fiery hair trailing behind her, and Nicholas could not resist her. He kissed her mouth to seal his pledge, while the crowd roared its approval, chanting the names of their lord and lady to the sky.

* * *

Nicholas strode to the solar, pausing abruptly on the threshold at the sight of his wife, nodding over her needlework. The forgotten piece lay abandoned on the roundness of her belly, and he sucked in a breath at the tranquillity of the scene. He had never expected to know such peace as he had these past few months.

He and Gillian spent more of their time at ease with each other and less of it arguing. Although they still quarreled, both of them knew that they would soon settle their differences in an elemental manner, and even the servants no longer fled in the wake of their shouts. Indeed, their contentment seemed contagious, for all at Belvry seemed more festive than usual as Christmas approached.

Yet, into this harmonious atmosphere, Nicholas must bring a note of discord. He frowned, unwilling to distress the woman who slumbered so sweetly, even though he knew that his news must do just that. Perhaps he should let her sleep on, for now, but even as the thought passed through his mind, his contrary wife fluttered her lashes and looked at him drowsily.

"Nicholas…" She said his name on a sigh, and he stepped forward, resolved to wait no longer.

"Darius has returned," he said. Her green eyes widened, and she sat up straighter, grabbing up her needlework before it fell to the floor. "I have not spoken to him, but I saw him approach and told Rowland to send him up directly."

Gillian nodded, her lovely mouth set in a firm line. She was preparing herself for ill tidings, and Nicholas could offer no comfort, for he knew what to expect from the Syrian's report. All he could do was take a seat beside her and wait for Darius's arrival, which was not long in coming.

When he appeared, it was obvious that the Syrian had come straight to the solar, for his clothes were still damp from travel over snow-covered roads. He, too, paused in the doorway, his gaze taking in Gillian's newly rounded shape, and he grinned. "My lady!" He came forward, and Gillian would have risen to greet him, but Nicholas placed a restraining hand upon her arm.

"Rest, wife," he said. And he told himself that it was her welfare that made him speak, and not a sudden recurrence of his old jealousy.

"Darius," Gillian said from her chair. "'Tis good to see you again. And returned in time for the yuletide."

The Syrian bowed low, his lithe body more elegant than Nicholas remembered. "'Tis good to see you, as well, and in such a delightful condition. May I tender my congratulations to you, and to you, also, of course," he added, inclining his head toward Nicholas.

In return, Nicholas nodded, though his mood was soured by the way Darius was looking at his wife. Undisguised approval, along with something deeper, more threatening, appeared on the Syrian's normally impassive face, and Nicholas's eyes narrowed as he leaned forward. "You have news?" he asked.

Darius lifted his brows slightly at Nicholas's peremptory manner, but said nothing as he settled himself on a patch of carpet that graced the floor by the hearth. When he turned again toward them once more, his features revealed nothing.

"I traveled to the marches in search of information about your brother, lady," he said. "He claims to have served under a Baron Mollison, but I could find no man by that name, nor any history of such, though I traveled far and wide and asked for him of many. Nor could I find anyone who had ever heard of Hawis Hexham."

Nicholas nodded. "The Red Knight was here and recognized him as a squire for a petty knight who fought with Edward in Wales."

Darius frowned. "I am sorry, lady."

Gillian lowered her head.

"I went back to the place of your birth and questioned many there, without much success, until I finally located an old woman who not only remembered your brother, but tended him at his deathbed, when he was a child."

Nicholas saw Gillian swallow. Although she did not struggle for air, he watched her anxiously. "Thank you for your information, Darius. I know it cost you dearly in this weather," she said. "Perhaps, in the spring, I can visit my brother's grave, knowing that he is truly there and at rest."

Darius turned to Nicholas. "And the impostor?"

"He is dead," Nicholas said, but his eyes were on Gillian. She was so brave and strong, he knew she would never weep in front of another. "Thank you, Darius," he said curtly. "You will want to rest after your long journey."

The Syrian lifted his brows again at the abrupt dismissal, but did not protest. He rose from the floor gracefully, bowed to Gillian, and left, closing the door behind him.

Alone with his wife, Nicholas felt absurdly helpless. He was not good with words, and could not easily form those that would give comfort to her. "I wanted you to be certain that 'twas not your brother who was killed here," he explained.

Gillian did not move her head, but looked down at her lap. "I think I always knew, in my heart, that he was not Hawis."

"Aye," Nicholas said since a response seemed appropriate.

"The heart is a wondrous thing, Nicholas."

"Aye," he muttered again.

"It sees truths that the mind does not."

"Aye."

"I have a big heart, Nicholas."

"Aye," he repeated, though he did not quite follow her.

"Although you will always be first and foremost in it, there is room there for others."

Nicholas, uncertain of her meaning, kept silent this time.

"There are corners enough for Edith and Willie, Aisley and Piers and little Sybil, and even Darius."

Nicholas's gaze shot to her face, and she turned slowly to meet it. Her green eyes were calm and clear. "And there is room, too, for our baby. Nicholas, I can love them all without loving you less."

Nicholas stared, too stunned by her pronouncement to reply. When, at last, he found his wits, his first impulse was deny what she was saying, but he could not. The rebuttal stuck in his throat, for his clever wife was not wrong.

A selfish bastard she had called him once, and it was true. He would hoard all her affection for himself, and resent that which she bestowed upon others. Even the child he had given her in a fit of pique, trying to bind her more fully to him. And he had sworn to protect her for all the wrong reasons, not for her own welfare, but for his own peace of mind.

"Love is giving and sharing, Nicholas," she said softly.

Although he refused to glance her way, Nicholas felt her hand upon his, lifting it and placing his palm against her stomach. "Feel that, Nicholas? 'Tis your son." Her voice broke. "Tell me that your heart is big enough for him."

Beneath his fingers, Nicholas felt movement, as the flesh of her belly stirred and swelled. He sucked in a breath, awestruck that the unborn babe could make itself known to him so surely. "I never realized . . ."

"See, Nicholas? He is giving you greeting!"

Kneeling before her, Nicholas laid his cheek against her belly. It rippled and rolled beneath him, and he was abruptly aware of the presence of another being in his wife, in his life, in his heart. And he knew, just as suddenly, that he would love it, as he loved Gillian.

He looked up again, to see her lashes wet with tears, her smile tremulous, and it seemed as if he had loved her forever. But that could not be possible. He had been empty for so long before she entered his life and filled him with her spirit, her warmth, her passion.

"I will love him, Gillian," he said, his voice suddenly hoarse. "Just as I love you."

"Good," she said, blinking rapidly while her smile grew. Then she laughed aloud, the husky sound that always stirred his soul. "Why, Nicholas, I have never seen you grin so broadly." She paused to study him, then cried out in delight, "I do believe you have a dimple!"

Nicholas paced back and forth in the passageway, unwilling to go down to the hall and face the prying eyes of his people, yet forced from the great chamber where his wife lay in childbed. He had not wanted to go, but the midwife had folded her hands across her withered chest, pronounced that a birthing was no place for a man and demanded his departure.

He had exited the room, only to linger outside, listening like a thief at the door, but the oaken panels were thick, and he heard nothing. So Nicholas stood in the dark, a seasoned warrior, helpless, frustrated, knowing nothing. Thwarted by an old crone. He fisted his hands at his sides, struggling with a desire to beat down the wall that separated him from his wife. What was going on in there?

The memory of Gillian's illness returned to haunt him, and he envisioned her lying cold and silent upon their great bed. The stomach that had long been healed lurched wildly, and his chest tightened with fear. When would they let him back in?

The first of her cries tore at his insides, and Nicholas began to sweat, despite the coolness of the surrounding stones. The next few screams made him lunge toward the door, but he stopped himself, striding back and forth again, trying to regain his composure. Once, he saw Willie's face at the top of the stairs, but one fierce look sent Edith's husband scuttling away. Nicholas wanted no comfort. Nor did he desire that anyone see him this way, his control rapidly slipping away.

The minutes ticked by impossibly slowly, and the longer he paced outside the door, the more frantic Nicholas became. Gillian's moans were a constant now, coming closer together, sometimes louder, sometimes softer, and he found himself straining to hear them, for they meant that she lived and breathed.

Still, Nicholas had seen his share of misery, and he knew how suddenly death could claim a man or woman. The thought made him pause, for he remembered all too well that dark time during her illness when Gillian had nearly slipped away from him. Only the force of his will had kept her with him then. He had ranted and raved and drawn her back from the very brink, and ever since he had watched over her vigilantly.

Except now. The realization that his wife might be dying in there, away from his reach, made Nicholas act at last. Striding to the door, he wrenched it open, and it banged against the wall loudly, startling everyone in the room, as he stood on the threshold, assessing the scene.

Gillian was lying back upon the bed, Edith at her side and the midwife at her feet. A cloth covered his wife's upraised knees, but the birthing stool stood to the side, unused. The old midwife, who had been present at his own arrival into the world, turned to face him, a scowl on her wrinkled face.

"My lord! You must leave here at once!" she protested angrily. Unaccustomed to anyone but his wife gainsaying him, Nicholas wondered if the crone was witch. He did not trust her.

"Why is she not on the stool?" he snarled.

"My lord, my lord," Edith said, bustling over to come between him and the hag. "'Tis not quite time yet. You must be patient." She clucked her tongue, trying to herd him from the room, but he would have none of it.

"Patient? I have been listening to her screams for nigh on an hour!" he said.

Instead of agreeing with this appalling charge, Edith chuckled. "And it may take longer still. Now you must go and wait. We will tell you the moment the babe arrives."

"Nay! I am not leaving until I find out how my wife fares!"

"Let him stay!" Gillian said, in a surprisingly strong voice. "Better yet, let him come closer, and I will show him how I fare!"

"Gillian?" he whispered, brushing by Edith to go to her side.

She was lying back on the bed, red-faced and panting, but she did not have the pallor of death that he had seen on her before. Still, she did not look well at all, and as he watched, her features contorted into a grimace.

"How do you feel?" he asked.

"Lean nearer and let me twist your privates into a knot, so you can know how I feel," she promised between breaths.

Her remark stunned him for a moment. Then he straightened, frowning down at her. "You are the one who wanted this baby! Do not lay at my door the blame for your discomfort."

"Discomfort?" she shrieked. "Discomfort? I shall give you discomfort, you fiend! 'Tis all your fault! You bedded me!"

"You seduced me!"

The two were shouting so loudly at each other that neither one heard Edith ask about the birthing stool or the midwife's soft reply that it would not be needed. "You may push now, my lady," the woman said, but Gillian was too busy throwing curses at her husband's head.

"Push, my lady!" Edith urged, louder, and finally she did, releasing a long, ragged breath before yelling at Nicholas.

"I am never doing this again!"

"Fine! At last we agree on something!"

She pushed again, her face a startling shade of scarlet, and Nicholas felt alarm race through him until she reviled him anew. "You are never to touch me again!"

"Then you must keep your fine hands off me!" Nicholas returned. "Do not think you can change my mind this time, with your wiles!"

"Stubborn man!"

"Mulish vixen!"

Nicholas's eyes narrowed at they stared into emerald ones alight with fury. Then, suddenly Gillian fell back against the pillows with a sigh and reached for him. Despite her threats, he took her hand immediately, and his fingers closed around hers, just as the sound of an infant's cries filled the room.

Stunned, Nicholas looked to the foot of the bed, where the old woman was handing a tiny form to Edith. "Poor wee thing, to be cursed with the blood of these two," the midwife muttered, "both of them as daft as can be."

Nicholas grinned slowly as he turned back to his wife. Oblivious of the old woman's slurs, she gazed up at him with shining eyes. "I did not mean any of it," she said softly.

"Nor I," he admitted, his smile too deep to ever die. He pushed back the damp hair from her face and saw her lips curve in response. For a moment, their gazes held, the love that was so strong flowing between them like a river, and then he looked up to find Edith handing him a small bundle.

"A boy," the old servant said, tears of happiness running down her face. "A de Laci heir."

Nicholas held out his arms to take his son, and he felt as if he would burst with the force of his own joy.

"Why, Nicholas," Gillian teased. "Your dimple is showing."

Epilogue

$\infty\infty\infty\infty$

Nicholas did not even bother to wait outside the door this time, for he had been through that before, and liked it not. Besides, it went against his very nature to give even token agreement to the demands of the old midwife, who by all rights ought to be dead by now. The woman looked to be a hundred years old, and her temper had not improved with age.

She did not even bother to scold when he marched into the great chamber, having learned her lesson well, but he soon heard his wife's shout from the bed. "Nicholas!"

He strode easily to her side and leaned over to kiss Gillian's flushed cheek. "Why is that old crone still alive? She grows scarier by the year," he whispered.

"Hush! I need her. Stop starting trouble with your foul moods! You are always causing problems. 'Tis your fault that I am here right now," Gillian grumbled.

"I do not seem to remember you being unwilling," Nicholas answered. It was an old game between them, one that kept them together and heartened during the worst of times.

"I am never going through this again! How many times do I have to tell you?"

Nicholas thought of his three strong sons and two lovely daughters. "I do believe this is the sixth instance in which you have told me."

"Well, I mean it now!" she cried, reaching for him, and Nicholas let her take his hand in a fierce grip that sometimes actually managed to hurt him.

And even though he had been through this experience before, the fear was always with him that something might go awry.... "Never again," he promised fervently. "I swear I will never touch you again."

"What? No fighting?" the gnarled old creature at the foot of the bed taunted them.

Gillian smiled. "We hardly have time for it anymore. Each child comes—" she paused to take a deep breath and give a great push "—quicker."

An infant's wail filled the room, and the old crone shook her head, as if baffled by the behavior of the lord of Belvry and his lady.

"A girl!" Edith shouted, and as if her words were a signal, the five children who obviously had been listening at the door burst in to greet their new sibling. They swarmed past the dismayed midwife to join their parents on the rumpled covers.

"We have a beautiful family," Gillian whispered, as the baby was placed in her arms and its sisters and brothers crowded around to get their first look.

"Aye," Nicholas said, his heart as full as the great bed.

* * * * *

Harlequin® Historical

Another spectacular medieval tale from
popular, award-winning author

SUZANNE BARCLAY

The next book in her ongoing
Sommerville Brothers series:

Knight's Ransom

Watch for this passionate story
of a French knight who captures
the daughter of his enemy for revenge,
but finds love with his captive instead!

Coming this October
from Harlequin Historicals

Harlequin® Historical

If you liked
SADDLE THE WIND
by
PAT TRACY

You'll *love*

Beloved
OUTCAST

Boston bluestocking Victoria Amory finds more than
she bargained for when she's left behind by a wagon
train and discovers Logan Youngblood locked in
an abandoned fort!

SEPTEMBER 1996
Harlequin Historicals

PTRACY

Harlequin® Historical

If you're a serious fan of historical romance,
then you're in luck!

Harlequin Historicals brings you
stories by bestselling authors, rising new stars
and talented first-timers.

Ruth Langan & Theresa Michaels
Mary McBride & Cheryl St. John
Margaret Moore & Merline Lovelace
Julie Tetel & Nina Beaumont
Susan Amarillas & Ana Seymour
Deborah Simmons & Linda Castle
Cassandra Austin & Emily French
Miranda Jarrett & Suzanne Barclay
DeLoras Scott & Laurie Grant...

You'll never run out of favorites.

Harlequin Historicals...they're too good to miss!

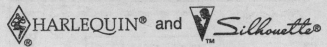

HARLEQUIN® and **Silhouette®**

are proud to present...

HERE COME THE GROOMS™

Four marriage-minded stories written by top
Harlequin and Silhouette authors!

Next month, you'll find:

Married?!	by Annette Broadrick
Designs on Love	by Gina Wilkins
It Happened One Night	by Marie Ferrarella
Lazarus Rising	by Anne Stuart

ADDED BONUS! In every edition of
Here Come the Grooms you'll find $5.00 worth
of coupons good for Harlequin and Silhouette
products.

On sale at your favorite Harlequin and Silhouette
retail outlet.

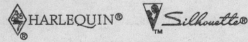

HARLEQUIN®   **Silhouette®**

HCTG996

Look us up on-line at: http://www.romance.net

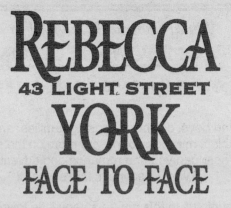

REBECCA
43 LIGHT STREET
YORK
FACE TO FACE

*Bestselling author Rebecca York returns to "43 Light Street"
for an original story of past secrets, deadly deceptions—and
the most intimate betrayal.*

She woke in a hospital—with amnesia…and with child.
According to her rescuer, whose striking face is the last
image she remembers, she's Justine Hollingsworth. But
nothing about her life seems to fit, except for the baby
inside her and Mike Lancer's arms around her. Consumed
by forbidden passion and racked by nameless fear, she
must discover if she is Justine…or the victim of some mind
game. Her life—and her unborn child's—depends on it….

Don't miss *Face To Face*—Available in October, wherever
Harlequin books are sold.

HARLEQUIN ®

®

43FTF

Merry Christmas, Baby!

★ ★ ★ ★

A romantic collection filled with the magic
of Christmas and the joy of children.

SUSAN WIGGS, Karen Young and
Bobby Hutchinson bring you Christmas wishes,
weddings and romance, in a charming
trio of stories that will warm up your
holiday season.

MERRY CHRISTMAS, BABY! also contains
Harlequin's special gift to you—a set of
FREE GIFT TAGS included in every book.

Brighten up your holiday season with
MERRY CHRISTMAS, BABY!

★ ★

Available in November at
your favorite retail store.

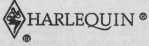